Lucy Christopher

SCHOLASTIC INC.

New York   Toronto   London   Auckland

Sydney   Mexico City   New Delhi   Hong Kong

This book was written with the grateful support of the Arts and Humanities Research Council. *www.ahrc.ac.uk*

ISBN 978-0-545-17094-9

12 11 10 9 8 7 6 5 4 3 2 1                    12 13 14 15 16 17/0

Printed in the U.S.A.                    40

First Scholastic paperback printing, January 2012

The text type was set in Adobe Garamond Pro.
The display type was set in JoeHand.

*Book design by Steve Wells with Christopher Stengel*
*Design of excerpt from untitled novel by Carrie Brewer*

*For Mum and Simon who helped,*
*and for the desert that inspired*

*You saw me before I saw you.* In the airport, that day in August, you had that look in your eyes, as though you wanted something from me, as though you'd wanted it for a long time. No one had ever looked at me like that before, with that kind of intensity. It unsettled me, surprised me, I guess. Those blue, blue eyes, icy blue, looking back at me as if I could warm them up. They're pretty powerful, you know, those eyes, pretty beautiful, too.

You blinked quickly when I looked at you, and turned away, as if you were nervous . . . as if you felt guilty for checking out some random girl in an airport. But I wasn't random, was I? And it was a good act. I fell for it. It's funny, but I always thought I could trust blue eyes. I thought they were safe somehow. All the good guys have baby blues. The dark eyes are for the villains . . . the Grim Reaper, the Joker, zombies. All dark.

I'd been arguing with my parents. Mum hadn't been happy about my skimpy top, and Dad was just grumpy from lack of sleep. So, seeing you . . . I guess it was a welcome diversion. Is that how you'd planned it — wait until my parents had a go at me before you approached? I knew, even then, that you'd been watching me. There was a strange sort of familiarity about you. I'd seen you before . . . somewhere. . . . But who *were* you? My eyes kept flitting back to your face.

You'd been with me since London. I'd seen you in the check-in line with your small carry-on bag. I'd seen you on the plane. And now here you were, in Bangkok airport, sitting in the coffee shop where I was about to order coffee.

I ordered my coffee and waited for it to be made. I fumbled with my money. I didn't look back, but I knew you were still watching. It probably sounds weird, but I could just feel it. The hairs on my neck bristled when you blinked.

The cashier held on to the cup until I had my money ready. Kenny, his name badge said; strange how I can remember that.

"We don't take British coins," Kenny said, after he'd watched me count them out. "Don't you have any bills?"

"I used them up in London."

Kenny shook his head and pulled the coffee back toward him. "There's a cash machine next to duty-free."

I felt someone move up behind me. I turned.

"Let me buy it," you said. Your voice was low and soft, like it was meant only for me, and your accent was strange. The short-sleeved shirt you were wearing smelled like eucalyptus, and there was a small scar on the edge of your cheek. Your eyes were too intense to stare into for long.

You had a bill ready. Foreign money. You smiled at me. I don't think I said thank you. Sorry about that. You took the drink from Kenny. The paper coffee cup bent a little as you grabbed it.

"Sugar? One?"

I nodded, too flustered by you being there, talking to me, to do anything else.

"Don't worry, I'll do it. You sit down." You gestured to where you'd been sitting, at a table between the fake palm trees, over by the window.

I hesitated. But you'd anticipated I would. You touched me gently on the shoulder, your hand warm on my skin. "Hey, it's OK, I won't bite," you said softly. "There's no other seats anyway, not unless you want to sit with the Addams family over there."

I followed your gaze to the empty chairs next to a large family. Two of the smaller kids were crawling over the table, the parents arguing across them; I made eye contact with a girl about my age. I wonder now what would have happened if I had sat next to them. We could have talked about kids' holidays and strawberry milk shakes. Then I would have returned to my parents. I looked up at your face, with the smile creases around your mouth. The deep blue of your eyes had secrets. I wanted them.

"I only just escaped my family," I said. "I don't want another yet."

"Nice work." You winked. "One sugar it is, then."

You guided me toward where you'd been sitting. Other customers were near your small table, making me feel more confident to approach it. It took me ten steps to get there. I walked in a kind of daze and sat in the chair facing the window. I watched you take the drink to the stand and lift the lid off. I saw you pour the sugar in, hair falling over your eyes as you bent your head. You smiled as you noticed me looking. I wonder if that was when it happened. Were you smiling as you did it?

I must have looked away for a moment, to watch the planes taking off behind the glass. There was a jumbo jet teetering on its back wheels, black fumes hanging in the air behind. There was another lining up to go. Your hands must have been quick, tipping it in. Did you use any kind of distraction technique, or was nobody looking anyway? It was some kind of powder, I suppose, though not much of it. Perhaps it looked like sugar. It didn't taste any different.

I turned to see you walking back, smoothly avoiding all the coffee-carrying passengers who stepped out in front of you. You didn't look at any of them. Only me. Perhaps that's why nobody else seemed to notice. You moved too much like a hunter, padding silently next to the row of plastic plants as you made your line toward me.

You put two coffees on the table and pushed one in my direction, ignoring the other. You picked up a teaspoon and twirled it idly, spinning it around your thumb, then catching it again. I looked at your face. You were beautiful in a rough sort of way, but you were older than I'd realized. Too old for me to be sitting there with you really. Early to midtwenties probably, maybe more. From a distance, when I'd seen you at the check-in line, your body had looked thin and small, like the eighteen-year-olds at my school, but up close, really looking, I could see that your arms were hard and tanned, and the skin on your face was weathered. You were as brown as a stretch of dirt.

"I'm Ty," you said.

Your eyes darted away then back again before you reached out your hand toward me. Your fingers were warm and rough on the palm of my hand as you took it and held on to it, but didn't really shake it. You raised an eyebrow, and I realized what you wanted.

"Gemma," I said, before I meant to.

You nodded as though you already knew. But, of course, I suppose you already did.

"Where are your parents?"

"They've already gone to the gate; they're waiting for me there." I felt nervous then so I added, "I said I wouldn't be long — just getting a coffee."

One corner of your mouth turned up again, and you laughed a little. "When does the flight leave?"

"'Bout an hour."

"And where's it going?"

"Vietnam." You looked impressed. I smiled at you, for the first time, I think. "My mum goes all the time," I added. "She's a curator — kind of like an artist who collects instead of paints."

I don't know why I felt I had to explain. Just habit, I guess, from all the kids at school who ask but don't know anything.

"Your dad?"

"He works in the city — stockbroker."

"Suited and booted, then."

"Something like that. Pretty boring, looking after other people's money . . . not that he thinks so."

I could feel myself starting to babble, so I took a sip of coffee to shut me up. As I drank, I watched a small trickle of sweat travel down your hairline. You couldn't have been hot, though; the air conditioner was beating directly onto us. Your eyes were flicking nervously all over the place, not always able to meet my gaze. That edginess made you seem shy, made me like you even more. But there was still something about you, hovering in my memory.

"So," you murmured. "What is it you want to do, then? Get a job like your dad? Travel like your mum?"

I shrugged. "That's what they'd like. I don't know. Nothing really seems right."

"Not . . . meaningful enough?"

"Yeah, maybe. I mean, they just collect stuff. Dad collects people's money and Mum collects people's drawings. What do they really do that's theirs?"

I looked away. I hated talking about my parents' work. We'd been talking about it on the flight from London, Mum going on and on about the paintings she wanted to buy in Vietnam. Right then it was the last thing I wanted to discuss. You half laughed at me again, your voice breathy. The teaspoon was balancing perfectly on your left thumb, hanging like magic. I was still wondering whether I should be there, sitting with you. But it was weird, you know, it felt like I could tell you anything. I probably would have, too, if my throat hadn't been so tense. Often I wish it had ended just then, with your smile and my nerves all bundled up tight.

I glanced around, checking to see whether my parents had come looking for me, although I knew they wouldn't. They would be happy enough waiting at the gate and reading the selection of journals they'd brought, trying to look intelligent. Besides, Mum wouldn't want to admit defeat over our clothes argument by coming to find me. But I glanced around anyway. There was a swarm of nameless faces slowly being drawn toward the drinks counter. People, people, everywhere. The grind and hum of the coffee machine. The squeal of small children. The smell of eucalyptus coming off your checkered shirt. I took a sip of my coffee.

"What does your mother collect?" you asked, your soft voice grabbing my attention back again.

"Colors, mostly. Paintings of buildings. Shapes. Do you know Rothko? Mark Rothko?"

You frowned.

"Well, that kind of stuff. I think it's pretty pretentious. All those endless squares." I was babbling again. I paused to look down at your hand. It was still on top of mine. Should it be there? Were you trying to pick me up? No one at school had ever done it quite like that. As I looked, you lifted your hand up quickly, as if you'd only just realized it was there, too.

"Sorry." You shrugged, but there was a twinkle in your eye that made me smile back. "I guess I'm . . . a little tense."

You put your hand down again, next to mine this time, inches away. I could move my little finger across to touch it. You didn't have a wedding ring. No jewelry at all.

"What do you do?" I asked. "You're not still in school, then?"

I winced as I said it. We both knew how stupid it sounded. You were obviously older than any other boy I'd talked to like this. There were tiny sun-wrinkles around your eyes and mouth, and you'd grown into your body. You were more confident than the awkward boys at school.

You sighed and sat back. "I suppose I sort of make art, too," you said. "But I don't paint squares. I travel a bit, garden . . . build. That sort of thing."

I nodded as if I understood. I wanted to ask what you were doing here, with me . . . if I'd seen you before. I wanted to know

7

why you were interested. I wasn't an idiot; it was easy to see how much younger I was than you. But I didn't ask. I was nervous, I guess, not wanting you to be weird in any way. And I suppose it made me feel grown-up, sitting there with the most handsome man in the café, drinking a coffee he had just bought for me. Maybe I didn't look all that young really, I thought, even though the only makeup I wore was lip gloss. Maybe you just looked old for your age. As you glanced out the window, I untucked the bit of hair from behind my ear, let it fall over my face. I bit my lips to make them redder.

"I've never been to Vietnam," you said eventually.

"Or me. I'd rather go to America."

"Really? All those cities, those people . . . ?"

Your fingers twitched then as you glanced at me, your eyes darting to the hair I'd just released. After a moment you leaned across the table to retuck it behind my ear. You hesitated.

"Sorry, I . . . ," you murmured, unable to finish, your cheeks reddening a little. Your fingers lingered on my temple. I could feel the roughness of their tips. My ear went hot as you brushed against it. Then your fingers moved down to my chin. You pushed it up with your thumb to look at me, almost like you were studying me in the artificial lights above my head. And, I mean, you *really* looked at me . . . with eyes like two stars. You trapped me there like that, kept me stuck to that spot of Bangkok airport as though I were something small drawn to the light. And I had wings fluttering away inside me all right. Big fat moth wings. You trapped me easily, drew me toward you like I was already in the net.

"Wouldn't you rather go to Australia?" you said.

I laughed a little; the way you'd said it sounded so serious. You moved your fingers away immediately.

"Sure." I shrugged, breathless. "Everyone wants to go there."

You were quiet then, looking down. I shook my head, still feeling your touch. I wanted you to keep talking.

"Are you Australian?"

I was puzzled by your accent. You didn't sound like any of those famous Aussie actors. Sometimes you sounded British. Sometimes it sounded as though you came from nowhere at all. I waited, but you didn't answer. So I leaned over and prodded your forearm.

"Ty?" I said, trying out your name, liking the way it sounded. "So what's it like anyway? Australia?"

You smiled then, and your whole face changed with it. It kind of lit up, like there were sunbeams coming from inside you.

"You'll find out," you said.

---

Things changed then. I slowed down, while everything around me sped up. It's amazing really, what a tiny bit of powder can do.

"How are you feeling?" you asked.

You were watching me, your eyes wide. I opened my mouth to tell you I was fine, but I didn't understand what came out. It was just a jumble of noises, my tongue too thick and heavy to form words. I remember the lights turning into blurs of blazing fire. I remember the air-conditioning chilling my arms. The smell of coffee smudging into the smell of eucalyptus. Your hand was tight around mine as you grabbed me and you took me and you stole me away.

I must have tipped your coffee cup when I stumbled to get up. I found a burn mark on my leg later, a pink stain running above my left knee. I still have it. It's turned a bit wrinkly, like elephant skin.

You made me walk fast. I thought you were taking me back to my flight, leading me to the gate where my parents were waiting. It was a long way, much longer than I'd remembered. When you dragged me along those moving sidewalks, it felt like we were flying. You talked to people in uniforms, and pulled me to you like I was your girlfriend. I nodded at them, and smiled. You led me up some stairs. My knees wouldn't bend at first, and it made me giggle. Then my kneecaps turned into marshmallows. Fresh air hit me, smelling like flowers and cigarettes and beer. There were other people, somewhere, talking softly, shrieking like monkeys when they laughed. You pulled me through some shrubs, then around the corner of a building. A twig caught in my hair. We were near the trash bins. I could smell rotting fruit.

You pulled me to you again, tilting my face and saying something. Everything about you was fuzzy, floating on the fumes of the bins. Your beautiful mouth was moving like a caterpillar. I reached out and tried to catch it. You took my fingers in yours. The warmth of you shot from my fingertips right up my arm. You said something else. I nodded. Some part of me understood. I started getting undressed. I leaned against you as I took off my jeans. You handed me new clothes. A long skirt. Shoes with heels. Then you turned away.

I must have put them on. I don't know how. Then you took your top off. Before you put a different shirt on, I stuck my hand out and felt your back. Warm and firm, brown as bark. I don't know what I was thinking, or even if I was, but I remember needing to touch you. I remember that feeling of skin. It's strange to remember touch more than thought. But my fingers still tingle with it.

You did other things, too, put something scratchy on my head and something dark over my eyes. I moved slowly. My brain couldn't keep up. There was a dull thud of something landing in a metal can. There was something slimy on my lips. Lipstick. You gave me a chocolate. Rich. Dark. Soft. Liquid in the middle.

Things got even more confusing then. When I looked down, I couldn't see my feet. When we started to walk, it felt like I was just walking on the stumps of my legs. I started to panic, but you put your arm around me. It was warm and solid, safe. I shut my eyes and tried to think. I couldn't remember where I left my bag. I couldn't remember anything.

People surrounded us. You pushed me into the middle of a crowd of blurred-out faces and color. You must have thought of everything: a ticket, a new passport, our route through, how to get past security. Was it the most carefully planned steal ever, or just luck? It can't have been easy to have got me through Bangkok airport and onto a different plane without anyone knowing, not even me.

You kept feeding me chocolates. That rich, dark taste . . . always in my mouth, clinging to my teeth. Before you, I loved chocolate. Now even the smell makes me sick. I blacked out after the third. I was sitting somewhere, leaning up against you. I was cold, and I needed your body heat. You murmured something to someone else about me.

"Too much to drink," you said. "We're celebrating."

Then we were crammed in a toilet stall. There was the shoot of air as the contents of the bowl were sucked away beneath me.

And we were walking again. Another airport, maybe. More people . . . the smell of flowers, sweet, tropical, and fresh, as if it had just rained. And it was dark. Nighttime. But not cold. As you dragged me through a parking lot, I started to wake up. I started fighting you. I tried to scream, but you took me behind a truck and pushed a cloth over my mouth. The world went hazy again. I sank back into you. All I remember after that is the numbed-out jolt and sway of being in a car. The engine grumbled on, forever.

But what I do remember is the waking-up part. And the heat. It clawed at my throat, and tried to stop me breathing. It made me want to black out again. And then there was the pain.

---

At least you hadn't tied me to the bed. Victims in films are always tied to the bed. Still, I couldn't really move. Each time I shifted my body even a little, sick rose in my throat and my head spun. There was a thin sheet over me. I felt like I was in the middle of a fire. I opened my eyes. Everything twisted and turned, beige and blurred. I was in a room. The walls were wood: long planks, bolted at the corners. The light hurt my eyes. I couldn't see you. I twisted my head around cautiously, looking. I tasted vomit in my mouth. I swallowed it. My throat was thick. Rasping. Useless.

I closed my eyes again. Tried breathing deeply. I mentally checked down my body. My arms were there, legs, feet. I wriggled my fingers. All working. I felt down over my stomach. I had a T-shirt on; my bra was cutting into my chest. My legs were bare, my jeans gone. I felt the sheet beside me, then rested my hand against the top of my thigh. My skin went hot and sticky almost immediately. My watch wasn't on my wrist.

I ran my hand over my underpants and felt through them. I don't know what I thought I would find, or even what I was expecting. Maybe blood. Torn flesh. Pain. But there was nothing like that. Had you taken my underpants off? Had you put yourself inside? And, if so, why had you bothered to put them back on?

"I haven't raped you."

I swung my head around. Tried to find you. My eyes still weren't seeing clearly. You were behind me, I could hear that. I tried pushing myself to the edge of the bed, away from you, but my arms weren't strong enough. They shook, and then collapsed me into the sheets. The blood was pumping through me, though. I could almost hear my body start to flow and wake up. I tried my voice, managed a whimper. My mouth was against the pillowcase. I heard you somewhere, taking a step.

"Your clothes are beside the bed."

I flinched at your voice. Where were you? How close? I opened my eyes a little. It didn't hurt too much. Next to the bed, a new pair of jeans was neatly folded on a wooden chair. My coat wasn't there. Neither were my shoes. Instead, underneath the chair was a brown pair of leather boots. Lace-up and sensible. Not mine.

I could hear you taking steps, coming toward me. I tried curling up, tried to get away. Everything was heavy. Slow. But my brain was working and my heart was racing. I was in a bad place. I knew that much. I didn't know how I'd got there. I didn't know what you'd done to me.

I heard the floorboards creak a couple more times, the sound shooting adrenaline into my veins. A pair of light brown cargo pants stopped in front of me. My eyes were level with the material between your knees and crotch, level with the reddish dirt stains there. You didn't say anything. I heard my breathing getting faster. I gripped the sheet. I forced my eyes to look up. I didn't stop until I reached your face. My breath faltered for a second then. I don't know why, but I'd half expected you to be someone else. I didn't want the person standing there, beside the bed, to have the same face I'd found so attractive at the airport. But you were there all right: the blue eyes, blondish hair, and tiny scar. Only you didn't look beautiful this time. Just evil.

Your face was blank. Those blue eyes seemed cold. Your lips thin. I pulled the sheet up as far as I could, leaving only my eyes uncovered, watching you. The rest of me was stiff and frozen. You stood there, waiting for me to speak, waiting for the questions. When they didn't come, you answered anyway.

"I brought you here," you said. "You feel sick because of the effects of the drugs. You'll feel weird for a while . . . shallow breathing, vertigo, nausea, hallucinations . . ."

Your face was spinning as you spoke. I shut my eyes. There were tiny stars behind my eyelids, a whole galaxy of tiny, spinning stars. I could hear you shuffling toward me. Getting closer. I tried my voice.

"Why?" I whispered.

"I had to take you."

The bed creaked and my body rose a little as you sat down on the mattress. I dragged myself away. I tried pushing my legs to the floor, but still they wouldn't go. The whole world seemed to turn around me. I was going to slide off. I pointed my head away and expected to be sick at any moment. It didn't come. I hugged my legs toward me. My chest was too tight for crying.

"Where am I?"

You paused before answering. I heard you take a breath, then sigh it out. Your clothing rustled as you changed your position. I realized then that I couldn't hear any other sounds, anywhere, other than yours.

"You're here," you said. "You're safe."

---

I don't know how much longer I slept. It's really hazy, this period, like a twisted kind of nightmare. I think you gave me food at some point, made me drink. You didn't wash me, though. I know that because when I woke again, I stank. I was sweaty and damp and my T-shirt stuck to me. I needed to pee, too.

I lay there, listening. My ears were straining to hear something. But it was silent. Weirdly so. There wasn't even the creak and shuffle of you. There was no sound of people at all. No traffic noises. No distant hum of a highway. No trains rumbling. Nothing. There was just that room. Just the heat.

I tested my body, cautiously lifting one leg and then the other, wriggling my toes. My limbs didn't feel so heavy this time. I was more awake. As quietly as I could, I pushed myself up and looked properly around the room. You weren't in it. It was only me. Me, plus the double bed I was lying in, a small bedside table, a chest of drawers, and the chair where the jeans were. Everything was made from wood, everything basic. There were no pictures on the wall. To my left was a window with a thin curtain covering it. It was bright outside. Daytime. Hot. There was a shut door in front of me.

I waited for a few more moments, straining to hear you. Then I struggled to the edge of the bed. My head was spinning enough to tip me, but I got there. I gripped the mattress and made myself breathe. Cautiously, I put one foot on the floor. Then the other. I made them take my weight, steadying myself by holding the bedside table. My vision blacked a little, but I stood, eyes closed, listening. There was still nothing to hear.

I reached for the jeans, sitting back down on the bed to put them on. They felt tight and heavy, and clung to my legs. The button dug into my bladder, making me need to pee even more. I didn't bother with the boots; it would be quieter with bare feet. I took a step toward the door. The floor was wooden, like everything else, and cool against my feet, with gaps between the planks leading to darkness below. My legs were as stiff as the wood. But I got to the door. I pressed down the handle.

It was darker on the other side. When my eyes adjusted, I saw there was a long corridor — wooden again — with five doors, two to my left, two to my right, and one at the end. All of them were shut. The floor creaked a little as I took my first step. I froze at the sound. But there were no noises from behind the doors, nothing to suggest that anyone had heard, so I took another step. Which door was my escape?

I stopped at the one to my right and grabbed the cold metal handle. I pushed down, holding my breath for a second before I pulled it toward me. Paused. You weren't in there. It was a dusky gray room with a sink and a shower. A bathroom. At the back was another door. Perhaps leading to a toilet. I was tempted for a moment, wondering if I could risk a quick pee. God, I needed to. But how many chances would I get to escape? Perhaps only one. I backed up into the corridor again. I could pee down my leg. Or outside. I just had to get out. If I could do that, then everything else would be OK. I'd find someone to help me. I'd find somewhere to go.

I still couldn't hear you anywhere. I pressed my hands against the walls to steady myself and aimed for the door at the end. One step, two. Tiny creaks each time. My hands ran over the wood, catching splinters in my fingers. I was breathing fast and loud, like a panting dog, my eyes scanning everything, trying to figure out where I was. Sweat was running from my scalp and down my neck, down my back and into the jeans. The last thing I could remember clearly was Bangkok airport. But I'd been in a plane, hadn't I? And a car? Or perhaps that was only part of a dream. And where were my parents?

I focused on taking small, quiet steps. I wanted to panic and scream. But I had to keep control, I knew that much. If I started imagining what had happened, I'd be too scared to move.

The last door opened easily. There was a big, dimly lit room on the other side. I cringed back into the corridor, ready to run. My stomach turned over, the pressure in my bladder unbearable. But there was no movement in the room. No sound. You weren't in there. I could make out a couch and three wooden chairs, cut rough and basic like the one in the bedroom, and there was a space in the wall that looked like a fireplace. Curtains had been pulled over the windows there, too, giving everything a dark, brownish light. There were no ornaments. No pictures. That room was as stark as the rest of the building. And its air was as thick and heavy, stuffy as a coat.

There was a kitchen to my left with a table in the middle and cupboards all around. Again the curtains were drawn, though there was a door at the end with a brightness through its frosted window. Outside. Freedom. I edged along the wall toward it. The pain in my bladder got worse, the jeans too tight. But I got to the door. I touched the handle. I pushed it, expecting it to be locked. But it wasn't. I gulped. Then I woke up and started pulling the door toward me. I opened it wide enough for my body to slip through, and I stepped straight out.

The sunlight hit me immediately. Everything was bright, painfully so. And hot. Hotter even than inside. My mouth went dry instantly. I struggled for a breath, leaning back into the doorway. I brought my hand up to shield my eyes and tried to stop squinting. I was blinded by all that whiteness. It was like I'd stepped out into an afterlife. Only there were no angels.

I forced my eyes open, made myself look. There was no movement anywhere, no sign of you at all. Besides the house, there were two other buildings over to my right. They looked makeshift, held together with strips of metal and wood. To the side of them, underneath a metal covering, was a beat-up four-wheel drive and trailer. And then, there was beyond.

I made a sort of choking noise. As far as I could see, there was nothing. There was only flat, continuous brown land leading out to the horizon. Sand and more sand, with tussocks of small scrubby bushes standing up like surprises and the occasional leaf-less tree. The land was dead and thirsty. I was in nowhere.

I turned. There were no other buildings. No roads. No people. No telephone wires or sidewalks. No anything. Just emptiness. Just heat and horizon. I dug my fingernails into the palm of my hand, and waited for the pain that told me I wasn't in a nightmare.

I knew as soon as I set off that it was hopeless. Where would I run to? Everywhere looked the same. I could see why you hadn't locked the doors, why you hadn't tied me up. There was nothing and no one out there. Only us.

My legs were stiff and slow to get going, the muscles in my thighs hurting immediately. My bare feet stung. The reddish earth looked empty enough, but there were spikes and stones in it, thorns and small roots. I gritted my teeth, stuck my head down, and jumped the ground cover. But the sand was so hot; that hurt, too.

Of course you saw me. I heard the car start when I was about a hundred feet from the house. I kept going, my bladder aching with every step. I even picked up my pace. I fixed my eyes on some distant point on the horizon and ran. My breath rasped, and my feet were bleeding. I heard the tires spitting up the dirt, coming toward me.

I tried zigzagging, thinking it might slow you down. I was half-crazy, gulping and sobbing and wheezing for air. But you kept coming, driving fast behind me with the tires skidding and the engine roaring. I could see you turning the wheel, spinning the car around.

I stopped and changed direction, but you were like a cowboy with his rope, circling me, stopping me everywhere I wanted to go. You were drawing me in, running me down. You knew it was

19

only a matter of time before I couldn't run any farther. Like a crazed cow, I kept going anyway, running away from you in decreasing circles. I had to fall eventually.

You stopped the car and turned off the engine.

"It's no use," you yelled. "You won't find anything. You won't find anyone."

I started crying then, great sobs coming out of me like they'd never stop. You opened the door and grabbed my T-shirt at the back of the neck. You pulled me toward you, my elbows scraping against the ground. I turned my head and bit your hand. Hard. You swore. I know I drew blood. I tasted it.

I got up and ran. But you were on me again, so quickly. This time you used your whole body to push me down. Sand grazed my lips. You were on top of me, your chest against my back, your legs against the top of my thighs.

"Give in, Gemma. Can't you see there's nowhere to go?" you growled into my ear.

I struggled again but you pressed harder, holding my arms tight against my sides, squeezing me. I was tasting dirt, your body heavy on top of mine.

It was then that I let go of my pee.

---

I screamed and struggled all the way back. I bit you again. Several times. I spat, too. But you wouldn't let me go.

"You'll die out there," you snarled. "Can't you see that?"

I kicked you hard, in the shins and in the balls and anywhere I could. It didn't loosen your grip, though. It just made you drag me faster. You were strong. For a thin-looking guy, you were bloody strong. You dragged me the whole way across the dirt, back to the house. I made myself go heavy, kicking and screaming like a wild thing. You pulled me through the kitchen and threw me into the murky bathroom. I hammered and yelled and tried to kick the door down. But it was no use. You locked the door from the outside.

There were no windows to break. So I opened the door at the back of the room. As I'd thought, there was a toilet there. I stepped down the two steps toward it. There was no floorboard around it, just bare ground which stung my feet again. There were no windows, either: The walls were thick, splintery planks with tiny cracks between them. I pushed against them but they were solid. I lifted the lid of the toilet. Inside was a long, dark hole, stinking of shit.

I went back into the bathroom and looked through the cabinet above the sink. I hurled everything I found in there against the door, as hard as I could. A bottle of antiseptic smashed and went everywhere, its strong smell filling the air. You were pacing backward and forward on the other side.

"Don't, Gemma," you warned. "You'll use everything up."

I screamed for help until my throat ached. Not that it was any use. After a while, my words just turned into sounds, trying to block you out. I banged my arms against the door until they had bruises all the way to the elbows, and bits of skin were coming off around my wrists. I was desperate. At any moment you could come into that room with a knife, or a gun, or worse. I looked for protection. I picked up a piece of glass from the antiseptic bottle.

The door jolted as you pressed your body up against it. "Just calm down," you said shakily. "There's no point."

You sat in the hallway, opposite the bathroom. I knew because I could see your shoes through the crack underneath the door. I sat back against the wall, smelling the antiseptic and the acidity of the piss in my jeans. After a while, I heard a soft clunk as you took the key from the keyhole.

"Just leave me alone," I yelled.

"I can't."

"Please."

"No."

"What do you want?" I was sobbing now, curled up tightly. I dabbed the blood on my feet, the scratches and mess I'd made from running.

I heard you slam your hand, or your head, against the bathroom door. I heard the rasp in your voice.

"I won't kill you," you said. "I won't, OK?"

But my tears only came heavier. I didn't believe you.

You were quiet a long time then, and I wondered if you'd gone. I almost preferred hearing your voice to the silence. I held the glass shard from the antiseptic bottle tightly in my hand, so tight it started to cut my palm. Then I held it up to the light from a crack in the wall. There were tiny rainbows in that glass. I turned it so a rainbow danced across my hand. I pressed my finger against it and a small bubble of blood appeared.

I held the glass above my left wrist, wondering if I could do it, then brought it down slowly. I slit a line into my skin, sideways. The blood started to seep out. It didn't hurt. My arms were too numb from banging against the door. There wasn't that much blood. I gasped as two drops fell to the floor, not quite believing what I'd done. You said later that it was the aftereffects of the

22

drugs that made me do it, but I don't know. Right then, I felt pretty determined. Perhaps I preferred to kill myself than wait for you to do it. I moved the glass to my left hand, and I stretched out my right wrist.

But you came in then. Fast. The door swung open and almost immediately you were taking the glass from my hand and bundling me in your arms, wrapping your strength around me. I punched you in the eye. And you dragged me into the shower.

You turned the tap a little. The water was brownish and came out in spurts, making the pipes groan. There were black things floating in it. I pushed myself backward into the corner. Blood from my wrist was mixing with the water, swirling round and round. I liked the water being there, though, separating us. It felt like a sort of ally.

You took a towel from a box near the door and put it under the water until it was thoroughly wet. Then you turned the tap off and came toward me. I stuck myself to the cracked tiles and screamed at you to leave me alone. But you kept on coming. You knelt in the water and pushed the towel to the cut. I pulled away quickly, hitting my head on something.

And after that, nothing.

———— ⸎ ————

When I woke, I was back in the double bed with a cool, damp bandage around my wrist. I was no longer wearing the jeans. My feet were tied to the bedposts with hard, scratchy rope. There were bandages wrapped around them, too. I pulled away, testing how tightly I was tied, and gasped as pain shot up my legs.

Then I saw you beside the window. The curtains were open a

little, and you were staring out. I saw the frown on your forehead. There were bruises around your eye. My handiwork there, I suppose. At that moment, with the sun turning your skin light, you didn't look like a kidnapper. You looked tired. My heart was hammering but I made myself watch you. Why had you brought me here? What did you want? Surely, if you'd wanted to do something to me, you would have done it already? Or perhaps you were making me wait.

You turned then, saw me looking. "Don't do that again," you said.

I blinked.

"You'll hurt yourself."

"Does it matter?" My voice was only a whisper.

"Of course."

You looked at me carefully. I couldn't hold your gaze. It was those eyes of yours. Too blue. Too intense. I hated the way they looked almost concerned. I lay back and looked at the ceiling. It was made of curves of metal.

"Where am I?" I asked.

I was thinking about the airport. My parents. I was wondering where the rest of the world had disappeared to. Out of the corner of my eye, I watched you shake your head slowly.

"It's not Bangkok," you said. "Or Vietnam."

"Then where?"

"You'll find out, I suppose, eventually."

You rested your forehead in your hands, pressing your fingertips softly on the bruises around your eye. Your nails were short and dirty. Again, I tried pulling my feet away. My ankles were sweaty and wet, but not slippery enough to pull them free.

"Do you want some water?" you asked. "Food?"

I shook my head. I felt the tears on my cheek again. "What's going to happen?" I whispered.

You took your head from your hands. Your eyes flashed at me for a moment, but they weren't icy. They'd thawed a little. They looked wet. For a second I wondered if you'd been crying, too. You saw me studying you and turned away. Then you went out of the room and came back several minutes later with a glass of water. You sat beside the bed and held it out to me.

"I won't do anything to you," you said.

———— ৽ ————

I stayed in the bed. The pillowcase got thin from my tears. The sheets sealed in my sweat. Everything stank. At some point you came in and changed the bandages on my feet. I was limp by then, melting away like my body heat.

You told me later that it was only for a day or two. It felt like weeks. My eyelids swelled from crying. I tried to think of ways to escape, but my brain had melted, too. I got pretty acquainted with the ceiling, the rough walls, and the wooden frame around the window. I drank the brownish earthy water left beside me, but only when you weren't watching. And once I nibbled at the nuts and seeds you left in a bowl, touching them gingerly with my tongue first in case they were poisoned. Whenever you came in, you tried to talk to me. The conversation was pretty similar each time.

"Do you want to wash?" you asked.

"No."

"Food?"

"No."

"Water? You should drink water."

"No."

A pause while you thought about what I would like. "Do you want to go outside?"

"Only if you'll take me to a town."

"There are no towns."

One time you didn't leave the room like you normally did. You sighed and went to the window instead. I saw that the bruises around your eye had changed color from deep blue to a jaundice-yellow; my only indication that time had passed. You looked at me, a wrinkle deep in your forehead. Then, quickly, you ripped open the curtains. Light flooded in, making me shrink back against the sheets.

"Let's go out," you said. "We can look at the land."

I turned away from the light and you.

"It's different out the back to out front," you said. "We'll go there."

"Will you let me go, out back?"

You shook your head. "There's nothing to escape to," you said. "I've told you. It's a wilderness."

You wore me down in the end. I nodded to say I'd go. It wasn't because you wanted me to, though. It was because I didn't believe you when you said there was nothing out there. There had to be something: a town in the distance, or a road, or an electricity pylon. Nowhere is a wilderness really.

You untied my feet. You unwound the bandages and pressed your hand against my soles. It didn't sting like I thought it would. You checked my wrist, too. The cut was scabby and brownish red, but there was no fresh blood.

26

You tried to lift me from the bed but I pushed you away. Even that small action set me shaking. I stretched across, and got out of bed on the other side.

"I can do this myself."

"Of course, I forgot," you said. "I haven't chopped your legs off yet."

You chuckled at your joke. I ignored you. My legs started to shake so much that it was hard just to stand up. I made myself take a step. My foot twinged with pain. I swallowed hard. But I knew I couldn't stay in that room forever.

You turned away while I put the jeans on. They'd been washed and dried once again, the stains from crawling along the dirt gone. I was desperately weak when I walked out of that room, ready to black out at any moment. I wished I had accepted more of the food you'd offered me. I walked down the corridor, and you followed. You didn't make a sound as you walked, not even the floor creaked. I turned toward the kitchen I'd found before, but you grabbed my arm. I flinched at your touch, couldn't look at you.

"This way," you said.

I shook off your fingers, left a few steps between us. You led me through the living room where the curtains were still drawn, and I had to strain my eyes to see. As I took a step, something pierced my foot. My eyes filled with water but I wiped them quickly, before you noticed. I lifted my foot and pulled out a small gold-colored hook, the kind used for hanging pictures. I wondered what it was doing there when there were no pictures to put up.

We went through a kind of porch area to reach the other side of the house. I squinted at the daylight as you opened the door. There was a veranda running the length of the building.

Then I saw the boulders. They were huge, smooth, and roundish, maybe two hundred feet from the house and almost towering over it. Two larger boulders were in front, with about five smaller ones hugging tight around them. They were glowing red, lit by the sun. They looked like a handful of hot marbles, dropped by a giant. As I peered closer I could see crevices worn into them, cracks sprouting spindly trees that clung hard to the sides. Those rocks were so different from the rest of the land; they stuck out of the ground like thumbs.

"The Separates," you said. "That's what I've called them. They look unlike ... kind of ... separate from everything else, around this area anyway. They're alone, but they're together in that, at least."

I hobbled to a wicker couch, tumbled onto it, and cradled my foot, rubbing the red mark from the picture hook. "Why didn't I see them before?" I asked. "When I ran?"

"You weren't looking." I felt you watching me. When I didn't look back, you moved across to one of the veranda posts. "You were too upset to see anything much then."

I scanned the boulders, looking for pathways, checking for anything man-made. There was a plastic pipe leading out from them and running all the way along the ground to the house. It fed into a large metal tank at the far end of the veranda, near where the bathroom was. There were wooden posts spaced evenly around the base of the rocks as if there'd once been a fence there.

"What's on the other side?" I asked.

"Nothing much. More of the same." You jerked your head sideways, nodding at the dusty ground around the house. "It's not your escape route, if that's what you're wondering. Your only escape route is through me. And that's bad luck for you, I guess, since I've already made my escape by coming here."

"What's the pipe?" I asked, thinking that if a pipe led to your house then there could be other pipes and other houses behind the rocks.

"I laid it. It's for water."

You grinned, almost proudly, and started feeling around in your breast pocket for something. Then you reached down into your pants pocket and took out a small handful of dried leaves and some rolling papers. My eyes lingered over your other pockets. Were there any small bulges? Could that be where you kept the car keys? You crumbled the leaves and rolled yourself a long, thin cigarette and licked up the sides.

"Where are we?" I asked again.

"Everywhere and nowhere." You leaned your head against the veranda post and looked across at the rocks. "I found this place, once. It's mine." You studied your cigarette as you thought. "It was a long time ago. I was small then, maybe half your height."

I glanced at you. "How did you get here?"

"Walked. It took about a week. When I got here, I collapsed."

"All by yourself?"

"Just me. The rocks gave me dreams . . . and water, of course. It's special, this place. I stayed here about two weeks, camping in the middle, living off those rocks. When I got home, everything had changed."

I turned away, not wanting to know anything more about you or your life. There was a bird circling high above us, a tiny *x* against the darkening sky. I wrapped myself up small, cradling my knees, gripping them tighter, trying to stop the fear inside me from opening up into a scream.

"Why am I here?" I whispered.

You patted your pockets, then pulled out a box of matches. You gestured toward the rocks.

"Because it's magic, this place . . . beautiful. And you're beautiful . . . beautifully separate. It all fits." You twisted the cigarette between your thumb and forefinger. Then you held it out to me. "Want one?"

I shook my head. None of this fit. And no one had ever called me beautiful before. "What do you want?" I asked, my voice cracking.

"That's easy." You smiled, and the cigarette in your mouth hung down, stuck to your lips. "Company."

When you lit up there was a strange smell to the cigarette, more natural than tobacco but not as strong as weed. You inhaled deeply, then looked back at the collection of boulders.

I followed your gaze and spotted a small gap through the middle of them. It looked like a pathway.

"How long will you keep me?" I asked.

You shrugged. "Forever, of course."

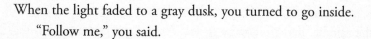

When the light faded to a gray dusk, you turned to go inside.

"Follow me," you said.

You paused in the porch we'd come through before, beside a bank of industrial-sized batteries. There were wires attached to them, leading up to the ceiling, passing through several switches on the way. On the shelf above your head was a line of six kerosene lanterns. What would happen if I tipped one off? Would the impact stun you? How much time would it buy me to get away? You bent down, checked something, then flicked a switch.

"Generator," you said, nodding at the batteries. "This powers everything in the kitchen and the few lights we have around the house."

But I was still looking at the lamps. You saw, and took one down, pushing it into my hands. I grasped its bulging middle, and the thin metal handle shook against the glass. You started explaining how to use it. When you turned to get another, I lifted it toward you, but my arms were shaking too much to touch you with it. So I just stayed there, lamp midair, looking stupid. You realized what I wanted to do, though, and put the second lamp back on the shelf pretty quickly, then reached out for mine.

"You can't get rid of me with that," you said, the corner of your mouth curling up.

You took it from me, poured kerosene inside, and lit it. Then you pushed me from the room. Holding the lamp out in front, you led me back to the bedroom where I'd been sleeping.

"This is your room," you said. You moved toward the chest of drawers near the door. "You'll find clean sheets here."

You opened the bottom drawer and showed me. Then you pulled open the two drawers above, revealing T-shirts, tank tops, shorts, pants, and sweaters. I ran my fingers over one of the

T-shirts. It was beige colored and plain, size medium, and felt new.

"It'll fit, right?" you asked.

I didn't ask you how you knew what size I was. I just kept looking at the clothes. Everything was beige and boring. There were no brand names, nothing fancy. It looked like it had all been bought from a cheap department store. You pointed at the top two smaller drawers.

"Underwear," you said. Then you stepped back. But I didn't look in that drawer, either.

"I've got skirts and a dress or two, if you want them. They're in the other room. They're green."

I narrowed my eyes. Green was my favorite color. How did you know all this? *Did* you know all this? You turned toward the door.

"I'll show you the other rooms." When you saw that I wasn't following, you spun back and stepped up close to me, so close I could smell the smoke from your cigarette still lingering on your clothes. "Gemma, I won't hurt you," you said quietly.

You turned again and left. In that semidarkness, I heard the walls moan, contracting as the day's heat dissipated. I followed the light from your lantern to the next room down. There was a low foldout cot set up along one of the walls, with a mess of blankets across it. There was a bedside table beside it, a wardrobe against the opposite wall, and a wooden chest next to that.

"I sleep in here, for now," you said. You avoided my gaze. I avoided the way your words hung, unfinished.

I already knew the bathroom. The next door beyond it led to a large closet. There was nothing much in there apart from a couple of brooms, a mop, and some metal boxes. I followed your lamp to the door opposite, the last room off the corridor. It was bigger than your bedroom, almost as big as the room you said was mine. There was a cabinet at one end, and an armchair. There were bookshelves down the entire length of one wall, though they weren't exactly full. You opened the cabinet and showed me the games on the lowest shelf: UNO, Connect Four, Guess Who?, Twister. They were all games we'd had at home, games I could remember playing with friends, or on Christmas mornings with my parents. But these versions were faded and old, as if they'd come from consignment shops.

"There's a sewing machine, too, a guitar . . . sports things," you said.

I glanced at the books, neatly lined-up on the shelves. In the lamplight, I could only make out some of the titles. *Wuthering Heights, The Great Gatsby, David Copperfield, Lord of the Flies . . .* books we'd studied at school. I couldn't see any modern books up there, just classics. I looked at the next shelf. This one contained mostly field guides: guides to desert flowers and animals, studies about snakes. There were books about tying ropes and making shelters, and others about rocks. I saw a dictionary of Aboriginal languages. As I looked over the titles, I realized something.

"We're in Australia, aren't we?"

A brisk nod from you. "Took you awhile," you muttered.

I remembered what you'd said to me in the airport, about whether I'd ever wanted to visit . . . and then your odd accent. It made sense. Apart from the fact that I'd thought Australia was all beaches and bush, not just endless red sand. But I felt a brief glimmer of hope anyway, a stirring that maybe everything would be OK. Australia was a civilized country, with a law system, and police and a government. People could be looking for me already, police hunting me out. The whole nation might be on alert. Then the glimmer faded. You'd taken me from Bangkok. Who'd guess to look for me in Australia?

"Who knows I'm here?" I asked.

"No one. No one knows either of us are anywhere. We're in the middle of the Australian desert. We're not even on the map."

I made myself swallow. "Nowhere is unmapped."

"This is."

"You're lying."

"I don't lie."

"How did you bring me here, then?"

"In the back of the car. It took awhile."

"Without a map?"

"Like I said," you hissed. "It took awhile."

"I would have remembered."

"I made sure you didn't."

That shut me up. Your eyes darted away from mine, and I took a step back. I remembered the chemical smell of that cloth over my face. The hazy jolt and sway of being in your car. The sickly sweet chocolates. I reached for more memories, but they wouldn't come. I shook my head, not really wanting them to, either. I took another step back into the darkness and leaned against the bookshelf. My head was reeling. I wondered what else you were hiding from me. What other horrible little secrets.

"Someone must have seen you," I whispered.

"Doubt it."

"There are cameras in airports . . . security cameras are everywhere now."

"Most of those cameras don't even have film in them." You lifted the lantern. Its light cast shadows onto your face and made dark hollows under your eyes.

"Someone will be looking for me. My parents will be looking for me."

"Probably."

"They're important, you know."

"I know."

"They've got contacts, money. They'll be on TV; they'll post my photo all over the world. Someone will recognize it."

"Unlikely." You moved the light toward me; I felt its heat. "You were in the trunk most of the way here, under the tent."

My chest tightened once more as I pictured my body curled up and contorted, thrown in like a piece of luggage. It was like a grisly horror film, only I hadn't made it to the knife scene yet. I crossed my arms over my chest. How could I not remember any of this? Why only just tiny glimmers? Were the drugs you'd given me really that strong? I took another step away from you, backed up toward the door.

"In the airport, someone will have seen you. . . ." I was speaking to myself, really. "Someone will have seen me. It's impossible you could have got past all that security without anyone . . ."

"If anyone saw you, they wouldn't have recognized you."

"Why not?"

"You had a wig on, sunglasses, heels, a different coat. The passport I used for you had a different name. I left your old one in the dumpster."

You moved toward me. Again, there was that intensity in your eyes, like you wanted something, and I remembered how you'd looked at me in the coffee shop. I'd fallen completely for that piercing look then. This time it was very different. I looked at the shelves; a guidebook to Australian mammals was inches from my face. I thought about chucking it at you.

"We left your backpack in the dumpster, too," you added. "Don't you remember getting changed, putting on a skirt? Don't you remember touching me? You thought it was all fun at the time."

Salty water built up in my mouth like I was going to be sick. You moved around, angling yourself between the door and me. I reached for the mammal guide.

"You're a new person now, Gem," you murmured. "That old you's been left behind. There's a chance out here to start again."

"My name's Gemma," I whispered. I held the book between us like a threat. Some weapon! "And I didn't let you do all that."

"You did, you enjoyed it."

You took the final step until you were standing right in front of me. I leaned back against the bookshelf, pressing my spine into it. You reached out and touched the side of my cheek. My skin went hot immediately. I held the book up, in front of my neck.

"You were pretty obliging back then, remember?" you murmured.

"No."

My cheek was burning up beneath your touch. My jaw was set hard as I looked back at you. But I did remember. And that made it worse. I remembered laughing as you tilted and angled something on my head. I remembered the clothes, your back. I remembered how badly I'd wanted to kiss you. I shut my eyes. A noise somewhere in my throat escaped and I was suddenly crouched over and huddled into the bookshelf. Your hand was on my back.

I lashed out, catching your chin. I used all my strength to push you away.

"I hate you!" I screamed. "I fucking hate you!"

You moved your hand away immediately, as if I'd suddenly burned it.

"Maybe that'll change," you said quietly.

You took the lantern with you, leaving me huddled against the bookshelf in the dark.

———————

I couldn't sleep that night, as usual. It wasn't the heat. It was never hot at night out there. And it wasn't the darkness. I'd pulled the curtain open, craving the light from the moon.

As the heat died and the wooden walls shrank around me, it sounded like there were wolves in them, growling, getting ready to pounce. I listened for you, angling my pillow so that I could see the door handle. I didn't turn over in case that little action muffled a noise from outside. The creaks in the walls sounded like your footsteps in the corridor. I was so stiff I got a headache.

A lantern was burning weakly beside my bed. I could grab it if I needed to. I could throw it as soon as that door scraped open. I imagined where I would aim. There was a black stain in the wood beside the door frame, about the right height for where your head would be. I was pretty sure I could make it. But after that? The doors could be locked, and if not, where could I run to so that you wouldn't find me?

You lay in the next room, only a few feet away . . . a thin wall between us. I tried to think about school, about Anna and Ben. I even tried thinking about my parents. About anything except you. But nothing worked. Everything came back to you. You lying there. You dreaming. You thinking about me. I pictured you, on that mess of blankets, eyes wide-open and imagining how you'd kill me. Perhaps you touched yourself and pretended it was me doing it. Or perhaps you had your eye pressed up close to a crack in the wall, watching me waiting for you. Perhaps it gave you a kick. I listened for the blink of your eyelash against the wood. But there was only the creaking.

In the end I did sleep, but I don't know how. It must have been nearly dawn when I did, my body just packing in, exhausted by the tension. When I did, I dreamed . . .

I was back home. Only I wasn't really; it was as though I could see what was going on, but no one could see me. I was leaning against the window in the corner of our living room.

Mum and Dad were there, too, sitting together on the white couch. There were two policemen talking to them, perching uncomfortably on the chairs Mum had brought back from Germany. There were cameras and cameramen. People everywhere. Anna was even there, standing behind the couch with her hand on Mum's shoulder. One of the policemen was leaning forward, his elbows on his knees, firing questions at Mum.

*When did you last see your daughter, Mrs. Toombs?*

*Did Gemma ever talk about running away?*

*Would you please describe what your daughter was wearing that day?*

Mum was confused, looking to Dad for the answers. But the policeman was impatient, shooting a glare at the cameras.

"Mrs. Toombs," he started. "Your daughter's disappearance is an important matter. You do realize you'll be in all the papers?"

When she heard that, Mum dabbed at her eyes. She even managed a thin smile.

"I'm ready," she said. "We must do all we can."

Dad straightened his tie. Someone shone a bright light onto them both as Anna was moved out of the shot.

I tried to cry out, to let them know I was there, in the living room with them, but no sound would come. My mouth just gaped open, the noise stuck somewhere in my chest. Then I felt my body being pulled backward, being drawn toward the window, going straight through the glass like a ghost. And I was on the outside, in the chilly night air.

I pressed against the window, trying to melt back through the glass. I was aching and cold, desperate to be back inside. Then I felt your strong arm around me, pulling me into your chest, your breath warm on my forehead.

"You're with me now," you murmured. "I'll never let you go."

I could see Mum pleading with the cameras, sobbing as the lights became brighter.

But your earthy smell filled my nostrils. And your body was smothering me. Your arms wrapped around me like a blanket, your chest thick as rock.

I woke, wheezing and gasping. Your smell was still there, in that room. It filled that space like air.

———— ⁊ ————

I lay, listening. But soon I needed to pee.

I didn't go back to bed after. I padded softly around the house instead. You weren't around. I started searching for car keys, house keys, anything that could be useful. I was looking for weapons, too. And of course, I was looking for a phone, any way of communicating with other people. There had to be something, a radio at least.

I started with the living room. I searched quietly, listening for you constantly. I looked in drawers, under the mat, along the inside rim of the fireplace. There was nothing. I moved to the kitchen. There were four drawers underneath the work surface. The first two didn't contain anything much, just a few cotton bags and some pegs. The third drawer had old, blunt cutlery. Possibly useful. I took a knife — the sharpest I could find (I tested them by scraping marks in the wood) — and I put it in my pocket.

The fourth drawer was locked. I pulled at it. The handle wobbled, but the drawer didn't budge. There was a keyhole in the middle. I placed my eye to it, but inside it was too dark to see anything. I stuck the knife in the keyhole and tried to open it that way. No good. I clattered around through your tea and sugar jars, looking for the key.

I searched the rest of the kitchen, opening the cupboards gingerly. I don't know what I was expecting, perhaps some sort of torture device or a huge knife. Whatever it was, I didn't find it, or the key. Those cupboards contained pretty much the same sort of stuff any other kitchen would: bowls, plates, cooking utensils. Nothing of use to me unless I hit you over the head with a frying pan. It was tempting.

Then I opened the big cupboard beside the door. Inside was a pantry full of food. Cans and boxes were stacked neatly on shelves, and barrels of flour and sugar and rice were lined up along the floor. I stepped inside. It was well organized, most of it alphabetically. Not far from the bags of lentils were bags of dried melon, then tins of mushroom. I stood on my tiptoes to see the top shelves. There were sweeter things there: cocoa, custard powder, and fruit-flavored gelatin mixes. All the way in the back was a whole shelf of orange juice cartons.

It was awhile before I came out. When I did, you were standing in the kitchen. I stepped back rapidly, away from you. There was brownish dirt smudged around your cheeks and red dust on your hands. Your expression was serious, waiting for me.

"What were you doing in there?"

"Just looking," I said. Instinctively I reached for the blunt knife in my pocket. You pressed your lips together tightly and glared. I felt my heartbeat quicken as I gripped the knife. "If I'm staying awhile, I thought I'd better get to know the place," I went on shakily.

You nodded. You seemed pleased with that. You stepped aside and let me pass. I breathed out, as quietly as I could.

"Did you find anything interesting?"

"A lot of lentils."

"I like them."

"There's a lot of food."

"We'll need it."

I stepped around the kitchen table away from you, relieved and feeling slightly braver. "Isn't there a shop here, then? Somewhere to buy more?"

"No, I told you."

I looked back into the pantry. How did you get all this here? And what would happen if I destroyed it all? Would you go out and find more? I ran my hand along the back of one of the chairs tucked under the table.

"How long will it last?" I asked. I was looking at the food, trying to calculate it. There was enough for a year, maybe. Perhaps more.

You shrugged. "There's more food in the outbuilding," you said. "Lots more."

"And when that runs out?"

"It won't. Not for a long time."

My heart sank. I watched you turn the tap slowly, until a small trickle of water bubbled out.

"Anyway, we've got chickens," you said. "And when you're —" You stopped to look at me before choosing the right word. "When you're *acclimatized*, we can go walkabout, pick up some bush foods. And we should catch a camel, too, sometime, maybe a couple. We can keep them in the boulders, stick a fence around."

"Camel?"

You nodded. "For milk. Or maybe kill one for meat, if you want it."

"Camel meat? That's mad," I said.

I caught the warning look in your eyes immediately, saw the

way your shoulders tensed. It made me shut up, made me grip hard on the back of a chair.

You washed your hands. The water ran a reddish brown, like blood. I watched it spiral down the drain. You used a scrubbing brush to get the dirt out from under your nails. As I said, I was feeling a little braver that day, for the first time since I arrived. Don't know why, but I wanted to ask you more. It didn't feel like you were watching me so intently all the time, either. I walked around the kitchen table, and stopped beside the locked drawer.

"Why's it locked?" I asked.

"For your safety. After your wrist trick . . ." Your words drifted away as you turned back to the sink and kept scrubbing. "I don't want you hurting yourself again."

"What's inside it?"

You didn't answer that one. Instead, when I started tugging on the drawer again, you stepped backward from the sink and lunged at me, wrapping your arms around my waist. You dragged me back, through the kitchen and down the corridor. I screamed and kicked out, but you kept going until you got to my room. You dropped me on the bed. Quickly, I crawled away from you. I felt for the knife in my pocket. But you'd stepped back to the doorway by the time I had it out.

"Lunch will be ready in half an hour," you said.

You slammed the door behind you.

———————— ≷ ————————

That night I lay with the blunt knife in my fist and the lantern beside my head. The curtains were open, the moonlight illuminating the door. One thing I was certain of: You wouldn't do anything to me without a fight.

---

I watched you carefully, learning your routine. If I was going to escape, I needed to know more about this place and I needed to know more about you. I watched where you put things and I looked for a pattern to what you did. I was scared, some days I was stupid with terror, but I forced myself to think.

I used the knife I'd taken to make notches in the side of the bed. I couldn't remember how many days had passed already, but I guessed about ten or so. I made ten small slits into the wood. Anyone else looking at that bed might think it was a record of how much sex we'd had there.

Your routine was pretty simple. You woke early, in the coolest part of the day, when the light was dim and purple-gray. I heard you washing in the bathroom. Then you went outside. Sometimes I heard you banging and hammering near the outbuildings, the sound echoing around. Other times I heard nothing. I strained my ears for the roar of an engine, a car or an airplane howling toward me. I found myself longing for a highway. But there was never anything. It was amazing how quiet it was. I wasn't used to it. I even spent a day or two thinking I had hearing damage. It was as if all the sounds I was used to had disappeared from the world. Compared to the bombardment of noise in London, the desert made me feel deaf.

After a few hours, you came back in. You made tea and break-fast, and always offered me some. It was a kind of porridge, nutty-tasting and watery. Then you went out again for the rest of

44

the day. I watched you walk the hundred feet or so to the nearest building. You closed the door behind you. I didn't know what you did in there for so long every day. For all I knew, you were keeping other kidnapped girls inside. Or something worse.

I found the darkest, coolest part of the house — in the corner of the living room, next to the fireplace. Then I sat and tried to think of ways to escape. I wouldn't let myself give up. I knew if I did, that would be it. I might as well be dead already.

You tried talking to me when you returned, but it didn't work too well. You can't blame me. Every time you even looked at me I stiffened, my breathing quickening. When you spoke, I wanted to scream. But I gave myself little challenges. One time, I made myself watch you. The next time I asked you a question. And on the thirteenth night, I forced myself to eat with you.

It was dusk when I stepped from the living room into the kitchen. Oil and pungent spices pushed into my nostrils. There was a weak light over the stove — one of the few in the house — with moths and other small insects bashing against it. You were using it to cook by. You were hunched over, throwing things into a pot, stirring quickly. The rest of the room was lit by a couple of lanterns and a candle or two, throwing shadows onto the walls. You smiled when you saw me, but the low light in the room made it look like a grimace.

I sat at the table. You put a fork next to me. I picked it up but my hand started shaking. I put it down again. I looked at the blackness on the other side of the window. You took bowls and dished out the meal. You did it carefully, extracting the best bits first. You placed a bowl in front of me. There was too much food, and it smelled heavily of white pepper. I coughed.

There was meat in it — maybe chicken, maybe not. Lots of fat and gristle, bits of bone, too. A leg stuck up vertically from the middle. Whatever it was, it was clear you'd used the whole animal instead of just parts of it. I pushed my fork around the bowl as I looked for the vegetables. I found some small pealike things, wrinkly and hard. My hand was still shaking. It was making my fork tap against the side of the bowl. I found something that looked like a bit of carrot and I chewed.

By then I'd given up on starving myself. If you'd wanted to poison me, you'd have done it already. But I can't say I enjoyed the meal. Of course, you noticed. Anything to do with my health you always noticed.

"You don't eat properly," you said.

I looked down at my shaking fork. My throat felt too choked up to swallow right away. Plus, it tasted as if you'd emptied a garbage can in my mouth. But I didn't tell you that. Course not. I kept quiet and watched you shovel your food between your lips. You ate like a street dog, wolfing everything down as if it were the last meal you'd ever have. You picked up a bone and gnawed at it, pulling strips of meat off with your teeth. I imagined those teeth biting into me, pulling my flesh apart. I pushed away the bones on my plate.

The moon was starting to rise already; a small beam of moonlight fell on the floor around my feet. Outside, crickets were beginning to creak their repetitive choruses. I imagined I was with them, in the dark . . . away from you. I swallowed the remnants of the carrot thing, and summoned up my courage.

"What do you do all day?" I asked.

Your eyebrows shot up in surprise. You almost choked on your meat. I wished you had.

"When you go outside," I continued, "when you go into that building, what do you do in there?"

You put your bone down, the grease on your cheeks shining in the candlelight. You stared at me wide-eyed, as if no one had ever asked you something like that before. I suppose they hadn't.

"Well, I . . . ," you started to say. "I suppose I make things."

"Can I see?" I said it quickly, before I changed my mind. I looked again at the window. If I could just get outside, to somewhere else . . . Anything had to be better than being in that house every day.

You looked at me for a long time. The tips of your fingers rubbed at the flecks of meat still stuck on the bone, pushing them back and forth. Your fingertips were greasy, too.

"If you come with me, I don't want you trying to escape again," you said.

"I won't," I lied.

Your eyes narrowed. "It's just . . . I don't want you getting hurt."

"I know, you don't have to worry," I lied again.

You glanced at the blackness behind the glass, at the stars beginning to appear. "I'd like to trust you," you said. Your eyes darted back to mine. "Can I?"

I swallowed, trying to think of something to convince you. That made me angry. I didn't want to stoop to your level for anything, let alone ask you for something.

"I know I can't go anywhere," I said eventually. "I know it's hopeless, trying to escape. I won't even try, I promise." I still don't think you believed me on that one, so I added, "Besides, I'd like to see what you do all day."

I even smiled as I said it. God knows where I dragged that from; I must have had some form of superhuman strength. I know my eyes weren't smiling, though; they were boring into yours, hating you.

Your eyes were wide as a child's. Your fingers picked at the meat. Then, with a little birdlike jerk, you nodded quickly. I think you wanted so much to believe me, to think that I was finally coming around. You turned to face the window again. Swallowing my pride, I made one more effort.

"Do everything you normally do," I said. "I just want to see."

I heard you cough before I opened my eyes. The light was thin and grayish. You were standing at the side of the bed with a cup in your hands. I backed up, away from you. It looked like you'd been waiting awhile. The cup made a dull thud as you put it on the bedside table.

"Tea," you said. "I'll wait in the kitchen."

For once, I drank it. You'd made it how you like it, though, with two sugars. Too sweet. I got dressed, even wore the beige clothes you'd bought for me. They smelled clean, a little like herbs. I laced up the boots, size seven and a perfect fit. Then I followed the smell of bread to the kitchen. You were waiting on the wooden crate that you used as a step, just outside the open door. I rubbed my hands over my arms, feeling the chill from a breeze. But it was good to see the world through the open door, even if it was full of nothing. The sun was bobbing on the horizon, just peeking over. Its light shimmered on the sand behind you, making your body look like it was glowing . . . like it had a kind of aura.

"I made damper," you said. "Eat."

You pointed to some lumps of bread resting on the countertop. I took one. It was the same size as a bread roll, but funny-shaped. It was too hot to hold comfortably. I tried shoving it in my mouth instead, but it burned my lip. You got me a glass of water.

"You ready?"

I nodded, stepping out into the sunlight. The heat wasn't so intense this time, but even so, sun rays began to tickle the back of my neck. I wobbled on the wooden crate, shielding my eyes and looking out. It was so big, that view. I'll never remember it perfectly. How can anyone remember something that big? I don't think people's brains are designed for memories like that. They're designed for things like phone numbers, or the color of someone's hair. Not hugeness.

You kicked the gravelly sand at the edge of the crate. It was a dark red color, like rust. It was as if it had been weathered from blood instead of rocks. It was nothing like the creamy sand of a beach. You took a few steps, running your finger through the dust that stuck to the side of the house, creating a wiggly line on the wood. I jumped off the crate and followed. You walked the couple of feet to the corner of the house, which, I noticed for the first time, rested on large concrete slabs. There was a dark and cool-looking space underneath it, just about wide enough to crawl into. You bent down onto your knees, and pushed a stick into the gap.

"Still under there," you muttered. "He's just too far in to catch."

"Who is?"

"Snake."

I leaped back from the building. "What kind of snake? Can it get into the house?"

You shook your head. "Not likely." You glanced up. "Just make sure you've got boots on if you're walking out here, OK?"

"Why? Is it dangerous?"

You shut one eye against the sun as you studied me. "Nah," you said. "You'll be all right." You stood up, your knees reddish brown. "Just wear boots, 'K?"

You leaned against the house, squinting as you looked down its length. I looked, too. The building was rough and untidy, like a large piece of driftwood. You jumped up, gripping the metal roof, and hauled yourself across the planks to look at a row of shiny panels.

"Our electricity," you said. "Our hot water, too."

I squinted.

"Solar power," you explained, then, when I still looked blank, added, "obviously we're not on a grid."

"Why not?"

You looked at me like I was some sort of idiot. "Out here the sun's strong enough to power Pluto. Using anything else would be stupid. I haven't had time to connect it all up properly yet, though." You wiggled some wires that disappeared into the walls, checking everything was secure. "But, in time, I can put more lights in the house, if you want them, that sort of thing."

I could feel beads of sweat forming on my forehead. Even though it was only early, the sun was starting to force its way through my T-shirt, making my armpits tingle. You dropped down from the roof into the sand, your feet making a soft *thump*.

"Want to see the herb garden?" you said.

You walked across the sand toward the outbuildings. I followed, my eyes scanning the landscape for anything, anyone . . . any sign of movement. You went to a small fenced-in area next to the four-wheel drive. The ground inside had been dug over and turned.

"This is it," you said. "Only it's not working too well."

I looked at your collection of shriveled-up stalks. It looked like the herb garden Mum had tried to grow once, in the terracotta planters on our patio. Mum had never been much of a gardener.

"It's not working at all," I said.

I knelt and stuck my hand through the fence. I touched the ground. It was hard as concrete. I'd taken over Mum's herb garden eventually. I'd made it grow parsley and mint . . . well, until the winter anyway.

"It was stupid to put it here, really," you said. You picked halfheartedly at the crispy brown stems. A leaf fell off in your hands. You glanced up at the rocks behind the house. "The garden in the Separates is better."

I looked up at those rocks, too. The sun was making shadows around them.

"What else is in there?" I asked.

"Vegetable patch, more herbs, lots of food . . . turtujarti trees, minyirli, yupuna, bush tomato . . . anything you could want. A few stubble quails come and go, lizard . . . there's chickens, too."

"Chickens?"

"Someone'd left a cage of them on the side of the road, on the way here, so I took 'em. Don't you remember them being in the back of the car when we drove here?" Your eyes glinted a little. "S'pose not, huh? They were half-dead, and you weren't much better." You reached into your pocket, took out a small hip flask, and sloshed some liquid onto the dried-out herbs. "Water," you explained. I wanted to grab the flask and give them more.

"They haven't had enough," I said.

You looked at me sharply, but you kept sprinkling until the plants got a few more drops. You stood. "The herbs in the Separates are healthier," you said again. "There's shade, you know? Some water."

I remembered the path I'd seen leading through those rocks. I thought about what might be on the other side.

"Can we go there?" I asked.

Your eyes flicked over me, assessing my intent. "Tomorrow, maybe."

You stepped away from the herbs and took a couple of steps into the sand. You looked out, away from the Separates, at that endlessness of rusty-colored land. It stretched before us in waves: a surging sea of dirt, with small green shrubs bobbing on its surface.

"There are no other people for hundreds of miles," you said. "Not really. Doesn't that just make everything better?"

I stared at you. You could have been joking, or saying

something to scare me. But I don't think you were. You had that faraway look in your eye, the look when your eyes went a bit misty and it seemed as if you were looking out even farther than the horizon. Just at that moment I wasn't scared of you. Right then you looked like a kind of explorer, looking out over the land, planning where to go.

"What's it called?" I asked. "This desert? Does it have a name?"

You blinked. The corners of your mouth twitched. "Sandy."

"What?"

You pressed your lips together, trying not to laugh. But you couldn't help it. Your shoulders started shaking, and then you bent your head to the ground. Your laugh was so loud and deep, it made me jump. Your body moved with the sound, until you kind of collapsed on the sand. You picked up some of the grains and gripped them in the palm of your hand.

"Good name for it, right?" you said, once you'd composed yourself. "It's the Sandy Desert, and it's sandy." You opened your fingers and let the grains go in an orange waterfall. "All just a load of sand hills. Come and see."

I took a step toward you, just one. You picked up another handful and held it out to me, pushing your fingers through the grains.

"This sand is the oldest in the world," you said. "Even the land I sit on now has taken billions of years to form, worn down from the mountains."

"Mountains?"

"Once there was a range near here higher than the Andes. This is ancient land, sacred, it's seen everything there is to see."

You pushed the sand toward me. "Feel the heat," you said. "This sand's alive."

I took the sand. The grains burned into my skin and I dropped them all in a rush. It was the second time you'd made my skin burn that morning. You ran your fingers over the place where they'd fallen, then buried your whole hand underneath. You shut your eyes against the sun.

"The sand's like a womb," you said. "Warm and soft, safe."

You buried your other hand, too. Your shoulders relaxed, and your body went still. It was similar to how people look when they've toked on a joint, totally blissed out. It was weird. I took a step backward, then another. You didn't stop me. After a few moments you slipped off your boots, and stuck your feet under the sand, too. With all your limbs buried in it like that, it was as if the sand had sprouted you. You snuck open your right eye and looked for me.

"You're thinking something," you said.

I nodded toward your feet. "Does it hurt?"

"Nah." You shook your head. "My feet are tough; everything has to be to live out here."

The sun burned the back of my neck. I thought I could see something in the far distance slightly to my left, some sort of shadow. Maybe more rocks, maybe just a heat haze. It hurt to look out at it for long. I walked forward a few feet to get a better view, but quickly gave up. Whatever those glimpses of shadow were, they were impossibly far away. It would take hours, days maybe, to get anywhere close.

I knelt beside one of the many clumps of grass that were dotted around the landscape. From a distance this grass looked spongy and soft, like giant balls of moss, but when I ran my fingers over it, its spikes pricked and scratched my skin. They were the needles I'd stood on when I'd tried to get away: the reason my feet had got so torn.

I heard you move up behind me. I heard you swallow. It reminded me of how we'd met in the airport. Then, you'd been close enough to brush against me. This time I moved away. When I looked at you, your hand was raised like you wanted to touch me.

"Don't," I said. "Please."

You touched the plant instead. You ran your fingers lightly up one of its long needle leaves. It didn't seem to sting you.

"Spinifex," you said. "When it's really dry, its leaves roll up. It closes in on itself." You glanced back at me, your eyes so pale in the sunlight. "Pretty good survival tactic, huh?"

I didn't want to look at your too pale eyes, so I looked at the shadows in the distance. Heat was starting to hover over the ground, making everything look shaky and unreal . . . making me feel sick.

———— ⌇ ————

You walked toward the outbuildings. I hesitated at your car, looking in the window to see if you'd left the keys inside. Orange rubbed off onto my clothes as I leaned against the door. The car was white beneath this dust. There were flecks of rust around the windows, a drum of gasoline or something on the backseat, and a piece of scrunched-up clothing in the front. There were two gearshifts below the dashboard. I rested my hand against one of the warm, fat tires.

You looked bored when I caught up with you. "I don't know why you keep trying," you said. "There's no way out."

You took a key from the pocket in your shirt and stepped up onto the crate in front of the first outbuilding. The key clunked as it went in the keyhole. You paused before opening the door.

"I don't want to take you in here if you're not ready," you said, your voice firm.

The door dropped on its hinges a bit as you opened it. The room was dark inside and empty-looking. I could make out a few shadowy objects farther in, but nothing else. Suddenly, I didn't want to go in. I froze, my breathing getting faster. I had this image of you killing me in there, killing me in that dark . . . leaving my body to rot. You had that weird smile on your face, too, like you wanted to.

"I don't know . . . ," I started to say, but you grabbed me quickly around the shoulders and shoved me inside.

"You're going to like this," you said.

I started to scream. You held me tighter and tighter, those strong arms of yours squeezing. I struggled against you, tried to get away. But your arms were fastened and solid: a python's grip. You dragged me farther into the room. It was so dark.

"Don't move!" you shouted. "Be still. You'll wreck it."

I bit your arm, spat at you. Somehow I loosened your grip. I fell away onto the floor, hitting my knee hard against it. You grabbed my shoulder and pushed me down, using your strength to keep me there.

"I said don't move!"

You were hysterical, your voice on the edge. I scratched at the floor, tried to grip on anything, tried to drag myself along.

"Don't hurt me!" I screamed.

I lashed out. My fist connected with something. You made a gasping noise. And then, suddenly, you let go. I was up and stumbling and running to where I thought the door was.

"Just stop . . . STOP!"

I tripped and hit the floor again. There was a wetness and stickiness against my palms, right where I landed. I crawled through it. It didn't end. The whole floor was wet. And then there were the other things . . . hard things, sharp things, things scratching at my legs. There were soft lumps of material. It felt like clothing, clothing from all the other girls you might have killed in there. The sticky stuff was stuck up to my elbows. It felt like blood. Had you hit me without me realizing? I touched my forehead.

"STOP! Please, Gemma, just stay where you are!"

I was crying and screaming, trying to get away. You were yelling, too. I could hear you thumping through the room, after me. At any moment I'd feel a knife in my shoulder, or an axe slicing my head. I kept bringing my hand up to check if I'd been hit already. I felt my throat. I didn't know where the door was. I slid over the floor, feeling along it, desperately searching for something to protect myself with. My shoes slipped in the wetness.

Then you pulled open the curtains. And I saw it all.

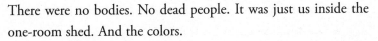

There were no bodies. No dead people. It was just us inside the one-room shed. And the colors.

I was sitting in the middle of it all. There was dirt and dust, plants and rocks . . . all of it scattered over the floor around me.

My arms were covered in blood. At least that's what I thought at first. Everything was red, all of my clothes stained with it. I touched my forearm. It didn't hurt, nothing did. I lifted my arm to my nose. It smelled like dirt.

"It's paint," you said. "Made from the rocks."

I spun around quickly, found you. You were between me and the door. Your face was wild, your mouth tight and angry as you looked me over. Your eyes were dark. I started shaking. I crawled backward, reaching behind for something solid to hold between us, but all I could grab were sprigs of flowers, needles of spinifex. I backed up until I reached the wall. Then I waited; every bit of me focused on you, on what you'd do next, on where you would move. My breath was coming in bursts. I wondered how hard I could kick you. Could I get past you to the door?

You watched me. You were wilder than I'd ever seen you, but you were still as stone. Just the sound of my breaths, getting faster and faster, hung between us. Your hands were clenched in fists. I saw the veins sticking out on the back of them and the whiteness of your knuckles. I risked a look back at your face.

Your eyes squinted tight, as if you were trying to fight something inside you, some deep emotion. You groaned. But the tears came anyway. They ran down your cheeks quietly, slipping over your jaw.

I'd never seen a man cry before, only on TV. I'd never even seen Dad close to crying. Those tears looked so odd on you. It was like the strength of you just seemed to sap away. The surprise of it stopped me being so scared. I took a deep breath and looked away. The walls were painted in large streaks of color. There were bits of plants, leaves, and sand stuck to them.

You took a step toward me, and instantly my eyes switched back to your face. You crouched down on the backs of your heels. You didn't move into the area that I was in, the area filled with sand and stickiness. You stayed on the edge, just looking at it all . . . just looking at me.

"You're sitting in my painting," you said at last. You leaned forward and touched a leaf. "I made all this." You moved your hand along the edge, stroking the sand. "There were patterns and shapes, made from the land. . . ." Your face went rigid and angry again as you surveyed the damage I'd done. Eventually you shrugged, sighing as your shoulders dropped down. "But you created a different pattern, I guess. . . . In a way, it's almost better. You're part of it."

I saw the line I had made as I'd crawled along the floor, the paint I'd spread everywhere. Shakily I got to my feet. A bundle of twigs tumbled from my lap. I looked at your face, with your red-veined eyes and tear tracks, at the tension in your jaw. You looked crazy then, someone mentally ill who didn't believe in taking his pills. I ran sentences through my mind, trying to figure out what to say to get out of that room without upsetting you further. How could I get to the door without tipping you over the edge? How were people supposed to act with madmen? But you were the first to break the silence.

"I didn't mean to scare you," you said, your voice level and reasonable again. "I was worried about the painting. I've been working on it . . . for a long time."

"I thought you were going to . . . I thought . . ." The images were too horrible to get the words out.

"I know." You ran a hand through your hair, turning parts of it red from the sand in your fingers. You seemed serious. Your face was tired and empty-looking, your forehead wrinkled up.

"Just relax," you said again. "Please. Just relax. For once. Neither of us can go on like this. Just trust that it's all for the best."

Your face was earnest, like you really did want the best for me. I stepped through that strange painting of yours and came up pretty close to you, closer than I wanted to be.

"OK," I said. My body was shaking again; it was all I could do to keep upright. I had to keep my voice light and friendly. I knew that much about crazy people. As long as the tone is right . . .

I summoned up the courage to look you directly in the eyes. They were wide, not so red as before. "Just let me go," I said. "Just for a bit, a little while. It'll be OK." I tried to make my voice soothing; I tried willing you to say yes. Again, I glanced toward the door.

The tears were running down your face again. You couldn't hold my gaze. Instead, you leaned your forehead against one of the piles of sand. The red grains stuck to the wetness of your cheeks. You gulped as you swallowed your tears. You brushed some of the sand, sweeping it into a neat line, and hid your face from me.

"Fine," you said. You said it so softly that at first I thought you hadn't said anything at all. "I won't stop you. I'll only save you when you get lost."

I didn't wait to hear it again. I stepped past you. I was so tense, waiting for you to grab me, waiting for those rock-hard fingers on my thigh. But you didn't even move.

The door opened easily. I pushed down the handle and stepped out into a white, hot blast of sunlight. You made a sort of sobbing noise behind me.

———————————————<br>

I started running, past the second building and toward the rocky outcrop of the Separates. I kept looking behind me, but you weren't following. Sweat was pouring off me before I'd even gone a few feet. I jumped over small bushes and stumbled over dry, exposed roots. I closed that hundred feet in about ten seconds, I think. I was glad for those leather boots.

I slowed down when I neared the boulders. Again, I noticed the wooden stakes sticking up from the ground, evenly spaced around them, and the line of plastic piping leading from the house. I could follow that. I looked down the small crevice where the pipe entered the rocks, the gap that had looked like a pathway from the veranda. But was it the right way? The other option would be to follow the edge of the boulders, skip going through the middle entirely, and get to the other side that way. But that would mean losing the pipe. And I still thought it was part of some larger water system, that it would lead me to another building on the other side.

I heard a thud from over near the outbuildings and made a quick decision. I would follow the pipe.

The path was rocky and uneven, getting narrower all the time. But it was cooler in there straightaway, as if the cool was radiating off the stone itself. My eyes took a moment to adjust to the shadowy light from the boulders towering above. The path became so narrow I had to walk with one foot on either side of the pipe. Soon the rock sides felt like they were starting to close in on me, pressing me like a flower. I stretched my arms out and laid my palms on the cool, dry stone, as if pushing it back. I tripped over the pipe as I hurried, using my hands to steady myself. The path got narrower still but I could see light at the end. Was it the other side already?

Another few feet and I got there. But it wasn't the end. Instead the path opened into a clearing. The light was brighter but greenish, filtered through vegetation. I stopped. The clearing was the size of a large room, but with thick bushes and trees around the edge, some growing up the rock sides and spreading out above. There were other pathways, too, leading deeper into the rocks. It was so different from the stark openness on the other side, a different environment entirely. It was the first real bit of green I'd seen for ages.

I took a few steps to the middle of the clearing. The pipe curved around to the right and down one of the larger pathways. There were some cages just before it. The chickens! When I walked toward them, they started clucking. I knelt and looked through the wire. There were six, scrawny like rags. There was another cage next to them with a rooster inside. I stuck my finger through the wire and stroked his black tail feathers.

"Poor feller," I murmured.

I pulled the lid of the hens' cage until it swung open. I stuck my hand inside and felt for eggs, thinking I could take them with me before I disappeared. But there were none. I wondered about setting the birds free, but I didn't want them to come clucking back to you and show you where I'd gone.

There was a thick patch of vegetation behind the chickens' cages. Strange yellowish berries hung from some of the branches, and small apple-shaped lumps peeked out from deep in the undergrowth.

I glanced back down the narrow path. I was taking too long. You could catch up to me any moment. So I left the chickens. The quicker I could get through the clearing, the better.

I followed the pipe. The path it went down was wider and flatter than the last, and I had to step through several patches of thick grass. I wondered about snakes. What would I do if I saw one? I saw a movie once where a man tied rope around his arm above a snakebite, but he tied it so tightly that later he had to have his arm amputated. I tried to push that thought out of my mind; it wasn't exactly helpful right then. I kept going, hoping I was traveling in the right direction. It seemed like I was walking in a straight line toward the other side. The sun was above me, beating down strongly, but it wasn't the same kind of stifling heat as near the house. The vegetation was getting thicker. Inside those boulders, it wasn't like the desert at all. I hadn't walked far before the path opened up into another clearing. It was smaller than the last and even denser with plants. I followed the pipe through the middle.

The pool was so closely screened by foliage that I almost walked straight into it. Instead, the thick arm of a tree caught me just in time.

Rock overhung the pool, sheltering it from the sun. There was a cave at the back, just above the water, with moss growing around the entrance. That dark hole could have been hiding anything. Snakes, crocodiles . . . bodies. I shivered.

I clung to the tree arm and stared out, faintly listening to the birds chattering somewhere above. The water was deep and dark, but it wasn't murky. I could see right down to the sand and weed at the bottom. I should have known there would be water at some point. Why else would all those trees be there? They certainly weren't surviving on rain.

I knelt at the edge and stuck a finger into the water, then gasped and took it back. The water was cold, ice-cold, almost. I wanted to jump in . . . jump straight in and drink it all up. But I just sat there, resting on my heels. I was so stupid. I was looking at all that water, dehydrating more every second, and not touching a drop. I didn't know if I could drink it, you see. I didn't know what was in it. All I could think about was a TV show where an explorer guy drank from a river and a tiny fish swam into his stomach and started eating his insides; then a doctor had to stick a long tube inside him to get it out. There were no doctors around that pool. And I didn't want a tiny fish in my insides, so I gave up on the water idea. I stood up and walked around it, trying to find where the pipe came out the other side.

But it didn't. The pipe stopped in the pool, not leading anywhere else. I ran my hands through my hair as I glanced around. You were right, it seemed. There were no other buildings using that water supply.

I tramped around the small clearing, looking for another way out, a way to get me to the other side of the boulders. There were two other pathways, but they were even narrower than the one I'd come in on, more overgrown, too. I stepped gingerly down the larger one. If I had been worried about snakes before, it was nothing compared to my thoughts about that path. The grass was up to my knees at points, and there were things moving and rustling around me. I thought I saw something in the rocks near my hands, something slithering away. Loudly buzzing flies were hovering around my head, too, being drawn to my sweat. I kept walking until that path turned into a dead end of rock and I had to turn back. I tried the second, smaller pathway, but that soon became too narrow.

I went back to the main clearing, but the other paths out of that were no better, either. I just got more lost, tangled up in the maze of the Separates. I don't know how long I spent trying to get out. It was hard to keep an idea of time in that place. It felt like forever. But one thing I did know, you hadn't followed me. Not yet. I clung desperately to the hope that you thought I'd run somewhere else. I tried another, smaller path, squeezing myself flat to fit between the rocks. But when I came back to the main clearing yet again, I realized I was going around in circles.

That's when I finally woke up and had my idea.

There was a tall, white-barked tree with thick branches growing against one of the boulders. I was glad of its strength as I swung myself up into it. I loved climbing trees when I was young, though I'd never done much of it. Mum was always too scared I'd fall out. It felt weird to be in a tree again, and I couldn't work out where to put my feet at first. But I soon got the hang of it. I hugged the trunk and pulled myself up its bark, using the branches as steps. The only time I stopped was when I saw a small brown spider scuttle away in front of me. It was pure determination that made me keep going after that.

It was annoying when I got to the top, though. There were branches and leaves everywhere, and I couldn't see out. I took a deep breath, closed my mouth and eyes, and tried to sweep the branches aside. Things fell on me as I did. I didn't want to know what they were so I brushed them off before I looked too closely, but it still felt like they were crawling on me. I could feel their legs in my hair. I clung to the uppermost branches and rested a foot against the rock face, dragging myself up it a little way.

And then I looked out.

I shielded my eyes. There was nothing but sand and flatness and horizon. I used the branches to turn myself around, grazing my leg a little on the rock. But there were no buildings on the other side, no towns . . . not even a road. It looked the same on that side as it had looked near the house. Long, flat emptiness. I wanted to scream, probably the only reason I didn't was because I was worried you would hear me. If I'd had a gun, I think I would have shot myself.

I sank down into the top of the tree and leaned my head against one of the branches, sticking the heels of my hands into my eyes. Then I wrapped my arms around the branch, and pressed my face into the bark. A rough part of it scratched at my cheek, but I kept pressing against it, trying to stop the sobs.

It sounds crazy, but right then all I could think about was my parents at the airport. What had they thought when I hadn't turned up for that flight? What had they done about it since? I leaned my cheek against the bark and tried to remember the last thing we'd said to each other. I couldn't. It made me cry even more.

I was almost calm again when I heard the car. Quickly, I scrambled back up the tree and out onto the rock. I grabbed a branch, nearly losing my balance. I looked out at the horizon first, then at the land beside the Separates. There! Your car was driving slowly across just underneath me.

It took me a little time to figure out what you were doing. At first I thought there had always been a fence. Then I realized you were putting it up, right then. My heart sank. So that was why you hadn't followed me — you'd been driving around the Separates the whole time, boxing me in, trapping me like an animal. I'd been so caught up in trying to get through the rocks that I hadn't even noticed the sound of the car.

I watched you make the fence. You had a long roll of what looked like chicken wire, and when you got to the wooden stakes, the ones I'd seen stuck in the ground earlier, you hammered the wire to them. You worked quickly, stretching to nail in the tops and then crouching to secure the bottom. It only took a couple of minutes per stake and then you were driving to the next one. It looked like the job was almost finished. I was already fenced in.

I leaned against the rock. Up there, above the trees, the sun was strong on my face, and I was suddenly exhausted. Beaten. I shut my eyes, wanting to block it all out.

When I opened them again, you'd stopped driving around. Instead, you were waiting on the other side of the fence, car stationary and the driver's door open, your boots resting on its wound-down window. I saw the smoke rising from a cigarette.

I held on to the branches and looked back at the house, at the desolate land around it. There was a slight breeze blowing about some bits of vegetation. In the far distance, I could still see those hill-like shadows. They were such a long way away, but still, they gave me a tiny spark of hope. Apart from those, the rocky outcrop I stood on was the only bit of height for as far as I could see. For the first time, I wondered how you'd found that place. Were there really no other people anywhere? Was it really just us? Perhaps any explorers had given up halfway, or died. There was something astonishing about being able to survive in that land. It seemed more like another planet than earth.

I felt my throat close up, and I wanted to start crying again. But I wouldn't let myself; I had to be stronger than that, otherwise I would just stay on top of that tree until I died of starvation, or thirst. Dad said once that dying of thirst was the most painful death of all, a person's tongue splits and then the internal organs pack up one by one . . . busting open as they expand. I didn't want that.

So I decided to make my way back to the main clearing. I'd wait until it got dark, then creep out to that fence and test it, see if I could get over it or under it. How difficult could it be? Then I'd run back to the house, get supplies and clothing if I had time, some water, and head off across the desert toward those shadows in the distance. Eventually I'd find a road, some sort of track. I had to.

It got cold before it got dark. My whole body was shaking long before the moon had risen. I curled myself into a small ball and sat hunched against the rocks, my teeth tapping against each other.

I hadn't been outside at night before. I knew it was colder at night than in the day, as I'd felt the temperature drop even when I'd been inside the house, but I hadn't expected that kind of cold. Right then, it felt colder than a winter night back home. It seemed crazy for the desert to be so stupidly hot in the day, and then so stupidly cold at night. But I guess there are no clouds out there; there's nothing to hold the heat in. The heat just disappears like the horizon. I suppose that's why it was so light that night, too: There was nothing to hide the moon.

I was glad of that. It meant I could still see my way around the rocks fairly easily. It meant I could watch the ground for snake-shaped shadows. I started pacing, anything to keep warm. Eventually, I couldn't wait any longer. I picked my way back along the thin pathway to the edge of the Separates.

From there I looked out at the fence you'd built. It was pretty tall but it didn't look that sturdy. I ran my hands over my arms, rubbing them. I was too cold to think much beyond getting warm again. Occasionally I heard the rumble of your car engine approach as you circled past on one of your patrols. One thing that was pretty good about this plan was that I could hear you coming for ages before you actually arrived. My teeth were clacking together so loudly, though; I was worried you would soon be able to hear them, too. I wondered what you were thinking: Did you know exactly where I was?

I wrapped my arms around me as tightly as I could, and stared up at the stars. Had I not been so cold and wanting to escape so badly, I could have stared at them forever: They were amazingly beautiful, so dense and bright. My eyes could get lost up there if I left them looking long enough. Back home I was lucky if I even saw the stars at night, what with the pollution and city lights, but in the desert I couldn't miss them. They swallowed me up. They were like a hundred thousand tiny candles, sending out hope. Watching them made me think that everything might be OK.

I waited until you next drove past me, and then I stepped away from the boulders. I was surprised when I took my shoulders from the rocks, surprised again at the cool of the air against my back. The rocks must have been soaking up the sunlight all these hours, becoming warmer. I took a couple of steps into the sand.

I felt instantly exposed, as if I were naked and you were watching my every movement. I ran quickly to the fence, with my head bowed. Those few feet felt so much longer than they were. All the time I was listening for your car, and I heard it, too, but only as a dull rumble on the other side of the rocks.

I stopped when I got to the fence. It was made of tightly stretched chicken wire, towering a few feet above my head. I couldn't get my fingers into its tiny holes. I tried sticking my boot in to get a grip, but it wouldn't hold, and I ended up sliding down the wire, skinning my fingers. I tried again with the other boot. No good. I kicked the fence. I pushed against it, but it just bounced me back.

I started shaking then, whether from the cold or the fear, I don't know . . . probably both. I forced myself to focus on the problem. I couldn't get over the fence so I'd have to go under. I fell down to the sand and started digging. But this wasn't normal sand, like on a beach. This was hard, desert sand with rocks and thorns and bits of plants stuck inside it. It was as tough and as difficult as everything else out there. I gritted my teeth, tried to ignore the way the dirt was scratching my hands, and kept digging. It was like being in a war movie, digging out of a prison camp. But things never work out like in Hollywood. The hole I made was only big enough for a rabbit to get under. It was hopeless. I crawled onto my stomach and tried lifting the fence from the bottom but it wouldn't budge. I got my fingers underneath, but that was it. The wire was pulled too tight. I lay flat out in the sand, nose against the fence. My heart sped and sped, my breathing, too. I got up and tried again to get over the wire. I was almost screaming in frustration. Everything was closing in on me: the fence, the rocks . . .

Then I heard your car.

I started running back toward the Separates. But you came around the corner before I'd reached their shelter. I went back to the edge of the rocks anyway, and waited.

You stopped the car and turned off the engine. You got out and leaned against the hood. You peered at the boulders, looking for me. You'd seen me running; I was sure of that. You could probably see me there, too, shivering against the rocks, trying desperately to soak in some of their heat.

"Gem?" you called.

After a moment, you went around to the passenger door and opened it. You took out a sweater, came back, and held it out.

"Come back to me."

I stayed quiet. I didn't want to go back to you. I didn't know what you would do. I pressed my arms into the rock and willed myself to stop shaking. The tips of my fingers were turning blue.

"There's no way out," you called. "I'll wait here all night if I have to, all week. You can't escape me."

You felt your pockets, took out a ready-made cigarette and started to smoke. The smell of burning leaves wafted toward me, hanging in that cold night air. I pushed myself against the rock, tilting my head away from the scent. I tried to curl my fingers into a fist, but they were so stiff with cold that it hurt.

Once again, I'd been trapped by you; it was only going to be a matter of time before you flushed me out. I slid down the rocks and sat on the sand, digging my hands into its still-warm particles, desperately trying to soak up heat.

You saw me move. You came right up to the fence, leaning your palms against it, and peered at me. Then you went to the car and came back with wire cutters. Moonlight fell on your skin as you worked, glowing on half of your face. You cut a small slit in the fence. Then you pulled the wire back until you'd made a hole large enough to step through, curling it like a wave.

———— ~ ————

I didn't struggle. I didn't do anything. My body went limp. In the house you wrapped me in blankets. You put something hot in my hands, which you made me drink. But my body and my brain and my insides had frozen solid and nothing would thaw them. I had slipped down, down into a dark, dark, empty place. You were saying something to me, your voice muted. I didn't want to surface. The truth was too hard to hear.

There was nothing on the other side of those boulders, only more of the same.

Wherever I went, you'd only catch me.

I couldn't get away.

I closed my eyes. Behind my lids it was dark and calmer and I sunk into it. I didn't move or make a sound. I retreated, stepping back through my mind, through the couch and floorboards, until I reached that dark, cool place underneath the house where I curled up in the dirt. There, I waited for the snake to find me.

There was nothing else I could do.

. . . only wait for the dreams.

I slept.

Mum was nearby, stroking my forehead and shushing me. She spoke quietly, her words a lullaby. She put something around my shoulders and wrapped me into her. I felt her arms surrounding me, her breath sweet like sugared tea.

The next time, I was older. I was home sick from school. Mum had her laptop set up on the kitchen table, her phone by her elbow. I was on the couch, wrapped up and warm. I didn't want to watch the Teletubbies and Mum wouldn't let me watch the talk shows.

"Can we play a game?" I asked her.

She didn't answer.

"Hide-and-Seek?"

After a while I got up off the couch and tiptoed to the utility closet. I scraped the heavy door across the carpet and stepped into the darkness. The air was warm and moist, and smelled like my school blazer when it got wet. I found a place in the corner and waited, imagining I was at the bottom of the sea. . . . I was in the belly of a ginormous creature.

I could hear the tap of Mum's keyboard through a hole in the wall. But at any moment she would stop typing and come find me. I knew she would. Sometime soon she would wonder where I was.

I sank farther down into the darkness of the utility closet . . . waiting. . . .

———————

Then I was in a hospital. There were machines plugged into me, beeping quietly. I couldn't open my eyes, but I was awake. People visited: Anna and Ben, people from school. Dad sat beside me and brushed the back of my hand. He smelled like smoke, just like he used to smell when I was little. There was a nurse nearby, saying it was important to keep talking to me. Another nurse dabbed my forehead.

I reached out at Anna, clawing at the air near her face. But she didn't see me. I tried to scream, tried begging them to stay, all of them. But my mouth wouldn't open, and the noise remained in my throat.

When I opened my eyes, they vanished. The only person left was you.

———————

I didn't talk to you. I just lay on that bed in the plain wooden room and looked at the walls. My voice had shriveled up and disappeared and I didn't know how to find it again. I forgot about the notches on the bed. I tried to forget about everything.

Sometimes you sat beside me. Sometimes you tried to talk, but I didn't look at you. I tucked my knees into my chest and clasped my hands around them.

Then I'd remember.

I'd start with waking up, with the feel of my thick down duvet around my shoulders and the softness of flannel pajamas on my skin. If I concentrated, I could almost hear the whir and the grind of Mum making her morning coffee. I smelled the bitter richness of the grains boiling on the stove, the way the aroma used to waft under the crack in the door and into my bedroom. The clunk of the central heating kicking into gear.

Then Dad was up and banging on my door. He always lectured me over breakfast, about getting good grades and about which universities I should start looking at in the summer. I shut my eyes and tried to see his face. I gasped a little when I couldn't. What shape were his glasses exactly? What was the color of his favorite tie?

I tried for Mum next but even she was hard to see. I could remember her red dress, which she liked wearing to gallery openings, but I couldn't remember her face. I knew her eyes were green, like mine, and her features delicate . . . but somehow I couldn't put the pieces back together.

It frightened me, this amnesia, and I hated myself for it. I felt like I wasn't worthy of being anyone's daughter.

But I could remember Anna. And I could remember Ben. I spent hours thinking about him, imagining he was there with me, my fingers in his floppy, sun-bleached hair. When I shut my eyes, he was in the bed beside me, keeping watch.

He was spending the summer surfing, in Cornwall. Anna had gone with him. That summer was the first one Anna and I had spent apart, ever. I wondered what they were doing in their beach hostel, sitting on the sand every day . . . such different sand from mine, so much softer. I wondered if they even knew I was gone.

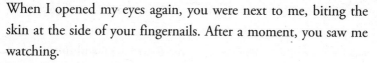

When I opened my eyes again, you were next to me, biting the skin at the side of your fingernails. After a moment, you saw me watching.

"How are you feeling?"

I couldn't answer. It felt like my body had turned to stone. If I even moved my lips, I would crack.

"I can make you food," you tried. "A drink?"

I didn't blink. I thought that if I stayed still long enough, you were bound to leave.

"Maybe . . . maybe we should change the sheets?"

You angled yourself a little toward me. You reached across and pressed the backs of your fingers against my forehead but I hardly felt them. Right then, you were a million miles away, existing in a parallel universe, some sort of dream. I was back home, in my bed . . . any moment I would wake up and get ready for school. It was Ben sitting beside me, not you. It couldn't be you. You sat back on the chair, watching me.

"I miss those words of yours," you said.

I swallowed; it hurt my dry throat. You looked at me, your eyes resting on my lips.

"I know how this works," you said. "I went silent once, too." You found some rough skin on the corner of your finger and moved it back and forth with your thumb. "People thought I'd never spoken, like I was . . . what do you call it? Mute. Some of them thought I was deaf, too." You chewed the bit of skin free. "That was right back after I found this place."

My eyebrow twitched then, and you saw.

"Got you interested now?" You rested your head back against the wall. There was a drop of sweat traveling down your cheek, running over your faint scar. "Yeah, that's right," you said, nodding, seeing where I was looking. "I got that when I was silent, too." Quickly you wiped the sweat away, your hand lingering on the puckered skin. Then your finger and thumb moved together and you flicked at your cheek. I jumped at the sound. "A net can hit skin so quickly," you said, "so easy to make a mark."

You stood up and went to the window. I shifted, turning my head a little so I could see you. You noticed.

"Not so dead, then," you murmured. "Not so gone."

Sometime later you put a thin, faded notebook on the bedside table. After you'd left the room, I picked it up and flicked through it. The pages were blank. There was a pencil on the table, too, its

lead sharp. I jabbed it hard into the soft skin between my forefinger and thumb. It hurt. I jabbed again.

———————⸙———————

I tried to draw them, all of them . . . Mum, Dad, Anna, and Ben. I
wanted to remember. But I've never been very good at art. The
faces I drew were shapeless strangers, a mess of lines and shades. I
scribbled jagged black lines over them all.

So I tried words. They were always more my thing anyway.
Mum and Dad could never understand it, how I was so good at
English and never very good at math or art like them. But even
words didn't flow too well, not then. They certainly didn't make
much sense. Anyone reading them now would think I was on
drugs or something, the way those words jumped about.

I tried a letter, but I couldn't get past "Dear Mum and Dad."
There was too much to say. And anyway, I didn't know whether
you would read it.

So I wrote the only words I could think of: *imprisoned,
confined, detained, constrained, incarcerated, locked up,
interned, sent down, abducted, kidnapped, taken, forced,
shoved, hurt, stolen . . .*

I scribbled lines over that piece of paper, too.

———————⸙———————

I couldn't sleep any more. There was a pain in my bladder, and
everything was stiff. I wanted to move. Cautiously, I tried bend-
ing my knees. I scrunched my toes tight and ran my tongue over
my dry lips. My arms felt weak as I pushed myself away from the
mattress, my legs shaking as I tried to stand.

I put on new clothes from the drawer. The shorts were loose on my hips, my stomach thin. I went into the bathroom and peed into the long drop. Then I turned the tap on. It chugged into life, spurting out hot, brown-speckled water. I washed my face, then stuck my head under the tap and gulped. In that tiny cracked mirror, I watched the water drip off me. My eyes were slightly swollen, my nose peeling from the little sun I'd seen. I looked older somehow.

You were in the kitchen. Your head was low to the table, looking at handwritten words on sheets of loose paper. You glanced up at me, then went back to what you were doing. Small glass vials were spread out around you; some of them with liquid inside, some empty. You picked up one with a yellow lid and squinted to read the label. You held the container to the light from the window, then wrote something down. The previously locked drawer was hanging open, but I couldn't see what was inside. There was something that looked like a needle on the bench nearby.

My stomach kind of flipped. Everything around you pointed to one thing: drugs. Perhaps drugs you'd used on me, perhaps ones you were yet to use. I stepped back from the kitchen. You didn't look up. For once you were more engrossed in something else.

I walked through the small porch area, past the batteries and boards lined up against the wall, and stepped onto the veranda. I looked at the floor while my eyes got accustomed to the brightness. When I could look out without squinting too much, I took a few steps and leaned against the rail. I stared across the sand to the Separates. The fence you'd made was still up, the boulders as still as ever within it. From where I stood, no one would guess at the greenness and life that those rocks contained; no one would believe the birdsong. Those rocks were secretive and strange. Like you.

I glanced at the cloudless blue sky. There were no planes up there, no helicopters. No rescue missions. Lying in bed, I'd had the idea of writing "help" in the sand, but I realized then, it was a pretty stupid idea if no one ever flew over anyway. I turned to see the rest of the view: horizon, horizon, Separates, horizon, horizon, horizon . . . nowhere to run.

I heard your steps on the wood and the snap of the door before I saw you on the veranda.

"You got up," you said. "I'm glad."

I stepped back.

"Why today?" You looked genuinely curious.

But I was full up with sadness. I knew that if I opened my mouth, it would all come spewing out. And I didn't want you to have anything from me, not even that. You kept trying, though.

"Nice day," you said, "hot and still."

I backed up into the couch. I grabbed its arm, making the wicker strands crunch.

"Do you want food?"

I stared straight ahead, looking at the craters in the rocks.

"Sit down."

I did; don't know why. You had that tone in your voice, I guess, that tone that would be stupid to argue with, the tone that made my legs weak with fear.

"Why don't we talk?"

I drew my feet up. A tiny breeze had started blowing the grains around. I looked at the sand that was starting to swirl in front of us, a few feet ahead.

"Tell me about something, anything — your life in London, your friends, even your parents!"

I flinched at the sudden loudness of your words. I didn't want to tell you anything, let alone about them. I clasped my arms around my knees. What would Mum be doing right now? How upset were they that I had disappeared? What had they done to get me back? I gripped my legs a little tighter, trying to force their faces from my mind.

You didn't say anything for a while, just stared out at the land. I watched you from the side of my eye as you pulled at your eyebrow with your forefinger and thumb. You weren't comfortable, hovering on the edge of the veranda. I knew what you were thinking, though; you were trying to come up with something new to talk about, something interesting to entice me out of my hole. Your brain was sweating with the effort. Eventually you leaned your elbows on the railing and let out a low sigh. You talked with a voice so quiet.

"Is it really that bad?" you asked. "Living with me?"

I opened my lips and breathed out. I waited at least a minute. "Of course," I whispered.

Perhaps there was something more to those two words . . . some sort of a need to connect, wanting to use my voice rather than risk losing it. Because that's what it felt like then, when that wind was up and blowing the sand around; it felt like it could blow my voice completely away from me, too. I was disappearing with those grains, scattering with the wind.

You heard my words, though. You nearly stumbled off the veranda with shock. You frowned as you composed yourself and thought about my response.

"It could be worse," you said.

You left your sentence hanging. What could be worse? Dying? It couldn't be much worse than being in the middle of nowhere, looking out at nothing . . . never able to get away from it. And, for all I knew, I was waiting to be killed anyway. I shut my eyes against it all and tried remembering life back home. I was getting better at that. If I took my time, I could easily spend a few hours imagining every tiny thing I used to do in a day. But you weren't letting me dream, not then. Soon I heard you kicking the tips of your boots into the railings. You started banging out a rhythm. I opened my eyes. This wasn't like you. Normally you moved like a cat.

"At least there are no cities," you said finally. "Out here . . . no concrete."

"I like cities."

Your fingers tightened around the railings. "No one's real in a city," you snapped. "Nothing's real."

I shifted in my seat, surprised at your sudden anger. "I miss it," I whispered. I buried my head into my knees as the reality of how much I really did miss everything set in.

You took a step toward me. "I'm sorry about your parents," you said.

"Sorry about what?"

You blinked. "Leaving them behind, of course." You perched on the other end of the couch, your eyes piercing into mine. "I would have liked to have brought them . . . if I'd thought it would make you happier, that is."

I moved away, as far into the other end of the couch as I could.

You scratched at the wicker strands. "It's better like this, just you and me. It's the only way it could work."

I scanned the sky again, trying to work out my thoughts. I swallowed my fear.

"How long had you been planning it?"

You shrugged. "Awhile, two or three years. But I'd been watching you for longer than that."

"How long?"

"About six years."

"Since I was ten? You've been watching me since then?"

You nodded. "On and off."

"I don't believe you," I said. But something inside me was telling me to think about it. There was something there, at the back of my mind that, if I thought about it a little more, might make sense of all this.

I searched my memory, trying to find your face anywhere in it. There was nothing specific, but there were hazy, half-remembered things; like the man my friends saw once waiting outside the school gates, and that time in the park when I thought I saw someone watching in the bushes . . . the way Mum was paranoid about someone following her home. Was that you, I wondered? Had you been watching me that long? Surely not. But there was something else, too, something else I couldn't quite remember.

"Why me?" I whispered. "Why not some other poor girl?"

"You were you," you said. "You found me."

I held your gaze. "What do you mean?"

You looked at me curiously. When I didn't give you the

response you were after, you leaned across the couch toward me. There was an intensity in your eyes. "You don't remember? You don't remember meeting me that first time?" You shook your head slightly in amazement.

"Why should I?"

"I remember you." You moved your hand toward me like you wanted to touch me, your bottom lip quivering slightly. "I really remember you."

Your eyes were opened wide. I tucked my chin into my chest, away from them.

"It didn't happen," I said. My voice was shaky and soft, hardly there. "It isn't true."

You reached across to me and grabbed my shoulder. I felt your fingers dig into my skin, forcing me to look at you.

"It happened," you said. Your face was set, your eyes unblinking. "It's true. You just haven't remembered it yet." You stared hard at me, at my left eye and then my right. "But you will," you whispered.

After a moment, I heard you swallow. Then your eyes clouded over a little, and you let me go. I fell back against the couch. You stood up and turned away. I heard you in the kitchen, slamming cupboards. I was shaking; there were even goose bumps on my legs, though I wasn't cold.

<hr>

I don't know how long I sat there, just thinking. My eyes moved repeatedly across the land in that time, looking for anything . . . anything different that could lead to escape. Orange streaks began to thread into the blue of the sky, and the horizon glowed pink.

You came out, squinting at the sunset. You carried a glass of water in each hand. You hovered in the doorway for ages, looking at me, waiting for me to look back at you. When I didn't, you stepped toward the couch. You held one of the glasses out to me. I didn't take it, although I desperately wanted it. In the end you placed it near me on the floor and you stepped away, sipping from your own glass. You kept watching me. I think you were waiting for me to talk again. I don't know why; you didn't seem like the talking type. I watched the wind instead, picking up random grains of sand. It was so arbitrary where it dropped them.

"Who are you?"

The words were more my thoughts than a question. I didn't even realize I'd spoken them until I saw how you were struggling to answer me. Your face was frowning, your forehead lined. You sighed.

"Just Ty," you said. You sat on the edge of the couch and rubbed your fingertips against your eyebrows. In the intense orange of the sunset, your eyes looked lighter than ever. It seemed as if there were flecks of sand in them, too, grains flung there from the wind. "I come from here, I guess."

Your voice was soft and hesitant, so different from how it usually sounded. It was more like a piece of spinifex being blown about. I felt like I should lean forward to catch your words before they were blown away completely.

"You're Australian?"

You nodded. "S'pose. I was called Ty after the creek my parents fucked next to."

You glanced at me, checking for a reaction. I didn't give you one; I just waited for you to start talking again. I thought you might.

There was something about you then, a kind of pent-up energy that you wanted to release.

"Mum was real young when she had me," you continued. "But then, she and Dad were never really together anyway. Mum was from this posh English family. As soon as I was signed over to Dad, they all packed up overseas and tried to forget about me. So Dad moved me to a piece of land with a few hundred acres and a handful of cattle. That was life."

"What happened?"

I watched you shift on the couch arm, struggling to answer. I enjoyed you being uncomfortable. It made a change. And part of me thought I'd be able to use those answers against you when I was rescued and you were chucked in jail. You chewed at a thumbnail, watching the sunset.

"Dad did all right at first," you said. "Guess he wasn't completely fucked back then. He actually had people working for him, ringers and some lady to look after me . . . can't remember her name now." You broke off and tried to think about it. "Mrs. Gee or something." You raised your eyebrows at me. "Who cares, right?"

I shrugged.

"She was kind of my teacher, I s'pose. Her, and the oldfellas and ringers."

"Oldfellas?"

"Local aborigines, the guys who worked on Dad's farm: the proper owners of this place. They taught me about the land, Mrs. Gee tried to teach me arithmetic or some shit, and the rest of the farmhands taught me about liquor. Good education, eh?" You half smiled. "It was all right, though, running about out here."

It sounded weird to hear you talk so much; normally you only said a few words at a time. I'd never imagined that you'd have a story, too. Until that moment, you were just the kidnapper. You didn't have reasons for anything. You were stupid and evil and mentally ill. That was all. When you started talking, you started changing.

"Weren't there other kids around? When you were growing up?" You looked across at me sharply. But I liked the way my voice sounded angry and demanding and the way it made you hesitate for a moment. I liked that tiny amount of power it gave me.

You shook your head. I don't think you wanted to talk about this anymore, but now that I was finally talking to you again, you didn't want to ignore me, either.

"Nah, I didn't see another kid until I left," you said eventually. "I thought I was the only one in the world. I mean, Mrs. Gee told me there were others, but I didn't believe her." Your mouth twitched into what was almost a smile. "I used to think that I had this special power that kept me smaller than everyone else. I never thought I was younger than anyone, just smaller."

"You never played with other kids?"

"No, only the land."

"What about with your dad?"

You snorted. "He didn't play with anyone, not after Mum left."

I was silent as I thought. When I was young, I was surrounded by kids. Or was I? When I went to school I was, of course, but before then? When I really thought about it, I couldn't remember being around kids then, either. I'd been a sickly child, and Mum had kept me pretty close. Before me, she'd had a sort of break-down. That's what Dad told me once. She'd had a miscarriage, a couple, I think; she didn't want to lose me, too. I grimaced then as I realized that's exactly what had happened in the end. Mum *had* lost me, eventually.

I looked back at you, hating you again. You had drunk all your water and were just staring out with the empty glass in your hand. You stayed like that for ages before you spoke some more. You spoke so quietly that I actually did lean forward to catch your words.

"After a while, Dad started going to the city, for work and stuff," you said. "Started selling stock, though he didn't sell 'em for money, just did it for drink and drugs, things to help him forget. His mind changed then. He never walked his property, never really looked after his cattle . . . never looked for me, either."

You glanced down at your glass. It looked like you wanted to wander off again to get some more. I don't know why exactly, but suddenly I wanted to keep talking to you. Perhaps it was the boredom finally getting to me, or that need to connect with someone else . . . even if it did have to be you. I don't know. Maybe I just wanted to find holes in your story.

"What were you doing?" I asked quickly. "All this time your dad was away, you must have been doing something?"

You frowned, trying to figure me out. "Don't you believe me?" you said. You tapped the edge of your glass against the wicker as you thought. You shrugged. "Doesn't matter."

You pulled out your leaves and papers, and rolled a cigarette.

The crickets started up, and you'd smoked almost half of your roll-up before you spoke again.

"If you want to know what I did," you said, your voice thick, "I ran wild in the bush mostly, tried living like an oldfella. I got thin and sick and slept under the stars. No one saw me for days, weeks sometimes. Once, I was desperate and had to kill one of Dad's calves; didn't tell him, though." You grinned suddenly, and your face went young again. "Most of the time I just ate lizard . . . if I was lucky." You looked up at the sky as if you were searching in it. "I could paint pictures with the stars up there, too, I knew them that well. Connect-the-dots masterpieces."

I remembered the stars from when I'd tried to escape, that night in the Separates. There could be worse beds than that, if it weren't for the cold that came with it, that is.

"How did you find water?" I demanded.

"Easy. If you look for the plants, you can find water simple enough . . . like the spring in the Separates."

I thought about that clear little pool, and my fear of it containing the stomach-eating fish. "That's drinking water?" I asked.

You tilted your head toward the glass at my feet. "How else've you got that? Where do you think that pipe goes?" You gestured to the long pipe leading out from the house. "I laid that."

"I don't believe you."

"You never believe me."

You slid off the arm and onto the couch properly, nearer to me. I recoiled instantly, more from habit than anything. You laughed a little at that. You leaned back on the couch, but didn't try to get any closer. After a while, you started talking quietly again.

"Once Dad found the city, and all the rest of it, that was it. . . . The farm didn't recover. He forgot about the land, forgot about me, too, laid off the stockmen and Mrs. Gee. I saw him sometimes, on the nights when I slept in my bed, but I'm not sure he really saw me, what with the drink and drugs flowing through him. We stayed like that for a while. Then one day Dad just didn't come back from the city." You glanced quickly at my glass of water. "Do you want that?" you asked.

I looked down at the brownish water with the black bits floating on top. I shook my head. You leaned across me to grab it. I watched you drink it down, your Adam's apple working like a piston.

"What do you mean he didn't come back?"

You rubbed your lips together, making them both wet. "Never returned. Disappeared. Fucked off!"

"How old were you?"

"Dunno, really," you said. "I didn't have birthdays much. 'Bout eleven or so, maybe. Everyone else had long left the farm; it was just me on it then. It was about a year, though, before anyone else figured it out and came to catch me."

"Catch you?" I repeated. You shrugged sheepishly. "Didn't you want someone to look after you?"

"Nah, why would I? Did it better myself." Your eyes narrowed. "I kept them trying for ages, too. They tried everything: tracking me, bribery, the priest. In the end they caught me with a net, just like an animal. They were making all these soothing noises at me, too. They thought I couldn't speak at first, or speak

English at least. Maybe they thought I was an oldfella . . . I was pretty dark from the sun." You smiled a little from the memory.

"What did they do with you?"

Your eyes clouded quickly and your mouth went tight, as though you were angry with me for asking. "They took me to the city, shoved me in the back of a truck . . . you know, one of those ones they carry criminals in? They took me to this kids' home place. They gave me a room without a window, bursting with other kids. They wanted my name but I wouldn't tell them; I wouldn't tell them anything. So they called me Tom."

"Tom?"

"Yeah, for a few months. They decided how old I was, what I was going to wear. Because I didn't speak to them, they tried to make me a different person. . . . Wish they'd never caught me."

I wondered what would have happened if they hadn't. Would you be running around your dad's farm still, wilder than anything? Would you have lost your language eventually? But maybe that wouldn't have mattered to you.

"When did you start speaking again?"

"When they tried to get one of them shrinks on me. I set 'em straight pretty fast then." You shrugged. "I learned to fight pretty good in that place."

"But they found you out anyway?"

"They found out my name," you snapped. "After a while, they figured Mum had gone overseas and Dad had died in a pub. By then the farm had been carved up for his debts." You were still glaring at me, gripping the couch until it started to creak. "Nobody knew who I was," you added. "Not really. When I went to the city, my whole life started again, from the dirt up."

A deep crease had formed in the middle of your forehead. Your shoulders were drawn up, too, tense around your neck. I realized I was beginning to read you, to understand when you were tense or angry, or upset. You ran your hand across your brow, smoothing your crease marks. I leaned a little toward you.

"So, they kind of stole you, too," I said softly. I kept my nerve and held your gaze. Your eyes turned to slits. You knew exactly what I meant. They'd stolen you, just as you'd stolen me. "Am I your way of getting back at them all?"

You were quiet for a long time. But I didn't drop my gaze. Once I could see you weren't going to get mad at me, I felt pretty brave. Eventually it was you who had to look away first.

"No," you said. "It's not that. I've saved you from all that. Saved. Not stolen."

"I wish you hadn't."

"Don't say that."

You glanced back at me then, your eyes wide, almost pleading. "This place is better than Dad's," you said firmly. "Nobody's bought this land, not even us. And no one's going to want it, either. It's dying land . . . lonely land."

"Like me, then," I said.

"Yes, like you." You chewed the corner of your lip. "You both need saving."

That night I couldn't sleep. But there was nothing unusual about that. I stared at the ceiling and listened to the creaks and groans of the house. It sounded alive. It was a ginormous animal lying in the sand, and we were in its belly.

I thought of ways to kill you. I imagined the gurgling you'd make after I stuck something sharp into the side of your neck. I imagined the blood gushing out, flowing over my hands and staining the wooden floor. I imagined your blue eyes turning still and hard.

But those images didn't send me to sleep. So I thought of things I would say to my parents if I could see them again: apologies, mostly.

*I'm sorry I broke Mum's favorite vase.*
*I'm sorry you caught me drunk that day.*
*I'm sorry we were arguing in the airport.*
*I'm sorry I got abducted.*
*I'm sorry, I'm sorry, I'm sorry. . . .*

And then I was in the park. I tossed and turned, trying to get myself out of that dream, but it was too late.

I was walking fast. The smell of warm, musty earth was clinging to my nostrils . . . the remnants of a balmy summer's day. Gnats were hovering all around, getting caught in my hair and flying into my eyes.

He was there, only a few feet away. Gaining on me. Following. I heard the rub of his jeans, the thud of his footsteps. I picked up my pace. I looked around at the trees and the bushes, hoping for something I recognized, but the trees were thick and dark, with their leaves rustling, rustling.

He was so close I could hear his breathing, heavy with a summer cold. I took a wrong turn and headed toward the pond. He sniffed. He was behind me, talking to me, telling me to slow down. But I started to run. It was stupid, really; I *knew* this guy. And anyway, it's not as if there was anywhere to go out there on that pathway — only the pond. My feet slipped on the wood chips, my breathing quick. And the water was so close, approaching so fast.

His shadow crept up on me, overtook me, covered mine with its darkness. I started to turn, tried to think of something to say . . . about schoolwork, or Anna, or something.

Then he stopped. And I saw him. Only it wasn't *him* this time, it was *you*.

You were wearing the checkered shirt from the airport, your arms outstretched. Your hands were shaking.

"Please, Gemma," you were saying. "Please . . . don't."

But I turned away from you and ran straight into the pond. I let the water cover me as I sank down, down, into the cold, dark deepness, and my hair got tangled up and caught in the weeds.

---

There was a thudding sound coming from the veranda, a steady thump of something being hit. I swung open the wire mesh door and stood for a moment, my feet bare on the wood. The morning sunlight was softer that day, not quite so intense. I didn't have to wait the usual couple of seconds before my eyes adjusted.

You were to the left of me, in a tattered pair of shorts and a thin, holey undershirt. A punching bag was swinging between your fists and the air. I hadn't noticed it before, so perhaps you'd only just put it up. You were on your toes, bouncing slightly, hitting the bag hard with your bare fists. Your body tensed before the impact, as rigid as the rocks behind you. Lines of muscle stood out under your ribbed tank top. There was nothing soft about your body, nothing unnecessary. You grunted slightly as you hit the bag, the skin over your knuckles red.

I don't think you knew I was watching. Your face was so focused, every muscle in your body geared toward hitting. I shuddered, imagining you hitting those rock-fists into me, imagining the *crack!* of my ribs breaking . . . the dark stain and spread of bruises.

You kept punching until your undershirt changed color from your sweat. Then you steadied the punching bag and dragged your shirt up to your face to wipe your forehead. I caught a glimpse of your stomach, smooth and muscled, like ridges of sand. You moved to a metal pole attached to the side of the veranda. You fastened your hands around it, then pulled your chin up and lowered it slowly. Your biceps swelled with each lift, stretching your skin tight enough to snap. You were the strongest man I'd ever seen. If you decided to, you could kill me so easily. Just a little push from your hands and I'd be strangled; just a little punch and my brain would explode. There'd be nothing I could do. One blunt knife under a mattress was no match against you.

---

Later I held the knife I'd taken from the kitchen. I tested its sharpness by cutting a shallow line across my finger. I imagined it was your throat I was sliding it across. A slit of blood appeared, dropping down to stain the sheet. Then I leaned over to the wooden base and cut more notches into it. I figured about sixteen days had passed, but I made an extra one in case I'd got it wrong. Seventeen days.

You were there when I woke.

"Are you ready to see the Separates?" you asked. "I'll take you today."

I frowned. "I've seen them."

I rolled over, trying to forget about my failed escape attempt, but you moved around the bed so you could see me wherever I turned. You were smiling as you watched me.

"You haven't seen them properly," you said. "Not with me."

Then you left. When I got up, quite a long time later, you were still waiting in the kitchen. When you saw me, you opened the door.

"Come on," you said.

So I followed you. I don't know why really. I could say it was because I had nothing else to do except stare at four walls, or that I wanted to try escaping again, but I think there was more to it than that. When I was trapped in the house, it felt like I'd already died. At least when I was with you, it felt like my life mattered somehow. . . . No, that's not really it; it felt like my life was being noticed. It sounds weird, I know, but I could tell that you liked having me around. And that was better than the alternative, that feeling of emptiness that threatened to drown me every hour of being in that house.

You led the way through the sand. At the fence you stopped to pull back the opening. You held the chicken wire away for me to step through. We walked in silence until we got to the edge of the pathway. You waited, your hand resting against the trunk of one of the trees that grew around the edge of the rocks. I hung back a little, keeping a few feet between us.

"You're not scared?" you asked. "Of going in?"

"Should I be?" I looked away. "What are you going to do?"

"Nothing, it's just . . ." You shook your head quickly. "One of Dad's stockmen told me something once. He told me there were spirits in the rocks near here, that the rocks had a reason for being, and a purpose. . . . He said that if I didn't respect them, they would fall down and crush me. Scared me shitless, those stories." You took a couple of steps until you were standing at the start of the pathway. You looked up at the boulders towering above you. "Since then I always greet these rocks first, before I enter. Take a moment to let them know I'm here."

You touched the rocks with your finger, scraping off a little dust. Then you rubbed it between your thumb and forefinger before touching your lip. You glanced back at me before you started down the path.

After a second or two, I followed. I kept a good distance. My legs trembled a little, making me unsteady. Again I held my palms out against those huge walls, and walked with my legs on either side of the pipe. I didn't like the low moaning of the wind whistling through. And I hated that the pathway into those rocks seemed to be the only way out, too. I felt like I was walking into a trap.

You went quickly, and were already leaning against a rough-barked tree when I got to the clearing. You were circling something small around your palm.

"Desert walnut," you said.

You held it out to me. It felt as tough as a small stone; it looked like one, too. I tapped my nail against its hard shell.

"They talk when they're cooked," you said. "When their shells pop in the fire, they're speaking to you. . . . That's what people say. The first time I cooked these nuts, I thought it was the spirits from the rocks, telling me I was about to die."

You smiled crookedly. Then you took the nut back and placed it in your pocket. You slapped your hand against the tree's bark again as you passed.

"Turtujarti . . . gives you sweets, salt, nuts . . . shelter, too. She's your friend out here if anything is."

You moved across the clearing toward the two chicken cages. You pulled open the lid of the main cage and placed a handful of seeds and berries in the corner, then checked their water supply. The chickens flocked to the food. You looked for eggs, tutting when you couldn't find any.

"They're not healthy yet," you murmured. "Still unsettled from the drive."

You ran your hand down their bodies, talking softly to them. I looked at the way your fingers felt gently about their necks. Just a little more pressure from your strong hands and you would strangle them. You shut the lid. I stuck my finger through the cage and touched the feathers of the orangey one.

You checked the plants behind the chicken cages next.

"Minyirli, yupuna, bush tomato . . ." You spoke to them all like friends, naming them for me. You turned over their leaves and fruits, picking off insects.

Then you stood and followed the pipe toward the pool.

You stepped confidently and noisily through the longer, scrubby grasses.

"Are there snakes?" I asked.

You nodded. "But if you make enough noise, they'll go away. They're scared, really."

I didn't want to, but I followed closer to you then. Every twig on the ground looked like a snake to me, until you stepped on them and snapped them.

At the pool, you leaned up against the tree arm that had caught me last time. You ran your hand over its smooth skin.

"Big Red," you said, as if you were introducing me. "This is the fella that helps filter the shit from our water."

You knelt down to the pool and dipped your hand under the surface, following the pipe down. Then, in one swift movement, you took your shirt off.

"Want a swim?" you asked. "I need to check the spring."

I shook my head quickly, forcing my eyes away from your chest. Every inch was firm and brown. I'd never seen anyone so toned, so perfect, before, but I knew this wasn't a good thing, your strength, and it made my heart falter as I thought about what you could do with it. I looked down at the ground instead. There were large black ants crawling around and over my boots. I shook one off as it tried to crawl up onto my leg.

"You can sit there," you said. You nodded toward the ants. "They probably won't bite."

You waded out into the pool. I glanced at you once more before you dived down under the surface. Your back was tanned and straight, muscles rippling with each movement.

Another ant tried to crawl onto my skin, but I flicked it away. A bird above me somewhere made a cry like a witch's cackle. Other than that, it was dead quiet.

On the way back, the only sound was our steps on the sand. I needed something to break through the quiet, the stillness of that place.

"Can I feed the chickens?" I asked. "Sometimes?"

You looked me over pretty slowly, sort of laughed, then nodded a little.

"Why not?" you said. "Maybe you'll make 'em lay."

Your shirt was draped across your shoulders, your body still wet from the pool. Beads of water clung to your skin. As we walked back to the house, I went ahead. I didn't want you to see me looking at you.

———————

Day Eighteen. You weren't waiting when I got up. I opened the kitchen door and sat on the makeshift step. I looked out at the sand and the sand and the sand. I waited; for what, I don't know. The day got hotter around me. The flies whined and buzzed about my ears. A heat haze blurred the sky.

Then, quite suddenly, a flock of tiny chattering things flew past. They pinged and squeaked, like children stepping on their plastic toys. I tried to focus on the individuals within the flock. Each bird was about the size of my clenched fist, with a gray back and a bloodred beak. They wheeled and circled around the house for a while before zipping toward the Separates. I waited for ages after that, hoping they'd return.

The next day you were waiting for me.

"Let's go," you said.

I followed. I was beginning to hate the silence of that house, beginning to hate the passive depression I was sinking into. But you didn't walk toward the Separates. Instead, you went toward the outbuildings. I hung back.

"I don't want to go in," I said when you stopped beside the doorway you'd shoved me through before.

"Come on," you said. "I need to show this to you."

You opened the door and went inside. I stood on the crate step and looked in from the doorway. You walked to the far end of the room and pulled open the curtains. Sunlight flooded in, illuminating the colors in that room: all the sand and flowers and leaves and paint. It looked like a mess at first, with everything strewn everywhere. Immediately my eyes scanned for anything that could harm me. The only thing I saw was a pile of rocks in one corner. As you walked over to them, I felt myself tense, ready to run.

But you didn't pick them up. Instead you unscrewed your hip flask and poured drops of water onto the rocks. You scraped off parts of their wet surface onto a small saucer, spitting and mixing in your saliva to make a dark brown paste.

"What are you doing?" I asked.

"Making paint."

There was a woven grass basket near me, containing leaves, berries, and flowers. You walked over and carefully picked out some small red berries. You ground them into a red paste. You worked quickly and methodically, taking different colored bits of the environment and turning them into paint. I could feel the sun starting to burn the back of my neck so I took a step inside the painting shed and leaned against the wall.

You sat, folding your bare legs in front of you. You took a paintbrush from behind the rocks, dipped it into a rusty-colored paste, and started painting your foot. You painted long thin lines, making your skin like the texture of tree bark. You frowned as you focused. I wasn't scared of you with your head down, concentrating, but I still watched you carefully. Right then, I almost believed you when you'd said you wouldn't do anything to me.

"How long are you going to keep me for?" I asked quietly.

You didn't look up from your painting. "I've told you," you said. "I'm keeping you forever."

I didn't believe you. How could I? If I'd let myself believe that, then I might as well have fallen down dead right then. I sighed. It was approaching the middle of the day, the time where it became impossibly hot, the time when to even walk a few feet became an Olympic event. I kept watching you.

Soon the paint on your foot stretched around your ankles and lower legs. You painted leaves on your shins and red, spiky grasses stretching up the backs of your calves. You smiled as you noticed me still watching.

"You don't remember meeting me, do you, that first time?" you asked.

"Why should I?" I said. "It didn't happen."

You finished painting your spikes, then filled the space between them with black charcoal.

"It was Easter," you began. "Spring. There was sunlight hanging in the branches. It wasn't cold; primroses were already in the hedges. You'd gone to the park with your parents."

"What park?"

"Prince's Park. The one at the end of your street."

I slid down the wall, once again shocked by what you knew about me. Your eyes were searching into mine, refusing to believe that I couldn't remember. You spoke slowly, as if by doing so you were forcing the memory into my head.

"Your parents were reading papers on a bench, in front of the rhododendrons. They'd brought a scooter for you to play with, but you left it lying on the grass. Instead you went into the flower beds nearby. I could hear you, talking to the daffodils and tulips, whispering to the fairies that lived inside their petals. Each separate flower had a different family inside it."

I hugged my legs tight to me. No one knew this. I hadn't even told Anna about these games. You noticed my shock, and looked a little smug when you continued.

"You walked carefully through the flower bed, greeting each flower family . . . Moses, Patel, Smith. I found out later they were surnames from kids in your school. Anyway, you walked right through until you ducked under the heavy rhododendron buds and came into the bushes . . . *my* bushes. You found me there, curled up with my swag and half a bottle of booze, half-wasted, probably. But I'd been watching you, listening. I'd liked your little tales." You smiled, remembering. "You asked me if I was looking for Easter eggs. We talked — you told me about your fairies and their flower houses. I told you about the Min Mins: the spirits who live in the trees around here and try to steal lost children. And you weren't scared, like most people were of me back then. . . . You just looked at me like a regular person. I liked that."

You were quiet as you drew an egg shape onto your thigh, then put little dots of brown paint in the middle.

"The robin's egg I gave you," you said, pointing at it. "I'd found it under an oak tree. It had a hole at the top where I'd sucked the yolk through earlier that day. I don't know why I'd been keeping it . . . keeping it for you, I guess." While I watched, you colored in the egg shape with a light sandstone color. "Fierce birds, robins," you said. "They'll defend their home to the death."

I could feel my heart racing. I knew this memory. Of course I did. But how did you?

"That was a tramp in those bushes," I said. "It was somebody thin and old and hairy and probably deranged. It wasn't you."

You smiled. "You said my roof of pink flowers was the nicest ceiling you'd ever seen."

"No! That was just a tramp I stumbled across. Not you. You've got it wrong."

You chewed on the corner of your thumb. "It's amazing what living on the streets in a city can do." You bit off a piece of your nail and spat it aside. "Anyway, you were a child then; I'd look old to you regardless, even if I was barely an adult myself."

I wiped my palms over my T-shirt. Every part of me felt clammy. You noticed, but you kept going anyway, enjoying my confusion.

"You said it was the best Easter egg you'd ever found. You carried it in your hand like it was the most precious thing. It reminded me of what I used to be like, when I lived out here. . . . It reminded me of finding something wild and knowing it was important somehow, to something." You drew another circle over your knee, then filled it in with specks. "It made me realize where I belonged . . . not in a city park with cheap store-bought spirits, but out here in the land I knew, with the real ones." You covered your kneecap with more circles, still not looking at me. "The next day I found the nest the robin's egg had come from. It was abandoned and tattered, but I knew you'd want it. Finding that, finding you . . . it was a sign."

"What do you mean 'sign'?" My throat had become so tight it was hard to get the words out. Because I did remember a robin's nest. I'd found it on my windowsill early one morning. I'd never known where it had come from. I tried to swallow. You were watching me, nodding slightly at something you saw in my expression.

"A sign that a person could do something different . . . ," you continued. "That they could be hooked by a drug more wild than alcohol. I got thinking about what I really wanted then, from life. And this is it . . . painting the land, living here, being free . . ." You swept your hand around the room. A fleck of color flicked from your paintbrush and landed somewhere. "So, meeting you . . . I guess it was the first step to making all this happen. . . . I got a job, learned to build, researched . . ."

A small, tight sound came out of my throat, stopping you midsentence. I clenched my fist against the floor, digging my knuckles into the wood.

"You're sick," I hissed. "You were obsessed with a ten-year-old girl, then abducted her six years later? What kind of freak . . . ?"

"No." Your mouth tightened. "That's not how it happened. I wasn't obsessed. . . ." Your face was set and hard, a murderer's face. "You don't know the whole story."

"I don't want to know."

You let the paintbrush clatter to the ground and crossed the room in three strides. I crawled back along the floor, toward the door. But you bent down and grabbed my leg.

"Let me go!"

You pulled me to you. "I'm not letting you go, and you will learn something about me." Your voice was even and steady, your jaw tense. I could smell the sour earth scent of your breath, feel your fingers tight around me. "I'm not a monster," you growled. "You were a child then. The moment I knew I wanted you came later." You blinked and looked away, suddenly hesitant.

I tried again to get free. I kicked out at your kneecap. But you pressed my arms against my sides like I was some sort of bird, stopping my flight.

"I've watched you grow up," you said.

I wriggled my shoulders. But you were so strong I could hardly move.

"Each day your parents pushed you into being like them," you continued, "pushed you into a meaningless life. You didn't want that, I know you didn't."

"What do you know about my parents?" I shouted.

You blinked again. "Everything."

I gathered saliva in my mouth. I spat it at you. "You're a liar," I said.

Your eyes narrowed as you felt the spit slide down your cheek. Your fingers gripped tighter. They were so tight around me, I thought my ribs were about to crack. My breath came in a rasp. But you still held me there, glowering.

"I don't lie," you said. "It's just the way things are."

The spit reached your chin, and you let me go to wipe it. I was up immediately and backing toward the door. But you turned anyway, ignoring me. You picked up the paintbrush and swept quick, angry streaks onto the back of your hand. For that moment, your blue eyes looked superhuman. The intensity of them made me take another step toward the door. But I wasn't finished yet. There was something else I needed to find out. I willed my legs to stop shaking. I clenched my fist, tightening it to control my fear.

"How do you know all this?" I glared at you, wanting you to drop dead from the power of my gaze alone. Then I turned around and slammed my fist into the wall. "You can't know all this!"

I could feel the tears in my eyes wanting to escape. The silence hung like the heat. Then you stood and came toward me.

"I've watched you a long time," you explained. "I was curious, nothing more. It was just, you were like me, when I was young . . . you never seemed to fit in." You sighed and moved your hand across your eyebrows. "Can't you remember me being there, ever?"

"Of course I can't! It's all just stupid lies." I slammed my fist into the wall again, flinching as I saw how red and raw my knuckles were turning.

"Gem," you said calmly, "I know you, I've seen you . . . every day."

I clenched my teeth, unable to look at you. I thought about

the times I'd walked around my house naked, knowing no one was home. I thought about when Matthew Rigoni came back with me after we'd got tipsy in the park.

"What did you see?" I muttered. *"How?"*

You shrugged. "The oak tree near your bedroom, the window in the garage, the neighbor's house when they were in Greece, and they were in Greece a lot . . . and the park, of course. It's easier than you think."

Your face was close. You were near enough to slap. Jesus, I wanted to. I wanted to slap and kick and punch you until you were a piece of lifeless shit on the floor. I wanted you to feel how I felt right then. But you stepped even closer to me. You reached out and moved my hand away from the wall. You ran your thumb over the sore, flapping bits of skin. My hand quivered immediately and I curled my fingers tighter.

"Don't touch me," I snarled.

You stepped back. "I know who you are, Gem."

I screamed then, and rammed my fist into your stomach. Hard. I drew back and punched you again. I threw all my weight against you, over and over, bashing myself into your solid, stiff chest. I didn't care what you did to me then. I just wanted to hurt you. But you didn't even seem to notice. You just grabbed my arm and held it behind my back, twisting it. You put your lips so close to my ear that, if I moved, I touched them.

"I know what it was like," you whispered, ". . . the nights you were in your parents' big house all alone, your parents working so late . . . your friends getting smashed off their asses in the park, and you not knowing whether to join them. Josh Holmes tapping on your bedroom window at one in the morning . . ." You let my arm fall to my side. "Were you really happy in the city?"

"Fuck off!"

You backed off a step. "I'm only asking," you said. "Did you really have a perfect life? Do you really miss it . . . your parents, your friends, any of it?"

You held my gaze. I nodded. "Course I do." But the words sounded like a cough.

You went back to where you'd been painting. I wrapped my left hand around my sore knuckles and tried to calm down. I hadn't realized how much I was shaking. You dipped a new brush into a saucer of green paint and started putting patterns on your toes.

"You know I'm right," you said. "Your parents are assholes. Their main concern is making money, making their house look like something out of magazine, and getting mentioned in the society pages. They were molding you all the way, too, training you to be a little version of them. I saved you from that."

"No!" I rammed my jaw shut, pressing my teeth into each other hard enough to break.

You shrugged at my reaction. "What? I've heard you say it to their face enough times."

"I'm their daughter."

"So?"

"I can."

You wiped the brush against your shorts, cleaning it. "Face it, Gem, they loved work and expensive things and influential friends more than you. They only loved you when you acted like them."

"That's crap."

You raised an eyebrow. "They missed that awards night at your school so they could pick up a new car instead."

"I wasn't getting an award."

"But you still had to go, and everyone else's parents were there."

"So were you, by the sounds of it."

"Course." You shrugged. You put tiny green dots on the base of your big toe. "But I can understand why they were like that. They just wanted recognition; they wanted to fit in . . . it's what most people want."

"Except freaks like you," I spat back.

Your eyes flashed. "I want freedom," you said simply. "You don't get freedom in your parents' lives, you just get fucked." The veins were pulsing in your throat. You swallowed, slowly, watching me. "I saw things you didn't see, remember?" you said quietly, your fingers tight around your paintbrush. "I heard conversations you never heard."

I slammed my hands over my ears. "You're trying to poison me," I whispered. "Trying to tell me you know my life better than I do."

"Maybe I do. Shall I tell you about it?" You rose, your face rigidly smooth. "First, I know your parents want to move away, without you . . . your mum talked to your dad about it. She said you could move into one of your school's dorms."

"That's not true," I whispered.

"OK then, what about Ben?"

"What about him?"

"Anna knew how you felt about him, she didn't like it . . . she didn't trust you because of it."

"No."

"And Josh Holmes?"

My breath caught in surprise.

"I know exactly what he wanted to do to you, how far he wanted to go. . . . I saw him follow you around, saw his creepy little text messages."

"You're lying."

You held my gaze. "Haven't I been right so far?"

I took a couple of steps backward until I felt the wall behind me. I steadied myself against it. That was the second time you'd mentioned Josh.

"He liked you, you know. I mean *really* liked you. He told Anna how much he wanted you."

"You followed him, too?"

"I followed everyone." You turned away, went back to your painting. "You didn't ever have to worry about Josh, though. Not really. I would have smashed his brains in before he'd even opened his fly."

I shook my head, thoughts reeling all over the place. I wished you had smashed Josh's brains in . . . then you would've been in prison, Josh would've been in the hospital, and I would've been at home. Perfect. I sank down against the wall, trying to work it all out. I still wanted to think that you were talking shit. But all this, all this you knew, it added up. I closed my eyes, wanting to shut you out forever.

Then I thought of something. I wondered if anyone had

suspected Josh when I went missing. He might have been the obvious suspect, although I doubt anyone would think he'd go to all the trouble you did to steal me. Perhaps he was interviewed, the police thinking he was a friend of mine, or a boyfriend. Perhaps they'd arrested him. I shuddered: Even though he was thousands of miles away, thinking about Josh still gave me the creeps . . . thinking about him playing the concerned friend in particular.

"Where did you live?" I asked.

"Kelvin Grove."

"You lived in the shelter?"

Your eyes flicked to mine. "Perhaps, for a time."

"That's near where Josh lives."

"I know." You didn't look up when you spoke, just kept focusing on painting. "Do you think he should have teamed up with me?" You laughed a little. "He might have had more luck catching you with me around."

"Did you watch him?"

"Of course."

"Talk to him?"

"Once."

"And . . . ?"

I stiffened, despite myself, anxious about what you might have said, or done.

"I said I was your guardian angel."

"You actually spoke to him, face-to-face?" My mind was racing overtime, thinking that if Josh had seen you, if he could describe you to the police, then that would have to be a lead. They could draw up one of those criminal sketches and stick your face on BBC's *Crimewatch*. They'd find you, somehow. They'd find us.

I thought about Josh a little more carefully, tried to figure him out. He was pretty gutless, but I didn't think he was dishonest. He wouldn't want to be a suspect. But would he come forward? At least he could describe your height, your voice, something. Right then he seemed like my only hope. It was strange to think of someone I hated as an only hope like that.

"They'll find me, you know," I said. "Eventually. You won't keep me forever."

Your forehead wrinkled a bit and you stopped painting.

"Or maybe you'll just let me go?" I continued. "Perhaps you'll get bored of all this?" I tried keeping my voice casual-sounding, trying a different tactic. "You know, I can get help for you, or money. Dad knows people, lots of people . . . doctors, lawyers . . ."

You didn't let me finish. You were up in a second. "You think that's what I want?" Your voice cracked. Then you pointed the paintbrush at me. "Do your hand now," you said firmly. It wasn't a request. You pushed a saucer of brown-earth paint toward me. I saw the pulse in your throat throbbing, your jaw tense. "Paint yourself. Now."

I moved my head into a tiny shake. "No," I whispered.

You pressed the paintbrush against my skin. "I want you to draw onto your hand," you said slowly, enunciating each word carefully. "Just like me."

When I didn't move, you leaned toward me and covered my right hand with yours, the paintbrush between your finger and thumb, your grip tight and rough. My hand crumpled like a piece of wastepaper. You were crushing me so hard, as though my skin were jelly. You moved the brush to the back of my left hand. A blob of cold, watery paint fell off onto my skin.

"No," I said again.

I wrenched my hand from your grasp. I tipped over the brown paint. It bled onto your foot, covering your patterns there.

"You little . . ."

You raised your arm, biting back the word "bitch." I shrunk away, watching your fist. But you kicked the fallen saucer, smashing it against the wall. Your eyes were iridescently mad. You wanted to hit me. Instead, you smiled. Or tried to. It was like your eyes and your smile were fighting each other. Anger versus control. Your clenched fist shaking.

"Shall we go for a drive tomorrow?" Your voice was singsongy and falsely happy, but your eyes were hard. "Maybe you can learn to appreciate all this? If you're lucky, perhaps we'll catch a camel."

You didn't wait for a response. Instead, you left me alone in your painting shed, the spilled paint seeping around me. I sat there, amid that sea of brown, shaking. It was a long time before I followed you back into the house.

———————⚡———————

There's a thing murderers always do in horror films: take their victims out on a long drive to a stunning location before they creatively pull them apart. It's in all the famous films, all the ones with murderers in the middle of nowhere anyway. When you woke me that morning, that day after you'd nearly hit me, I thought about that.

"We're going on a drive," you said. "To catch a camel."

It was very early. I could tell by the pale pinkish-white light and the cool in the air. I got dressed and put the knife into the pocket of my shorts. I could hear you moving and creaking around the house. Then you went outside and started the car. You were surrounding me with noise. I wasn't used to it. I took my time getting ready. I knew two things: On the one hand, a trip like this could mean a greater opportunity for escape. On the other, it might mean I'd never return.

You were loading the car, packing box after box of food and equipment. I didn't want you to flip out again, like the night before. So I decided I'd talk.

"Where are you going?" I asked.

"The middle of nowhere."

"I thought this was it."

"Nah." You shook your head. "This is just the edge." I watched you coil a rope into a tight circle and lay it on top of a cooler. You reached for another rope, started to coil that, too. "I'm not leaving you behind, you know."

You slotted three huge containers of water into the trunk, puffing as you lifted them in.

"How long you going for?"

"Just a day, but you never know out there . . . could be a sandstorm, fire, anything." You patted the last container. "Anyway, the camel will need water."

"I thought they carried that on their back."

You shook your head. "Fat."

"What?"

"They carry fat there . . . strength reserves. They need water like any other animal."

You tried to slot a bucket into the trunk, but it wouldn't fit. I pictured myself lying underneath everything: contorted, squashed, suffocated. It made me shake a little. I went around to the front instead. You stuck your head around the side of the car and kept an eye on me.

"This time the front seat's all yours," you called.

I opened the door, but I didn't get in. Inside, there was a musty smell: dirty, stale, and unlived in. Fine red dust covered everything. It looked like the car hadn't been used for fifty years. It freaked me out, made me wonder whether I'd been in the house with you for longer than I'd thought. The dust had even settled on the scrunched-up chocolate wrappers on the floor. It would be all over my shorts when I got out . . . *if* I got out.

The key wasn't in the ignition. I wondered if it was hidden somewhere else in the car, covered in so much dust it was impossible to see. I reached into the car and moved things around, vaguely hoping to find it. I turned the rearview mirror so that I could watch you. You were moving fast, loading things into the trunk, then taking them out and loading them in again in a better position. I could hear you humming something tuneless. You were happy, excited even.

When you'd finished, you came to see me. With your mouth smiling and your eyes crinkled at the corners, you looked a little like how you'd looked at the airport three weeks ago; almost handsome. I had to turn and look at the ground. It made me feel sick then, thinking of you like that.

"I don't want to go," I said.

"Why not? I thought you wanted to go someplace else."

"Not with you. Not with all that stuff you have in the back."

You leaned against the car. "Well, we could walk it if you like, but we'd be gone for weeks. We'd have to live off the land — that means eating lizards for food and frogs for water. Are you ready for that?"

I shook my head, no escape option there. Besides, the thought of walking with you out in the wilderness was worse than being with you near the house. I remembered what the teachers had told us on field trips: *If you get lost, stay where you are, someone will find you eventually.* Perhaps there was more chance of rescue where I was.

"I thought you wanted to catch a camel," you tried again.

"No."

"*I* want to."

"Well, *you* go, then."

You laughed. "I want your beautiful face where I can see it. Come on."

I stayed where I was. You sighed, and tapped the side of the car as you tried to figure me out.

"You're not still worried I'm going to hurt you, are you?"

I kept quiet, kept looking at the sand. You walked around the car so that you were standing beside me. "Look, I thought you understood this now. . . . I'm not going to do anything to you, not like that." You squatted so you were looking up at me. "Whatever you think of me, your body, well, it's yours . . . your choice what to do with it."

"You wouldn't let me kill myself."

"That's different. You weren't thinking straight."

"Because you drugged me!"

"I had to." You face wrinkled as you looked toward the sun. "Look, I'm sorry. I didn't realize all this would be so hard."

You were frowning into the horizon. I wanted to ask what

you meant by "all this." I wanted to ask whether you thought kidnapping me would be as easy as a walk in the park. But you turned quickly and stared at me.

"I promise I won't hurt you," you said.

"How do I know you're not lying?"

"You'll have to trust me, I guess. You're with me now, so you kind of have to."

I avoided your gaze. "I don't *have* to do anything," I whispered.

"I know that," you said gruffly. "But sometime you might want to." You picked up a handful of sand. "Especially when it will be exciting." You opened your fist and showed me. "Look, I'll swear on this that I won't do anything. How's that?"

"That's a crap thing to swear on, a piece of dirt."

"This sand is older and truer than everything . . . surely that's the best thing to swear on."

I snorted.

"It's truer than us," you said softly. You let it go and wiped your hands together. Then you pressed your palms to the earth, and stood. "Come on," you said. "Let's find a camel." You pulled your shirt up and wiped dust from your forehead. Your shirt turned red instantly.

"Are you going near a town?"

"Not nearer than this."

I swatted at a fly buzzing around my face.

"But I'm going near other things." You leaned against the car. "Better things."

Another fly was crawling around my knee, its legs itching my skin. "You won't do anything to me," I said quietly.

"Relax. I promise."

You held open the car door. You grinned your thanks as I stepped in. You shut it after me. My head spun. I wound my window down and a pile of dust fell on me. You got in and wound your window down, too. I shuffled away from you, as far as I could without jumping out.

"I guess you want me to put my seat belt on? Or would you rather just tie me to the seat?"

You shrugged. "Whatever. I've got rope in the trunk if you want, lots of it."

You laughed out loud then. It was a sound you didn't make very often and a sound that didn't suit you. It was too abandoned. Perhaps the wildness of it shocked you, too, because it didn't last very long. You quickly closed your mouth and stared back through the windshield.

You revved the engine and we pulled away from the house, making our own track through the dirt. I could feel the sweat forming in the palms of my hands, at the back of my neck. I rested my head on the door frame and took a big breath of the dry breeze rushing past. My mouth filled with dust.

---

The ground was rough and it jolted me around. You didn't drive fast; I don't think it was possible on that shrubby, soft land. The wheels spun through the sandier parts, and you revved the engine hard to get out of them. You stopped a couple of times to pull grass from the radiator. I soon got a headache. There was dust in my eyes and ears. A small desert had settled inside my mouth. I reached for the radio.

"Doesn't work," you said immediately.

I turned it on anyway. Only a faint hiss came out.

"Told you. We'll have to sing instead. Can you sing?" You were looking at me, genuinely interested.

"I joined the choir for six months in seventh grade. Don't you know that already?"

You shrugged. "I wasn't around all your life. I had to get money. Sometimes I was here, getting this ready."

You flung your hand toward the collection of buildings disappearing behind us in a cloud of stirred-up sand.

"Did you really build all that?" I asked.

"Sure did," you said proudly.

"I don't believe you. There must have been something here first."

"No way." You frowned. "I built it all."

I couldn't help looking at you scornfully.

"Well, OK, maybe there was an old farm building or something. . . . I did the rest."

"How?"

"Slowly."

"How did you get the money for materials?"

You smiled mysteriously. "Quickly."

"Tell me."

You shrugged. "Another time."

You turned back to the front, scanning the land.

"Do you know how long I've been here?" I asked.

"A vague idea."

The car slowed again as it hit another thick patch of sand. I thumped my head back hard against the seat, suddenly frustrated by it all. "I think it's my twenty-first day, but I'm not even sure. . . ."

I bit my words back quickly, looking at your wide grin, instantly wishing I hadn't told you.

"We should celebrate, then," you exclaimed.

I swallowed, cringing inside. "What do you mean?"

The car tipped down onto stonier ground. As you felt the change in texture, you pressed your foot flat and spun the wheel. The back of the car twisted sideways, the engine groaning as the wheels struggled to keep a grip. You started laughing as I was flung into your shoulder. I saw sand and spinifex spin past in a blur. I scrabbled frantically for something to hold on to.

"Whoo-hoo!" you screamed.

As the car twisted again, you spun the wheel the other way. I was pushed into the door this time. I stuck my arm out the window and clung on to it. Clouds of dust flew up and into my face but I could hear you, still laughing, as you wrenched the hand brake and we skidded to a violent stop. Your eyes were shining as you rested your cheek against the steering wheel.

"What are you doing?" I shouted.

"Having fun? Celebrating?" You looked out at the openness, grinning. "I mean, no one's going to stop us, are they?"

I looked out, too, noticing the giant skid marks cutting through the untouched land behind us. "It doesn't mean you have to kill me," I said, immediately regretting my choice of words. When I looked back at you, you were thoughtful, your eyes sad.

"Just want you to have a little fun."

I snorted. "Then you should have left me in England."

When you took off, more gently that time, I looked at what you did. You stuck your left foot down on the clutch and put the stick shift nearest you into first gear. You didn't touch the other stick. As you eased off, you pressed down on the accelerator. Dad had tried teaching me to drive once, in an abandoned railway yard behind the supermarket, but after I'd scratched his Mercedes along a hedge, he hadn't tried again. You saw me watching.

"You wanna learn?"

You laughed, and shook your head slightly before pressing your foot flat to the floor again. My head stuck to the headrest and sand spurted everywhere. Some of it came through the window and settled in my lap. When the speedometer hit seventy, you yelled for me to pull the hand brake. There was a mad grin on your face as the tires snaked and skidded through the sand. I started screaming for you to stop.

"Pull the hand brake, then!"

I put my hand on the hand brake and pulled. Immediately, the car swung hard in an arc. I'm sure it went up on two wheels for a second or two. I was flung so hard into you that I couldn't move away. The warmth of your shoulder slammed up against my forehead, and your body vibrated as you laughed.

———————

We'd been driving for over two hours. I'd been looking for signs of a town, signs of anything. In all that time, there wasn't even a road. It seemed crazy to drive for so long and to still be nowhere. Sure, the scenery had changed a bit during the journey; it had gone from being scrubby and pebbly and flat to being sandier and redder. Instead of the knee-high spinifex bushes, there were more spindly blackened trees. There was the occasional green splash of a eucalyptus, and jagged rocks pierced through the landscape like spears. There were other mounds, too, pointing up like crooked red fingers.

"Termite mounds," you said.

It was nothing like being in England. When Dad drove us west for two hours last year we'd ended up in Wales, another country. But there, in that desert, two hours was like driving farther into fire. The more we drove, the hotter and redder it became and the more I feared I'd never be able to get out.

You pulled up slowly, near a small splattering of trees. "See 'em?" you asked.

"See what?"

"Them! Right there!" You pointed at the trees. "Look for when their ears move, then you'll see them."

I looked at the trees. Suddenly, something twitched. An ear. I traced it down till I found the head and the long nose. I saw its big brown eyes, closing in the heat.

"Kangaroos," I said.

You nodded, grinned a little. "Tasty ladies."

"What?"

You pointed your first two fingers like a gun and, resting your arm on the steering wheel, you mimed it going off.

"You're going to shoot them?"

"One of those flyers would taste good in my stew, don't you think?"

I swallowed. I didn't know you had a gun in the car. It scared me. You shifted in your seat toward me, thinking I was upset about what you'd said about the 'roos.

"It's OK," you said. "I won't shoot them, you know. We have plenty of food."

I looked back at the three of them. The nearest kangaroo was licking the hair on her forearms.

"She's keeping cool," you said. "Her blood vessels are near the surface of her skin and she licks them to lower her body temperature. Pretty good method, right?"

You licked the back of your hand as if to try it for yourself, then scrunched your face at the taste. You smiled crookedly. Just then, one of the 'roos reached up to nibble a low-hanging leaf.

"Aren't they thirsty?" I asked, aware the dryness in my own throat.

You shook your head. "Don't need water, or much of it; they get moisture from the trees."

You were smiling as you watched them, with a look on your face that I recognized. It was like you wanted something, needed something, from the kangaroos, too.

"Bye, pretty ladies," you said as you eased the car away.

We drove on without speaking. I watched you from time to time. Your eyes were continuously scanning the land, never content with watching the sand in front of the windshield.

"How do you know where you're going?" I asked.

"I follow the way the sand's been blown. I look for markers."

"Do you know how to get back?"

You nodded absently. "Course."

"How?"

"It's got stories, this land. It sings."

"I'd rather have the radio."

"Nah, Gem, I'm serious. There are songs out here, the oldfellas know 'em, I know some of them . . . they're like maps, they help you find the way. You sing 'em and they show you the landmarks. There's a whole silent music out here: dirt music."

I ignored you and stared at the horizon instead. You didn't speak again. You could have been thinking about the land singing or, just as easily, something more sinister. Your face revealed nothing. I'd never imagined what kidnappers thought about before. I mean, who does? Did you think about your family? The places you left behind? What exactly did you think about me?

My stomach flipped when I imagined that and I presumed the worst. The more we drove, and the more I thought about what you could be thinking, the tenser I got. If you killed me then, out there in the middle of nowhere, no one would know. No one would dig for a body in that endlessness. It would be like trying to find a certain grain of sand.

You stopped the car with a skid. "Camels," you said. You pointed at something that looked more like specks on the windshield than a bunch of large animals. I raised my hand to shield my eyes. You leaned across me to the glove compartment, then dropped binoculars into my lap. "You'll see better with those."

I lifted them to my eyes. "It's blurry."

You reached over and twisted the knob on top. You were too close to back away from. A faint sweat smell clung to your chest.

"I can do that myself." I moved the binoculars from you and focused until the image was clear.

Five camels, four large ones and a slightly smaller one, were walking slowly, loping across the horizon. With the heat haze behind them, they looked like moving streaks of sand, twisting with the wind.

"I didn't believe you when you said there were camels."

"They're feral," you said. "Imports, like you. They were brought over to make the railway."

"Railway?"

"Yeah, long way away." You nodded. "And it doesn't run much anyway. Nothing much runs anymore, out here."

"Why not?"

"Everything's moved out — the rocks are mined, animals extinct, oldfellas gone. It makes everything quiet, too quiet. Can't you hear it?"

"What?"

You turned the car off.

"Silence."

You shielded your eyes and watched the camels.

"Aren't you going to try to catch one?" I asked.

"They're too far away to chase. They run pretty fast, you know? Hopefully they'll get curious and come to us. Either that or we'll need some firmer sand to drive on, to get the speed to catch 'em. We'll have to wait, see what they do."

"For how long?"

You shrugged. "However long it takes. Few hours, maybe." You opened your door. "Hungry?"

I shook my head; food was the last thing on my mind.

"I'll get the ropes ready, then."

You got out and went around to the trunk. You rustled in there. I turned in my seat and watched you pull out a coil of rope. I stiffened, imagining you wrapping that rope around my body.

The keys were still in the ignition.

I could do it. I could get to them, if I was quiet. I could slither up and over the hand brake and into the driver's seat — easy. Then I could speed off before you stopped me, before you even realized. Surely, it wasn't that hard, driving. I'd done it before; I knew how to change gears. I could leave you out there, perhaps running you over as I went.

I watched you in the rearview mirror. Your head was down, your hands shifting things around in the trunk. I moved my leg up so that my knee was resting on the seat, beside the hand brake. All I had to do was stretch my leg across to the driver's side, then maneuver my body over. I lifted my leg above the hand brake. Slowly, slowly, inch by inch, I started to move into your seat. I didn't make a sound, not so much as a chair creak. The only thing I could hear was my heartbeat. I lowered myself onto your seat. I put my hands on the steering wheel. Even with my legs stretched all the way out, my feet couldn't quite reach the pedals. I shuffled forward until I was on the edge of the seat. I moved my hand to the keys. Silence. I realized then that I hadn't heard your rustling for a while. I glanced in the rearview mirror.

Something moved to my right. My breath caught as I realized what it was. Its silvery head was resting on the edge of the open window, no more than a hand's width away from me. Its beady amber eyes were staring back at mine, its tongue flashing in and out. It was smelling the air, smelling me.

I took my hand from the keys and pushed myself back into the chair, pressing my body as far away from it as I could. The snake stopped. It turned its head sideways. I knew it was about to strike at me. I couldn't look. Quickly, I scrambled back across the hand brake. But my foot caught. I fell into the passenger seat, hitting my head and shoulders hard against the door. I checked my body. Nothing hurt. Had it got me without me even feeling it? Its silver-brown head was still there, watching, resting on the sill.

It was then I saw your hands. They were also on the sill, holding the snake just under the head. Your face moved into the window frame, too, inches from the snake's.

"Pretty snake, hey? Found her near the wheels. We nearly ran over her . . . lucky we didn't."

I don't know whether you saw the look of terror still in my eyes. Or whether you knew I'd been in the driver's seat, trying to get away. For all I knew, this was your sick way of punishing me.

"It's harmless," you said. "Pretty much. If that's what you're worried about. . . . 'Bout the only one out here that is."

"Why do you have it?"

"To show you."

"To scare me?"

"Nah." You looked fondly at the creature. "I thought we'd take it back to the house. A pet. You can name it."

"I'm not driving anywhere with that thing in the car." I spoke breathlessly, the words coming out in starts.

"We'll attach it to the camel, then." You grinned. You took the snake away. Again I could hear you clunking things around in the trunk. I hoped it wasn't the snake going in there. I had to keep swallowing to stop the vomit rising in my throat. I breathed in three deep breaths, as deep as I could make them with my heartbeat racing. I shut my eyes tight and imagined I was back home, sitting in our hot airing cupboard. When I heard you get back in the car, I kept them closed.

"I'm sorry if it scared you," you said quietly. "I just wanted you to see it. I forgot you don't like snakes yet." You turned the engine on. "Come on, I'll try to make it up to you."

Then you started driving. You didn't speak again for some time. My body swayed and my head was pressed back into the headrest as the engine roared and struggled with the land.

---

After more rough driving, you stopped the car. I heard your door shut and the trunk snap open. When I finally opened my eyes, all I could see was sky: bright blue, cloudless sky, with a large bird circling in it. I sat up. We were parked somewhere high up. Through the windshield I could see the desert stretched out before me like a map, an endless blanket of brown and orange and flatness. There were small squiggles of green — the spin-ifex — and humps of gray — rocks — and long dark worms of dry riverbeds.

There were trees around the car with red-black trunks, and ants crawling up them. I even heard birds somewhere above me: small birds, chattering like kids on a school excursion. There were rocks around us, too, with swirls and patterns in their texture. Tiny flowers grew out of their crevices, and a slight breeze made their petals sway. Considering the barren land all around, this place was a kind of oasis.

You'd spread a picnic to the left of the car, under one of the larger trees. You sat at the edge of a faded tartan blanket, chopping some sort of fruit. The seeds oozed out as your knife cut in. Flies were settling on the rolls you'd made earlier. You didn't brush them away.

There was a bottle of sparkling wine. It seemed so out of place standing up in the sand that I couldn't stop staring at it. I got out of the stifling car, drawn to the promise of a breeze more than anything. You poured me a glass, then poured yourself a smaller one.

"Just as well I brought it."

"Why?"

"Your twenty-first day! It's special. You must think so, too, or you wouldn't have said."

Once again I wished I'd kept that information to myself. I looked down at the glass in my hand. "Have you drugged this?"

You knocked yours back in one annoyed movement. "I won't do that again, I told you."

I shook the glass slightly as I studied it. Some of the liquid fell over the top and onto my hand. It was warm. Back home, my parents hid alcohol in a locked glass cabinet. Instead I'd get drunk with my friends in the park on someone else's booze. But out there, with you, I didn't want it. I tipped the liquid into the dirt. You poured us both another glass right away.

You handed me a roll. The damper bread was hard as rock and the tomato slice inside looked like it had melted. You caught my expression and shrugged.

"Best we have."

"If you're trying to impress me with a picnic, it's not going to work."

"I know," you said gravely. "I forgot the strawberries."

You took your shirt off and wiped your forehead. Then you knocked back your second glass and lay your head onto the T-shirt, staring up at the tree branches. Something was shaking the leaves up there, and you frowned as you tried to figure out what. Sweat beads formed on your chest, settling in the hollows of your muscles. I took a tiny sip from my glass. It was like hot fizzy tea. I recognized a sweater from the dresser back at the house sitting folded on a corner of the blanket; I grabbed it and stuck it on top of my head. The sun was beating down through the branches and leaves, making the landscape lazy.

"Listen," you said.

"To what? There's nothing."

"There is. Maybe not shopping centers and cars, but other things . . . buzzing insects, racing ants, a slight wind making the tree creak, there's a honeyeater up there, scuttling around, and the camels are coming."

"What?"

You nodded toward the land below, a slight smirk on your face. "Go see."

I stood and glanced down at the flatness. Sure enough, there was a bunch of hazy black dots down there, becoming bigger as they moved closer to our small hill. I no longer needed binoculars to see they were camels.

"You didn't *hear* them coming . . . you'd need Superman's hearing for that."

"Who says I'm not Superman?" You were looking at me with one eye closed against the sun. I shrugged.

"You would have rescued me by now if you were Superman," I said quietly.

"Who says I haven't?"

"Anyone would say you haven't."

"*Anyone's* just looking at it wrong, then." You pushed yourself up a little, onto your elbows. "Anyway, I can't steal you *and* rescue you. That would give me multiple personalities."

"And you don't have them already?" I muttered.

I ate the roll, and forced down more sparkling wine. When your eyes closed against the sun again, and I had nothing else to look at, I glanced quickly at your chest, curious, really. I'd only seen chests like that in magazines. I wondered if that's how you'd got all your money . . . modeling. I looked down at my stomach. I grabbed at it, seeing how much fat I could lift up in a roll.

"Don't worry," you said, one eye open again like a crocodile, watching me. "You're beautiful." You tipped your head back. "Beautiful," you murmured. "Perfect."

"You wouldn't know. You're built like some sort of super-model." I bit my lip, wishing I hadn't complimented you like that. "Or a stripper," I added. "Prostitute."

"I wouldn't want you to think I'm repulsive," you said, half smiling.

"Too late."

You opened your other eye to squint at me. "Will you ever give me a break?"

"If you give me your car keys I'll think the world of you."

"No chance." You shut your eyes again and leaned your head back into your T-shirt. "You'd only get lost and die."

"Try me."

"Maybe next week."

You lay there for a few more lazy minutes. You looked almost peaceful, with your eyes closed and your lips parted slightly. A fly landed on your cheek, then crawled to your bottom lip. It stopped halfway across and cleaned itself with your saliva.

After a while, you packed away the picnic, and we drove back down the hill. The car was almost vertical on parts of the decline and several times we hit rocks that sent the steering wheel spinning. The landscape shrunk as we descended, and when we hit the bottom I'd almost forgotten the view of endlessness that had spread out before me at the top.

You parked in the shadow of the hill. It was too hot to wait in the car so you told me to get out and stand in the shade. The camels came eventually. After ambling slowly toward us for several minutes, the camels picked up the pace, their body shapes getting larger as they came closer. They must have been traveling fast. You fixed your binoculars on them.

You turned and yelled, "Get in the car! They've seen us. They're going to turn before they get here."

There was a distant drumming of hooves on hard sand.

"Come on!" You waved me toward you. "Quick, or I'll leave you behind."

It was a tempting suggestion. But even though I pretended not to be, I was excited, too. I wanted to see how you were going to capture one of those huge creatures. You screeched off at top speed, even before I had the door closed, glancing over to check I was in.

"Sit down and hang on to something!"

The speedometer shot up as we raced toward the camels, the car going faster on the harder sand. Things were clunking and smashing in the trunk. I hoped the snake wasn't still in there, getting flung around, about to ricochet in my direction at any moment. I could feel the tires skidding. The car swung wildly sideways more than once. Your face was intent, fiercely concentrating.

"This isn't safe!" I shouted. My head hit the roof as we soared over a sandbar.

You glanced behind as your binoculars flew across the backseat, smashing into the door. "Maybe not."

You laughed as you pressed your foot flat to the floor. I gripped the door handle tightly. The speedometer stuck on just about 35. We were almost level with them. You were right; they had turned before they got to us. Now they were running full tilt toward the horizon. Their necks were stretched and low, their legs taking impossibly huge strides. I'd never seen a wild camel before. It was scary how much they towered above the car. One well-timed kick and a leg could go right through my window.

"Get the pole from the backseat!" you yelled. "Quickly!"

I turned and reached for the long wooden pole with the roped noose at one end. I tried to get it to you, but it was difficult in the small space. It wedged itself against the frame, and I couldn't pull it through the gap between the seats. You glanced at the pole, then back at the camels, trying to keep the car straight and level with them.

"I need it now!"

"I'm trying!"

You reached around to yank at it. As you pulled it free, it hit you in the face. The car swerved alarmingly to the right and toward the camels. I screamed. Your hand lashed out at my shoulder.

"Shut up! You'll scare them."

You pulled the pole over your lap and out of your window. The noosed end was pointing at the camels. You were looking them over carefully. Sweat was pouring off your face. It was pouring off mine, too, despite the breeze rushing past me.

"I'm going for the young female," you shouted. "The one nearest to us. You OK to drive for a moment?"

You started to lean out of your window.

"What are you doing?"

"Take the wheel!" you ordered.

You didn't give me much choice. As soon as you shouted it you were gone, leaning dangerously out of the car, which started to bank toward the camels. If it kept going like this, your head would probably crash into the back end of one of them. I was tempted to let it.

"Take the wheel now!"

I reached over. I could hear the camels grunting with the effort of running. I could hear you breathing hard, too. I took the wheel. It was hot and sticky from your grip. Your left foot moved over to be on the accelerator instead of hovering near the brake. Your right leg was resting on the door frame. There was only the hand brake to stop the car if we needed to.

"Keep driving in a straight line!"

I tried not to look at you or the camels. Whenever I did, I started veering toward them. I looked at the sand in front. I swerved to avoid a spinifex bush, nearly sending you headlong out of the window.

"Jesus! You're a worse driver than me!" You laughed into the wind.

You hooked your right leg behind your left one, and leaned farther out. You held the pole steady, drawing out the line of rope that was trailing behind it. Your thigh was pushing into my arm; I think you were holding it there to keep your balance.

"When the noose is over her head, get out of the way. The rope will rip through the car. Duck down if you can. If you get tangled in the rope, it could snap you in half. I'm serious."

I looked at my body stretching over from my seat and at my hands clamped tight around the wheel, and wondered how it would be possible for me to get out of the way of anything. The car jerked and shuddered as you pressed the accelerator. You were ready to throw the noose. Your whole body was tense and concentrated, your leg pushing harder against my arm.

I forced myself to keep breathing. Your arm was up and ready to throw. You leaned farther out, your long torso stretched to its limit, every muscle tight. If I pushed you, would you tip right out? You circled the pole around your head, gathering speed and momentum.

Then you let it go.

I caught a glimpse of the noose heading toward the camel's head, the rope flying fast behind it. The end of the rope whizzed through the car, past my arms, burning my skin as it went. It whipped over your bare stomach, too, branding you with a deep red streak. You almost plunged out of the car as you struggled to hold on to it. And then, suddenly, the car was banking hard, turning of its own accord. I felt the back swinging around to the left. I tried desperately to spin the wheel the other way.

"Leave it!" you yelled. You dropped back into the driver's seat, almost sitting on top of me. With one hand, you grabbed the wheel. You spun it toward the camel.

"Hang on!"

Your left foot stopped pressing the accelerator and went straight onto the brake. And then the car really did start to spin. I tumbled into my seat, trying to grab at anything, and shut my eyes.

You were out of the car fast. The camel was making this awful sound, a deep, desperate moaning. It echoed around the desert.

I came to look. "Have you hurt her?" I asked.

"Just her pride."

Her long neck was circling around and around, her eyes white with fear. I reached up and touched the hairs on her thigh. "Poor thing."

Quickly, you wound rope around her legs. Then you took a bucket from the trunk, and one of the large containers of water.

Grunting a little, you lifted the container up so it rested against your leg, then carefully poured the water into the bucket.

You tried to encourage the camel to drink, murmuring, "There now, easy, girl."

You were stroking her neck, trying to make her calm. But the camel was just looking over her shoulder at her disappearing herd. She moaned and moaned. She tried moving toward them but you were tightening the rope around her front legs. She kicked out one of her back legs, missing me by inches.

"Careful," you warned. You sprung beside me, wrapping the rope above the camel's knee. "Go over to the other side."

You chucked the rope over her hump. "Pull that," you said. I pulled. "Harder."

I hated every second. Each pull made the camel grumble and gurgle and look around at me with her desperate eyes. You were pulling from your side, too. Eventually the camel's front legs buckled and she knelt into the sand.

"Enough!" you shouted.

You threw yourself onto her hump, pressing your whole body weight down on her. You leaned into her until her back legs crumpled underneath and you were sure she wouldn't get up. Then quickly, you wound rope around the camel's knees, tying them so tightly she couldn't move them.

"That's cruel," I said.

"Do you want a brain hemorrhage from a kick to the head?" You scratched the skin above one of the camel's knees. "There are crueler ways of doing this, believe me."

I did. You probably knew crueler ways of doing most things. The camel's moan had grown in volume and desperation. It sounded too loud to just be coming from her; it sounded like the whole desert was joining in. I wondered if anyone else could hear. The rest of the herd were just dots on the horizon again, almost impossible to see. She was still moving her body toward them.

"You're dreaming if you think you're going to get away, girl," you muttered.

All her legs were hobbled and she was tied to the car. It did seem pretty unlikely that she was going anywhere. I wished she could, though. I wished she could break her ropes and gallop after her herd, calling loudly all the way.

"Would you take me with you?" I whispered to her warm, panting side.

I moved around so I could look at her face. Even scared, she had beautiful eyes. Dark and brown with soft-looking eyelashes. She stopped searching for her herd to glance at me.

"You're trapped, too, now," I told her. "Don't bother thinking of escape. He'll only come after you."

She dropped her head. Her eyes were on me, watching. It was like she understood. I nodded.

"You and me," I whispered. "You and me, girl."

In her moment of stillness, you stepped toward her. You reached up to grab at her face. You had some sort of halter in your hand. As soon as she saw you, she reared her head away, far out of your reach. She roared this time. The sound was monstrous and guttural. You put your hand on her neck, trying to pull her head down.

"Hey, girly," you murmured. "Hey, pretty girl. Don't do that."

The camel hated it. She roared and gurgled and swung her

head madly. You just kept pulling her toward you, your strength even winning against a camel. She looked briefly at me again, blinking her long, lovely eyelashes. Then she turned to you, and was sick on your head.

---

There's nothing like camel vomit. That greenish-brown, lumpy goop that smells like dog shit and sewers and piss all mixed together. It's undoubtedly the worst thing I've ever smelled in my life. Worse than Dad's farts. Worse than baby poo. Worse than anything. And your head was covered in the stuff. As I watched, you spat some out of your mouth. You wiped it off your cheek with the back of your hand. You used your fingers to scoop it out from your eyes. Then you leaned over and threw up some of your own.

I wasn't far behind you. As soon as I caught a whiff, I let go of my stomach. I'm hopeless like that, always sick when someone else is. I had to sit down in the sand and stick my head between my knees, it was that bad. And the sound of you being sick didn't make it any better. I kept throwing up for ages, longer than you, even. The camel stopped moaning sometime in the middle of all this. She was probably pretty satisfied with herself, probably laughing at us. I wouldn't blame her. Or maybe it was just the moment when she gave up hope, when she realized her herd was gone forever and there wasn't any point in moaning anymore.

I rolled over and leaned against a tree. The smell of rotten puke was everywhere. The flies had already latched on to it; they were buzzing relentlessly, dropping down onto the sick and then trying to land on my face. The heat only made it worse, making my head spin. I looked at the sand stretching for miles, but it was hard to focus on it.

The journey back was the worst of my life. Worse even than the one where I was stuck in the trunk, which I can't remember anyway. Even with all the windows down, the smell was still there, infecting every corner of the car with its foulness. When the sick dried on us, it smelled even worse. Something like foot odor meets sour milk. It didn't help that the smell was mixing with the squashed-fruit smell from the picnic, which was now spread all over the backseat from your mad driving. We drove with our heads out the windows.

The camel trotted along behind us, obliging on her rope. It was as if she had got us back in some small way, and was happier. I threw up more than once, down the side of the car . . . thin white dribbles of bile.

———————————⁊———————————

The next day you were out with the camel, training her, in a pen you must have made the night before. You'd stuck more fence posts in the ground and wound rope around them, linking this all to the chicken-wire fence already around the Separates.

I came out to watch. You had her head in a halter attached to a rope, and she was following you. She was calmer now, almost resigned. She carried her head lower, and she'd given up on moaning. You were talking to her softly and gently, in words I couldn't hear or understand. She seemed to like it.

"What do you want to call her?" you said when you noticed me.

"Stolen," I said. It was the first thing I thought of.

"That's not much of a name."

"But she is, though, isn't she? Stolen from her herd." I felt bad that I'd helped.

"She'll learn to love us," you said quietly. "Did you feel the same about your cat when you chose him from the animal shelter?"

"That's different."

You walked over to where I was standing and pulled on the camel's rope. She lowered her head so that I could pet her. You placed your hand against her stomach, thinking. "We should call her Wobbleguts," you said.

"That's a crap name."

"It's accurate. Took me forever to clean the side of my car." Your eyes were soft as they stayed on mine for longer than they needed to. You moved the rope toward my hand. "Here. Do you want a go at leading her?"

I stepped carefully into the pen, taking the rope without needing to touch you. I patted her front shoulder, trying to reassure her. I thought calm words, tried to let her know I wasn't going to hurt her. She towered over me, all legs and muscle. There was still a faint smell of sick about her, mixed with something else . . . something dirt and desertlike. She smelled like sand.

"Just walk straight, she'll follow."

I took a few steps and the camel came with me. She lowered her head and sniffed gently at my shoulder. I could feel her lips touching the collar of my T-shirt, her warm breath on the back of my neck. Her feet were clomping heavily next to mine.

"You are a lovely girl," I whispered to her. The bottom of her jaw worked around in a circle, chewing on something. I was surprised at her gentleness, her willingness to give in. It didn't seem like she was wild only the day before.

"We need to teach her to whoosh down next."

"To what?"

"Sit. Here, go through the fence again."

You took her rope from me and pushed me toward the fence. I ducked through it and you shoved her rope back into my hand.

"Just hold it there, firmly. If you're on the other side of this fence, she shouldn't be able to kick you."

Then you tied another rope to one of her front legs and ran it over her hump.

"We need to pull down together," you said. "She'll soon get the idea."

As soon as we pulled, the camel started moaning again. I shook my head at you. "I don't like it."

"Camels just make a lot of fuss." You ran your hand up her neck, and spoke gently to her once more. Her ear flicked back to listen to you. "As soon as she understands what we want, she'll do it. Camels are like that."

I wondered if you thought the same thing about me.

———————— ~ ————————

My scalp began to burn. I went back to the veranda and lay on the couch. I watched you with the camel, getting her to sit and then stand again, over and over. The sun was warm but not oppressive through the veranda roof; it made my eyelids heavy. Like that, half-asleep, edges of memories came: Anna's face when she first told me she was going out with Ben, Mum arriving through the door with takeout for dinner, Josh asking me on a date.

I heard the tuneless notes of your whistle. I snapped my eyes open and forced my body into a sitting position. You were walking toward me.

You leaned against the veranda post with a sigh. Your cheeks were slightly red, strands of hair stuck to your forehead. You took out rolling papers and rolled yourself a cigarette. Quickly, you licked the edges. I took my time that day, studying your face, my eyes lingering over your pronounced cheekbones and jaw, your small scar and longish hair.

"I *have* seen you before, haven't I?" I said. "I mean, after when I was ten."

You took a drag on your roll-up. There were so many half-remembered things in my head right then: vague images of seeing you around the neighborhood, in the park somewhere, sometime . . . something else, too. I remembered the way you'd seemed familiar at the airport.

"Why do I recognize you?"

"I told you, I've been following you."

"That's just creepy."

You shrugged.

I leaned forward on the couch. "But *I* recognize *you*, too. And that's creepier. Why?"

You smiled. "I lived nearby."

"Yes, but something else . . . that moment when I saw you in the airport, I knew . . . I knew I'd seen you before."

My brain hurt with the effort of thinking. I wiped the sweat off my forehead and from the corners of my eyes. I unstuck my thighs from the couch and shifted them to a cooler part. Your broad shoulders were blocking the sun, your T-shirt hanging floppy over the small of your back. You took another drag.

"I met you in the park, remember?"

"How often were you there?"

"All the time. As you know, I lived there for a while . . . Number 1, Rhododendron Gardens." You smiled. "Later I worked there."

"Worked?"

"Yeah, after I'd met you and decided to get my act together. I got a little job as a groundskeeper — maintenance, digging. . . . I saw you there with your friends."

"How long ago?"

"Maybe three years ago. I did it for a couple of years . . . on and off. I liked it."

I thought back to the park. I could remember where the trees and flower beds were, exactly where all the benches were, too . . . and the thicker bushes that were good for smoking out of sight. Sometimes I wondered if I knew that park better than my own house.

But I couldn't remember you in it. Or could I?

"You had long hair then?"

You nodded, smiled slightly. And then it came back: the quiet skinny boy, always on the edge of things, hair falling around his face, the boy who was consumed by his work in the dirt beds.

"That was you?"

"Perhaps, at some point."

"We used to talk about you. Anna said you were good-looking."

You laughed. "But what did *you* say? You were the one I was watching."

I could feel the heat in my cheeks. I hate the way I always blush so easily. I unstuck the backs of my knees from the couch again and bent them. I rested my head down so you couldn't see my face.

"That's just weird, you watching me like that."

"Not always. Sometimes it was good."

The blush disappeared. And instead, that sickness was in my stomach again, the nausea that always arrived when I thought about what you'd done to me. I wanted to know what you'd seen in the park over the years — I'd certainly done some stupid things — but at the same time I didn't want to know. I certainly didn't want to ask.

So I got to thinking about the park instead, the times I used to go there. First of all it had been with my parents. We used to go most Sundays, for a year or so, when the weather was nice, anyway. Mum and Dad read the papers on the bench, and I played around them. Mum brought me toys, but I preferred to wander in and out of the flower beds, making up tales about the fairy kingdom. It was a good memory, one of the happiest I have about my parents. Mum hadn't gone back to full-time work then, and Dad seemed more relaxed somehow. In my head, we are this normal, happy family. It's nice. That must have been the year when I first met you, that summer.

Had you seen all that? Were those rare blissful family moments part of the pull that drew you to me? I looked back at you. You were picking at a loose nail in one of the veranda posts, trying to work it from the wood. I watched you tugging it back and forth, trying to get your finger under it. It took your complete concentration. Hunched over like that, you looked smaller than you were. I leaned back into the couch and changed my focus to the sky. That blue, blue sky, so endless and empty. But there were a few clouds that day, wisps of cotton candy scudding across the blue. I tried to find faces in them.

How many times did I lie in the park with Anna, doing the same thing? We always found Ben — he was the large cloud with the swirly, smiley edge. Anna said she saw Josh up there once, looking down on me.

I'd watched for Josh after that. I'd even talked to him, trying to find out whether he was really as bad as I'd thought. It only encouraged him. He started following me around then, skulking on the edge of our group. Anna didn't mind, which was odd, because anyone could see that Josh was desperate to go out with me. But perhaps she wanted me to be with him. Then she'd have Ben all to herself.

I cringed. There was a thought drifting up there with the clouds that I didn't want to think about. I switched my gaze and tried concentrating on you instead. But the thought wouldn't go away. A warmish summer night. Almost two years ago. The park. *That* night.

You got one finger under the nail, and pulled at it.

Josh had been there that night, hovering at the edge of our group like some sort of bat. There'd been a bottle going around, strong stuff. A little bit of alcohol from each person, all mixed together. Anna was laughing and Ben was feeling her up, right there in the park, right there in front of everyone. I heard the rip of her zipper going down. I heard the elastic snap of her panties.

Jay and Beth were joking about them losing their virginity right there, right in front of us, but we were all just jealous, really. We skipped Anna and Ben on the drinking circle, and everyone else drank more. After a while, the rest of us stopped talking. Then Jay and Beth disappeared into the bushes. And I was left there, sitting next to my best friends, who were practically fucking beside me.

But Josh was still there, in the shadows, just behind. I drank more. Stupidly, I hoped Anna and Ben would stop soon, and we could all walk home together. I glanced over at them. And Anna looked at me, over Ben's shoulder, and I knew exactly what she wanted me to do. So I took off. I stumbled through the park and the darkness, heading for the exit. I don't know where Jay and Beth had gone, but I didn't see them. There was this thick smell in the air, earthy and heavy. There were tiny gnats flying around my eyes.

Josh followed.

I didn't see him at first, but I heard his footsteps when I was about halfway to the exit. They were hesitant but quick. I could hear the shuffling rub of his jeans as he walked. I turned. And I saw him, about ten feet back, coming up on me. The look in his eyes, well, it was nasty. Like he'd been waiting all those months for that moment. Just to get me by myself, like that and drunk. It had been his goal all along. As I watched him, my head started spinning. I had to steady myself against a tree.

That's when I got lost. When I turned back to the path I went the wrong way. I didn't notice it straightaway, either. That's because Josh started to talk to me, started to come closer. All I could concentrate on was walking a little faster. I heard him laughing then, low and soft.

"Gemma, wait," he was saying. "I only want to talk."

I was in a part of the park I didn't go to much, near the ferns at the back. There was a pond somewhere ahead of me. That's all I could remember. To get to the right path, I needed to go back the way I'd come. But Josh was on that path. And he was getting closer. It was so shadowy, I couldn't even see how close he was.

"Get lost, Josh," I said. "Another time. Just go home."

"But it's still early."

I glanced around me for a branch or something solid I could hold between us. I tried to remember where the pond was exactly. Did the path go around it? Did it lead anywhere afterward?

"Come on, Josh," I tried again. "What are you doing? You know I don't want to go out with you." My voice was shaking, my throat tight, barely letting the words escape. "Just leave me alone."

"I don't want to."

Josh was only a few steps away. I could almost see the pond, directly in front of me. The plants around it stood up like shadowy spears. I could feel the sudden damp in the air, the ground softer under my feet. I heard Josh's jeans swishing through undergrowth behind me. I saw the path leading off to my left, circling around the pond.

I was moving toward that path when it happened.

My eyes snapped open as I thought of something. You were still there working on the nail, though you'd just about got it out by now. I looked at your back hunched over it. I listened to the way you grunted.

"Were you there that night?" I asked quietly. "That night in the park with Josh?"

Your mouth twitched, and you seemed to hunch further into yourself, your shoulders curling over your chest. I shut my eyes again, just for a second.

The sound was easy to remember: the sharp, quick scuffle that I thought was Josh slipping in the grass. And then there were the shadows. There were two shadows besides mine, both cast over the path: one tall and one short. I looked back quickly. Someone else was there. Someone in a dark gray hoodie. Someone pushing himself into Josh, pushing him away from me. I heard Josh start to shout something before his voice got muffled by someone else's: a low, deep, urgent-sounding voice. I thought it was one of Josh's weird friends fooling around, someone catching him in a headlock, tackling him, pulling him into the bushes to smoke dope or something. Or maybe it was Ben or Jay.

I didn't stick around to find out. I ran past the bushes Josh had disappeared into. I ran all the way home. I didn't stop until I had the key in the lock and the door shut behind me.

You kept wriggling the nail away from the wood, until eventually it came free. You tossed it in the air a couple of times. You glanced back at me, and somehow I managed to hold your gaze.

"You were that guy in the hoodie, weren't you?"

You glanced back at the nail in your hand, then tilted your head up to look out at the land. The sun was beginning to go down. The light was spreading out over the Separates, turning the rocks to gold.

"What did you do to him? After you dragged him into the bushes?"

You looked at me then. A flash from your eyes told me you knew exactly what I was talking about.

"Nothing," you said. "I did nothing."

"He left me alone after that."

"I know."

I uncurled my knees and leaned toward you. I saw the sweat beads on your neck, but I felt only cold right then. I looked at your wide eyes, wondering something. "Do you think you saved me from him?"

"What do you think?" You took a step toward me and crouched down on your heels. Your eyes moved across my face, trying to read me. "Aren't you glad I was there?" You rested your hand on the couch, the edge of it brushing against my thigh. I frowned, confused.

"And in case you were wondering," you began softly, ". . . *that* was the moment."

"What moment?"

"The moment I first knew I wanted you . . . the moment I knew I had to bring you here. Not when you were ten — that night. From then on, this was all geared toward you. I worked harder to make sure it was finished, trying to rescue you as quickly as I could."

———— ≥ ————

The next day I sat in the dust at the side of the pen. You were gentle with the camel, and slow. Whenever she did something you wanted, you rewarded her with a branchful of dry leaves, which she nibbled with her soft, elastic lips. You spoke to her constantly, murmuring sweet nothings into the side of her neck. When she didn't do as you asked, you simply raised your hands and came toward her as if you were going to strike. Her fear of you was enough for her to learn. She slid sideways immediately, away. She walked back to you soon enough, though, with her head bowed and her jaw chewing slowly. It was a battle of wills, only it looked like the camel had already given in.

I leaned back on my elbows. My arms were already so brown, browner than they'd ever been. When I lay them down against the ground they almost blended in. I felt a tickle as a large ant crawled over my pinkie finger. I wasn't bothered enough to brush it away, despite its large-looking pincers. Strange: A couple of weeks before I would probably have stomped on it. It crawled over my next three fingers, then disappeared somewhere underneath my back. I didn't move, afraid I might crush it.

I watched you entice the camel toward you with the branches, then, when she was near enough, lay a strip of rope across her back. At first she skidded backward, afraid, and you let the rope slide off her. But as you persisted, she started to get used to it.

"I'm training her for a saddle," you called across to me.

I sat up slightly. The camel saw my movement and stepped sideways. The rope thudded on the sand. "You want to ride her?" I asked.

"Sure." You turned away from the camel, avoiding her eye contact, and, after a moment, she came toward you. "When the gas runs out we might need to get around."

"When will it run out?"

"Not for a while, a long time, but we've got to be prepared. Anyway, this girl will be useful for more than just transport, much more."

I glanced across to the outbuildings, my eyes lingering on the one next to the painting shed, the one I hadn't been inside yet. Was the gas there? I had an image then of locking you in the house and pouring gasoline all around it, setting fire to the veranda and watching you burn inside. I ran my eyes down your clothing for the billionth time. Without knowing where you kept your keys, my chances of escape, or even of burning you to death, were impossible. That second building was locked. I'd seen the padlock on the door. My eyes flicked back to the camel.

"When will you be able to ride her?" I asked. "Today?"

"Nah!" You scratched the camel's neck. "Not a chance. But it's always like this with camels . . . baby steps. Just one tiny thing at a time until she learns to accept."

You tried holding the rope against her back for longer each time. She evaded it easily. But sometimes she let it sit there, too.

"So you're forcing her to do what you want? Breaking her spirit?"

"It's not quite like that." You clicked your tongue at the camel and moved toward her, head-on. This time when you threw the rope over her back, she didn't move away. Instead she turned her long neck around and sniffed at it. "I'm giving her faith in me," you said. "Once she trusts me, and she's accepted me, she'll like it better this way. Camels work in herds, you know. She'll feel safer once she's got someone to follow, a leader. Then she doesn't have to worry about being scared anymore."

You spoke with your eyes entirely on the camel. You pressed your hands against her side, leaning your weight into her, pushing her to accept you. She didn't move away. Instead she nibbled at the leaves you offered.

"Good girl," you said. "Good, beautiful girl. That's what we want."

You stopped pressing. Then you lifted the rope from her back, picked up another branch of leaves, and started the whole process again. After doing this a few more times, you ran your hands over her, starting with her neck and working your way down to her feet. She gurgled softly, and you murmured in reply.

"Enough for now, baby," you said. "We'll do a little more tomorrow."

While she nibbled another branch, you cut farther into the chicken-wire fence that attached her pen to the Separates, widening the previous opening until it was camel-sized. You pointed her toward it, trying to encourage her to move in the direction of the boulders.

"You won't be able to catch her . . . ," I started to say.

But the camel wandered after you anyway, her head reaching for your shoulder. You ducked between the ropes that ran around her pen, and came to join me. You flopped down beside me, your body sprawling into the sand, shutting your eyes against the sun. You were pretty close, but for once I didn't shift. I was still worried about the ant crawling underneath me, not wanting to crush it or for it to bite me. And I was too hot and lazy. One of your eyes snuck open to look at me.

"We're getting there," you sighed. "Baby steps."

After a while you sat up and wiped your hand across your forehead.

"Let's get a drink," you said. "Too hot out here."

I followed you back to the veranda, but didn't follow you inside. I wanted to think for a moment, about our conversation the day before, about whether it really had been you in the park that night. Sometimes I thought it made sense, other times it didn't.

You'd left the door open and I heard you in the kitchen, gulping thirstily from the tap. You returned with two full glasses. You handed one to me. I took it, but didn't drink. I watched your shoulders tense when I put the glass on the floor. Then I sat on the edge of the couch. You were about the right height to be the guy in the hoodie. But this story of yours, this way that you knew me . . . it was too big, too crazy. And there were still so many things that didn't make sense. Why then? Why follow me all those years? Why me?

"Why did you leave Australia?" I asked. "Why even go to Britain in the first place?"

You didn't answer. You stepped slowly up to one of the veranda posts and leaned your forehead against it. You tried shutting your eyes. But I kept pressing, wanting to find you out.

"Why?"

You shook your head, your fingers tight around your glass. Then, quickly, you turned to me.

"I got a letter," you said. "OK?"

"What letter?" I watched your fingertips turn white from their grip. "What did it say?"

Your mouth opened as if to tell me, but you took a sharp breath instead. "I don't know. . . ." Your fingers were clenching so tight around the glass, I thought it would crack. You followed my gaze and looked down at them, too. "I don't know how she found me."

I shifted on the couch, suddenly interested. "Who found you?"

You thumped the glass down hard on the railing, and it smashed inside your hand. Your eyes opened wide as you looked at the jagged pieces in your palm.

"My mum, OK?" you whispered. "She found me."

A trickle of blood ran down over your wrist. You watched it, and the glass fragments made a dull *clink* as you dropped them on the floor. I looked at the four even-sized pieces before looking back at your hand. You had curled it up, but there was still blood leaking between your fingers. Your eyes remained wide, confused. You reached down to pick up the pieces but then saw me looking and flinched away again, quickly putting your hand in front of you where I couldn't see it. You turned your face away, too, your shoulders raised up, tense. One more word and you might explode. I waited awhile before speaking, and when I did my words were hesitant.

"I thought you said your mum disappeared, after you were born?"

"She did." You hunched over your fist, uncurling it, checking the damage. "But she found me," you whispered. "I don't know how. Not long after I turned seventeen she sent me a letter."

"Why?" The word was quieter than a breath. But it hung between us. Your back was as stiff as the post you were leaning against. Nothing about you moved.

"She said she wanted to see me. She gave me her address: 31-a Elphington Street. London."

"That's near me."

"I know."

"So you came to see her."

"I tried. My foster parents lent me the money."

"What happened?"

"They were glad to be rid of me."

"I meant with your mum."

You turned. Your face was contorted from the emotions you were wrestling with.

"You really want to know this?"

I nodded. In three strides you were across the veranda, slamming the door behind you. Then I heard you in the house, walking heavily, opening a drawer. I waited, tense. The door swung open again, bashing hard against the house wall. You pushed something into my hands: an envelope.

"Read her letter," you barked.

I fumbled with the envelope, my hands suddenly shaky as I pulled out the thin pages inside. A photograph fell out, too, landing in my lap. I picked it up.

It was faded and old, slightly crumpled around the edges. It was of a girl, a girl about my age, holding a baby tight to her chest. She was staring boldly at the camera, as if challenging the person taking it. I gasped a little as I studied her long dark hair and green eyes. She looked a little like me. The baby she was holding was tiny, wrapped up tight in hospital blankets. But his eyes were as blue as oceans, the one curl on his head golden.

I looked back at you, my eyes lingering on the blond hair falling in your eyes.

". . . You?"

You slammed your hand against the veranda post, making the whole structure shudder.

"I wanted you to *read* it!" You snatched the pages from my lap. "Give it back if you're not going to."

You took the photograph, too, though you were careful not to bend that. You placed it gently inside your shirt pocket, and put the pages in after. You talked quietly, like you were talking to yourself.

"She wrote to ask me to live with her," you explained. "She said she'd been alone too long."

"And what happened?" My voice was barely a whisper.

You leaned over me. Carefully, you uncurled your fingers and stretched them to my face. I saw the dark blood on your palm, hardening already. I turned my face away, but you pulled it back toward you, forcing me to look at you, your palm cupping my chin, your fingertips in my hair.

"Thirty-one-a Elphington Street was a squat," you sighed. "Shit on the walls, and dead sparrows in the fireplace. Some dealer almost killed me when I knocked."

"And your mum?" The words were hard to get out between the tight grip of your fingers.

"She wasn't there. Apparently, she'd left the week before I arrived." Your eyes darted away, remembering. "I tried to get another address for her, but no one would give it to me. . . . They said she was involved in too much shit, they didn't want to know her anymore."

I tried escaping from your grip. You wouldn't let me. Just gripped tighter, and moved your lips closer to my face, your breath sour like your rolled cigarettes.

"Eventually I got a number I could reach her on. I held that scrap of paper in my pocket for days before I had the guts to call, until I knew the numbers off by heart. When I did, I got this old woman asking if I had any money, and when I said no, she said she didn't know who I was talking about. But that voice of hers . . ." You took a breath. ". . . It sounded half-dead: drunk, or drugged, or something . . . like Dad had sounded sometimes." You paused. "You know, I often wondered if it was really her that answered, if that was her voice."

I held your gaze. Slowly, I tried moving my face back, away from you a little.

"I kept hunting, though," you continued, not noticing my movement. "Kept searching in those squats and shelters, trying to find her. Fuck! I'd never seen snow before I got there, I fucking hated it after the first day. I didn't have any money to get home, or anything else to do, or anyone, so . . ."

You broke off then, finally letting me go. I moved my jaw around, testing the damage. Your face was concerned when I glanced up. You stretched your fingers toward my cheek as if you wanted to touch it again.

I shook my head. No. Your face twisted up, and you slammed your hand down hard into the cushion next to me. We both watched it there. It was only a few inches away from me, and it was shaking. After a moment, you took it back and put it in your pocket. You moved away, back to your post looking out at the land.

"Is that when you found me?" I asked quietly. "Back in London, after you couldn't find your mum?"

You didn't answer. Instead you stomped across the veranda and jumped down into the sand. You threw a punch at your punching bag, then crouched over into yourself and threw several more. You growled as your injured hand connected. Then you slammed both arms against the bag and headed out to the Separates. I listened to the rhythm of the bag bouncing back and forth before it slowed, then stopped entirely. Sometime later, from inside the rocks, I heard an echo of a sound that could have been your scream.

———— ⋛ ————

It got to late afternoon, the time when you normally fed the chickens; you still weren't back. I picked up the box of seeds and nuts from the porch area, and went to do it myself. I had to go through the camel's pen to get into the Separates. It was the first time I'd been in there without you. The camel was resting, her legs bent underneath her. She raised her head when I entered.

"There now, easy girl," I said, trying to sound like you.

She was so big that it was hard not to be a little nervous around her. I stepped carefully through the pathway to the rocks. I wondered if you were still in there. And, if so, where? I had the feeling you were watching me.

I got to the clearing. It was noisier there, with the wild birds beginning their late-afternoon gossiping. A lizard basking on a rock retreated quickly to the shade as I made my way to the cages.

I went to the hens first, leaving the rooster until last. He was strutting around his cage like he was gearing up for a fight. I yanked open the lid to the hens' cage and stuck the food in. They clustered around my hand, their warm feathery bodies soft against my skin. I liked the way they clucked and gurgled. They sounded like the two old ladies who were sometimes on my bus home from school; those ladies twittered and murmured, too, only instead it was about their favorite TV shows. I missed those old ladies. I wondered if they'd noticed I was no longer on their bus.

I decided to name the chickens. The two fat gray ones I called Ethel and Gwen, after the bus ladies. The thin red one was Mum. The fatter red one was Anna. The large orangey one I called Ben (yeah, OK, so it's a boy's name), and the sick, whitish one was Alison, after Granny. I called the rooster Dick, after you.

After I'd stroked the hens for a while, I shut the lid to their cage and moved across to the rooster. His beak was between the cage wires, trying to peck at me. I flicked a bit of dirt in his direction, then tried opening the latch. He was onto me immediately, drilling his beak sharply into my fingers. I stepped back, throwing him off.

I heard your laugh from over near the fruit trees. You were leaning against the rock, your legs propped up on a tree. You were as still as the sandstone behind you.

"You need to pick him up when he does that," you said. "Carry him until he calms. Either that, or hold him upside down."

"I'd like to see you try."

You shrugged, came over. As you knelt in front of his cage, Dick tried to peck you, too. He leaped into the air, thrusting his sharp feet toward you.

"Ninja chicken, isn't he?" You grinned at me, rolling your sleeves up. "We'll see about that."

You reached into the cage. Instantly Dick was onto your hand, clawing at you, biting chunks out with his beak.

"Goddamn rooster!"

You tried dropping him. But Dick clung on. I turned my face to the side, hiding my smirk. You flung your hand around, trying to shake him off, but that rooster dug his claws in like his life depended on it. He tore a deep gash over your knuckles. You tried to pull him off with your other hand, but Dick kept fighting. He screeched and squawked, enjoying the carnage. You yelled back. It was a full-on battle all right, like the ones on nature shows between the dominant males of two herds. I felt like I should be cheering the rooster on, enjoying each scratch he gave you.

Finally, you managed to get your other hand around his wings. You pinned him like that. I waited, wondering if you would squeeze any tighter, whether you would really get back at the mad bird. But you just dropped him into the cage, chucked the food at him, and shut the lid quickly. You kicked the wire with your boot. Dick flew at the roof, whacking himself against it and plummeting back to the ground, squawking wildly.

Your hands and arms were bleeding and swollen from the scratches, your eyes wide.

"You're right, he's a killer," you said. "A rooster with some serious issues."

You shook your head, perhaps surprised that another creature could beat you like that. You held your injured hands out in front of you like a small child might. Blood wept from the gash over your knuckles and ran over your wrist. A couple of small chest feathers were stuck in it. You tried mopping up some of the bleeding with your other hand, but that only opened up a scratch on the back of that one, too.

"Ow," you said. Then you looked up, really turned those big blue eyes on me. "I think you're going to have to help me clean these," you said.

I ran the water, but I made it pretty hot. You sat on the dusty living room floor and waited for me to bring you the bowl. You winced when you dipped your hands in. I smiled. Simple pleasures, small retributions. I picked out an old, scratchy sponge from the sink, one you used for washing dishes.

"This be OK?" I asked innocently.

"You want me to have no skin left?" You rolled your eyes. "Actually, don't answer that one."

I brought it over anyway. I crouched on the other side of the bowl. As you swished your hands around, the water turned redder.

"Doesn't that hurt?" I said.

"Yep."

"How do you keep them in there?"

"I'm stubborn." You grinned. "Stubborn as a waddywood. And anyway, pain means it's healing."

"Not always."

The blood kept coming, swirling and curling around your fingers.

"Damn rooster," you muttered.

You hadn't started on your arms yet. There were scratches there, too, some of them going up to your elbows. You sighed, took your hands out, and rested them on the side of the bowl. They were pink, puffy as marshmallows.

"You're going to need to help," you said. "Please?"

I looked at you. "Why should I?"

Your forehead wrinkled. "Because if I can't use my hands, then we're both fucked." You breathed out quickly, frustrated. ". . . And I can't wash them properly myself." The corner of your mouth slid into a smile as your eyes pleaded with me again. ". . . And it hurts, Gem."

You held your hands stiffly out toward me, the same way you'd done earlier. They dripped pinkish water onto the floor. One drop landed on my knee, then started to slide off, leaving a dull brown trail behind it.

"What will you do for me?" I asked quietly.

You watched the drop sliding off my knee, too, keeping silent as you thought. "What do you want?"

"You know what I want."

"You're not going anywhere." You turned your right hand over, and watched the watery blood run down it in streaks. "I mean, what do you want from me, right here, right now?"

You looked back at me. That small action made your hair fall over your eyes. Your sun-bleached strands had grown almost to your mouth. You blew at them and they stuck to your lips.

"Please," you said. "Anything that's not about leaving here. Come on, just ask me. I'm happy to oblige." You leaned forward, curious as a cat. I pulled away. "But first," you whispered, "before anything, can you get me a towel? They're in the box in the bathroom."

"I know."

I opened the battered tin box beside the bathroom door and got you the towel. As I walked back, I thought about all the things I wanted to know about you . . . hundreds of things. But to ask them felt like a crime, some sort of betrayal. So I knelt with the towel on my lap, thinking. I was ready to give it to you when you asked, but instead you lay your arms straight down against it, over my knees. I felt the material go damp and warm from your watery blood. Your face was close to mine, but I looked at your arms instead. My legs were tense, tight, like an animal ready to run.

"I want to know how you built all this," I said eventually. "Where you got the money. If that was you, like you said, in those bushes years ago . . . then how did you go from that to this?"

I glanced around the room, noticing the cobwebs clinging to the roof. They wound down toward the curtains in such tiny threads, such fragile pathways of life. You rolled your arms over the towel, nodding at the sponge.

"Wash my arms? Please? I'll tell you then."

I dipped the sponge into the water and ran it over the scratches. It opened up the gashes further, scouring your skin. You flinched as your brown skin fell away to a pinker, softer skin beneath. I rubbed a little harder. Bits of sponge were getting stuck in the wounds. You were biting on your lower lip, dealing with the pain.

"I got the money a lot of ways," you said. "I stole at first; I was pretty good at taking handbags from pubs, that sort of thing. But then someone caught me and threatened me with prison."

You caught my look. You knew that if I had my way you'd be going to prison someday soon anyway. You ignored it.

"I even begged for a while," you continued. "Stuck my plastic McDonald's cup on the floor like the rest of them and felt like shit."

I stopped rubbing. "But begging isn't enough to make this." Again, I looked around the room. It was rough and basic, but it must have cost more than some loose change to make it happen . . . a lot more. "What else?"

You nodded. "I sold things."

"Sold what?"

"What I had." You winced badly, and it wasn't from the pain in your arms. I wasn't even rubbing you then. "I sold myself for this place."

"You mean . . . like a prostitute?"

"Like someone selling his soul." Your face contorted at a memory. You shook your head, trying to shake it away. "I just did what everyone else did in the city," you said, your eyes far away. "I chased money, pretended to be someone else to get it. It got easier the longer I did it . . . but that's the trap, see? When the deadness gets easier, you know you're sinking deeper, becoming dead yourself." You started dabbing at your arms with the towel, pressing the scratches to stop the blood. "Then I hit the big time."

"A high-class prostitute?" I smirked.

"Almost. I worked for Fantasyland."

"What, like Disney characters?"

"I could have been one of those, if they'd wanted it." You smiled ruefully. "I worked as a fantasy escort. I was a professional dater. I went out with whoever wanted me, and I was whoever they wanted me to be: James Bond, Brad Pitt, Superman. . . ." You paused, checking my reaction. "See, I told you I could be Superman."

"That's crazy."

"Yes, but that's the city — everyone loves to pretend. Especially the rich. Anyway, it's easy to be what people want: give them something to stare at, nod and smile, tell them they're gorgeous." You flashed me your best charming grin before you added, "The three steps to money."

Again, you smiled. But it wasn't your charming one this time. It was smaller and sadder.

"And your money? Do you still have it?"

You threw your hands out to the house. "All buried into this wood somewhere, into this place . . . what other use is there for it?"

"So," I began, "when you leave this place, you'll have nothing? No money, no family, no future . . . ?"

Your smile stopped. "I'm not going to leave this place. Ever."

You stood up, your healing done.

———— ❧ ————

I didn't sleep again that night. I'd gone to bed with too many questions. I heard your voice just before dawn, murmuring. I tiptoed down the corridor and pressed myself against your door, listening. But you didn't make another sound. Maybe you were dreaming.

I found you in the kitchen, with the morning sun flooding in through the window and over your skin. You were soaking rags in a bowl of dark brown paste that smelled like eucalyptus and dirt. Your hands were scabby; swollen, too. You took out a rag and asked me to help. As I wrapped it around your wrist, you looked out of the window, impatient to get on with something.

"Gonna be a hot one," you said. "Maybe even get some rain, one of these days, if we're very lucky . . . if it keeps building like this."

"If what keeps building?"

"The pressure. When the air gets heavy like it is now, it'll burst at some point. It'll have to."

I'd felt the pressure, too. For the past couple of days, the air had felt alive, clinging to my ears like it was trying to get inside and pressing its heat against me. I wondered, sometimes, if I stood outside with my arms open wide and waited, whether the air would press me all the way back home.

You took your hand away from me and tested how tightly I'd tied the bandage.

"Good," you murmured. You opened a drawer and dug around in it.

"How did you get this here?" I asked. "All this wood and equipment?"

You pulled out a small metal clasp. "I had a truck."

"That's all?"

"And time." You motioned for me to attach the clasp over the bandage I'd tied, securing it further.

"What else?" I stretched the small elastic of the clasp, digging its metal ends into the bandage. Then I kept hold of your wrist until you looked back at me.

"All right." You sighed. "There is somewhere else. . . . It's a shell of a place, really, not too far. Old mine site. I kept stuff there before I needed it. Then I just started building. I started years ago, when I first had the idea, before I even knew I wanted to bring you here, too."

"Can we go there?" I asked quickly. "This mine site?"

"There's nothing there."

"Must be more than here."

You shook your head. "The land there's been raped and taken, everything's dead."

I coiled away from your words.

"I'm serious, Gem. There's only a hole in the earth that's eaten everything up. It's repulsive." You opened the door to outside. "You coming?"

I shook my head, my heart quickening a little. If I could only get to your keys, maybe I could find this shell of a place you mentioned. If it was a mine site, there must be people there. . . . There must be something.

I watched your back as you walked away, toward the out-buildings. Then, for the billionth time, I searched through your kitchen. I was becoming more convinced that you carried the car key on you.

I went to the spare room. I ran my finger down the spines of the books and pulled out a few. There were no maps in them, nothing to tell me where I was. I looked at a book called *The History of the Sandy Desert* and flicked through some of the photographs: the different landscapes and the pictures of aborigines you'd said were once here. I traced their faces, wishing they'd never left.

I pulled out the next book: a field guide to Australian flora. Then I had a brain wave. Perhaps I could figure out where I was from identifying the vegetation around me. I thumbed through the pages. Some plants looked familiar, like the ones in the section on spinifex. I read a line: *Spinifex triodia dominates the vegetation of more than 20 percent of Australia, and occurs in all states except Tasmania.* Brilliant, I thought, I really could be anywhere . . . except Tasmania.

I opened the cabinet. There was a stringless guitar and a saggy football on the bottom shelf. I pushed them aside and something black and leggy scuttled away, disappearing into the darkness at the back. A thin thread of spider-life hung from the corner. I didn't look any farther in there.

There was a dirty sewing machine on the middle shelf that looked older than me. I turned the knob on the side and watched the needle move slowly up and down. I wished it would magically sew out some sort of map, telling me how to get home. I pressed my finger to its tip. It was rusty but it was still sharp — surprising, really, considering how old it looked. I twisted the needle until it snapped off in my fingers. I ran it across my palm, tracing my lifeline. I stopped in the middle of my hand, testing myself. Could I push it straight through? How much would it hurt? How much damage could this thing really do?

I heard the kitchen door slam and the sound of you marching through the house. I closed my hand over the needle and shoved it into the pocket of my shorts, quickly shutting the cabinet door and heading back to the bookshelf. I pulled out *The Adventures of Huckleberry Finn* and waited. You came into the room. Lately you'd stopped asking me what I was doing all the time, and that day was no exception. You just looked at me for a moment before you started pacing, pacing around the room as if it were a cage. You threw your bandaged hands into the air as though appealing to some sort of god.

"I can't do anything with hands like these," you said gruffly. "Do you want to go for a walk or something?"

I nodded, thinking of the mine site.

---

You took a basket. It was an old red plastic supermarket basket, with the words *Property of Coles* fading on the side. You held it at your side, swinging it as you walked. You greeted the camel as we stepped through her pen. As we got into the shadow of the boulders, you stopped and looked closely at the vegetation growing around its edge. You touched the leaves of a small, shrubby plant that looked a bit like spinifex. I thought about the plant guide I'd seen and wondered if its similar gray-green leaves could provide me with some sort of clue. I asked you what it was.

"Saltbush," you said. "Grows everywhere."

"Shame." I touched the diamond-shaped leaves. "I thought it might be special, like rare or something."

"He is special." You squinted at me. "You could fill books about this fella — he's tasty if you cook him right, and he helps

171

with swelling, toothache, digestion. . . ." You grabbed some of the thin, scaly leaves, putting slender branches of them into your basket. "He's one of the few plants that can not only handle all the salt in this earth but thrives on it," you added. "So that makes him pretty useful."

"What are you using it for?" I ran my finger over a leaf.

"These!" You held up your bandaged hands. "Plus, I thought we could have some for dinner."

I tried to pull the leaf off, but it just crunched in my hand. "It doesn't look tasty, it looks dead."

"You hear that, Saltbush?" You spoke to the plant, not me. "You're dead. Dead as a doornail. Quick, snap out of it!" You laughed as you turned to face me. "Out here things pretend to be dead, Gem. It's their survival tactic. Underneath, they're bursting with life. Nearly all of a desert plant's growth is below the soil." You took the crumbled leaves and touched your tongue to one of them. "I guess it's a bit like us in the city, or the city itself . . . dead to look at, but underneath, it's tingling. See, look at this." You took a step to point out a root growing in a gash in the rock. "This doesn't look like much, does it?"

"Dead as the rest."

"But it's just dormant, ready to come alive again." You ran your finger over it. "Next time we get rain, this root will grow and flower. Then, a few weeks after that, it'll have fruit — a kind of desert raisin. Amazing, right, for something to lie silent so long . . . ?"

You didn't go into the Separates, just continued walking around them. After you'd put some more leaves into your basket, you sat and leaned against the matted black trunk of a large tree. You reached behind and stroked its side.

"And this one is desert oak," you murmured, "the largest, and most tragic, of them all."

Saltbush, desert raisin, desert oak . . . there must be clues within those simple names. I repeated them over in my head, trying to imprint them there. I picked up a fallen leaf, crisped by the sun, and stuck it in my pocket with the needle. I sat down, opposite you. The needle stabbed a little into my thigh as I bent my knees. I put my hand in my pocket and pressed again at the tip. As you kept stroking the tree trunk, I rolled the needle in my fingers. I watched how your throat moved. When you swallowed, your Adam's apple moved like a target. You reached up and took some of the tree's whispering leaves in your hand.

"Some say this tree has the spirit of the dingo," you continued. "Or that he's an ancestral being with flowing white hair. . . . Some say when the wind is right, he can take out his roots and move across the landscape. But to reproduce himself, he has to die first." You crushed the leaves and then rolled them on your palm as if you were a reporter on TV talking about grain or seeds. "You see, his seedpods won't open until a fire rips them apart. After the fire, the seeds inside scatter on tiny wings and the tree's range extends." You dropped the leaves and patted the tree's bark. You smiled, pleased I was listening, thinking I was interested. "I've seen trees like him burning," you continued softly. ". . . Burning like torches, destroying everything around them with their chaos, but making new life, too." You leaned back against the bark, and the blackness of it rubbed off on your neck and hair. A small beetle fell onto your shoulder.

The needle was so tiny I could hardly feel it in my hand. I clasped my fist tighter until I was sure of its thin, hard steel. I looked back to your face, to your evil and beautiful eyes. I knew what I wanted to do. I leaned toward you, assessing how far it was from me to you. Three feet? Four? You thought it meant that I was interested in your story, so you kept talking, grinning like a kid.

"When most things die in a bushfire," you continued, "the oaks survive . . . in a way. They benefit from going through the flames, or their children do."

"And the rest of the plants?" I said, stalling for time to think.

"The fire kills off everything so the oaks can live. It's clever, very human, actually . . . to wait until everything's killed off before moving in."

You shut your eyes tight then and wrapped your arms around the tree behind you, hugging it to your back. I opened my fist and looked down. The needle glinted in the sun. I watched the sunbeams dancing on your face, turning you sluggish. I chose that moment, tipping forward toward you. My knee made a twig crack. I froze, crouched like an animal. But you stayed as you were.

"Maybe, when it all ends, it will be us and the desert oaks," you murmured, "battling it out."

I was only inches from you. You must have heard me there, but you kept your eyes closed. Maybe you thought I'd changed my mind about you. Maybe you were imagining that when you opened your eyes I would be right beside you, wanting to touch my face to yours. You even licked your lips, putting moisture into those dry cracks and hollows, ready.

I spun the needle between my finger and thumb. I held it out toward you, my hand trembling. But I carried it to your eyelid. I stopped breathing, trying to steady the needle. I lined up my hand. Then I brought the tip down until it pricked your delicate skin.

You stiffened immediately.

"One move and I push," I said. "It will go right through your eye and into your brain."

"What is that?" You frowned. "It's from the sewing machine, isn't it?" Then the corners of your mouth moved, and you started laughing. "Does that mean you've stitched me up?"

I jabbed the needle into your eye, not hard, but enough to let you know I was serious . . . enough to stop your laughter. You flinched away, bashing your head back into the tree.

"I want the keys to your car," I said. "Give me them now and I won't push any harder."

"Of course, you want to escape. I thought we were getting over that." You sighed. "Let me come with you."

"No."

Cautiously, you opened your other eye. You found my gaze. "You'll die out there, Gem. Let me come."

"Why would I take you? I want to get away from you."

You kept looking at me. I wondered if you were going to try to scare me, try to threaten me with what you would do if I didn't do what you wanted. I kept a firm pressure on your eyelid.

"Tell me where that mine site is."

"Trust me," you whispered. "It can't be like this."

"Yes it can. Tell me where it is, where are the people?"

With my other arm, I felt down your shirt, checking your

chest pockets. Then I went for your shorts. You didn't resist. Maybe you liked me feeling you up, or maybe you didn't have the strength to argue that day. I found a single car key resting against your left thigh, in the bottom corner of your shorts pocket. I grasped it tightly. I didn't know what to do then. Should I keep holding the needle to your eye and make you walk me to your car? Stab you with it for real? Or should I just run?

In the end you decided it for me. You started laughing again. You reached up and grabbed my arm. Before I realized it, you'd dragged the needle away from your eye. You looked at me, with both eyes, your hand gripped tight around my wrist.

"Don't be pathetic," you said, your words clear and controlled. "If you're really that desperate, Gem, just go. See how far you get."

———— ჳ ————

I was gone before you'd finished the sentence. I held that key so tight, thinking you'd be after me at any moment, pushing me back down to the ground with those strong arms. I didn't look back. I ran straight through the saltbush, the spiky leaves scratching against my legs. A sprig caught on my shorts and I took it with me. I hardly felt it. I leaped over a small termite mound. I could see your car, parked next to your painting shed, with its hood pointing forward to the desert. I just hoped you'd left some things in the trunk . . . water, supplies, gas. I hurtled through the opening to the camel pen. The camel got up and trotted toward me. But I sped past her.

"Bye, girl," I panted. "Sorry I can't take you, too."

She ran beside me for a few yards, her loping stride worth about three paces of my own. I wanted to let her out but couldn't risk the time.

I got to the car and jammed the key into the door. It didn't turn. Too stiff. Or I had the wrong key. I wrenched it from side to side, almost snapping it off. Then I realized the door wasn't locked anyway. I pulled it open, and it creaked loudly, stiff on its hinges.

I looked back. Bad move. You were walking from the Separates toward me, your arms and the red basket swinging by your sides. You weren't hurrying. I don't think you thought I could drive, you seemed convinced I couldn't escape. But I knew I could. I pulled myself up into the driver's seat. Slammed the door. Shoved the key in the ignition. My feet were a long way from the pedals, but the chair lever was too clogged up with sand to correct it. I sat on the edge of the seat. The steering wheel was so hot I couldn't hold my hands against it for long. There was no air in that car. Just heat. I tried to remember what Dad had said: Turn the ignition, foot on the clutch, gear in neutral. Or was it gear in first? I glanced back at you. You were walking faster, shouting something to me, but I couldn't make it out. You were through the camel pen.

I turned the key. The car lurched into life and made a huge hop across the dirt. And that moment when the car surged forward, I thought I had done it. I was leaving! Then my foot slipped, and it stopped. Stalled. My chest bashed into the steering wheel.

"Come on, come on!" I shouted, thumping it. You were about thirty feet away, less probably. "Just move!"

You were shouting something, too. I pumped my foot against the pedals, rocking my body, almost willing the car forward. Something wet was running down my cheeks, sweat or tears, blood for all I knew. You were holding your arms out toward me in some kind of plea.

"Why, Gemma?" you were saying. "Why do this?"

But I knew why. Because it was my only chance, because I didn't know when I'd leave this place again. I shifted back into neutral. I turned the key. I don't know how I was remembering how to do it all. It was like a different part of me had taken over, a more grown-up, logical part that remembered these things. I pressed the accelerator, not too much. And the car didn't stall; it just rumbled, waiting. When I'd watched you the other day, you'd eased the clutch off slowly. I tried to do the same, while pressing down farther on the accelerator with my other foot. The car roared back. I gripped the steering wheel, keeping me balanced on the edge of the seat. You were coming.

You suddenly realized that I might actually do it. You started running toward me, your face twisting into an angry shout. You threw the basket at the car and it clunked against the roof. Sprigs of plants spilled down the windshield. But the car was still roaring, straining like a dog on its leash, waiting to escape. I eased off the clutch. I tried to be gentle, tried doing it like you had done, but I screeched off into the sand with a wheel burn that would have made my friends proud. I screamed so loud then, I'm surprised the search parties didn't hear.

But you heard. Your face was right beside the window, your hands pressing against the glass and clawing at the door, your eyes hard. I pushed the accelerator farther down, and the car bunny-hopped in the sand. I felt the tires spinning. You dived at the car, your hands scrabbling at the side mirror. You got a grip and hung on.

"Gemma, don't do this," you were shouting, your voice firm and commanding. "You can't do this."

I swerved, but you didn't loosen your grip. You pulled at the door handle, and the door opened a bit. I reached around and slammed the lock down. You thumped your hand against the window in frustration. I pressed on the accelerator again, and you started running beside the car, still grasping on to the mirror. You pulled at it, as if you thought you could stop the whole vehicle with just your strength. I put my foot flat to the floor. That was enough. With a shout, you tumbled back into the dirt, leaving the side mirror hanging by some wires, bashing against the car. I heard you screaming behind me, your voice hoarse and desperate.

And then there was wide, open space in front of me. I turned the wheel and headed toward the shadowy hills on the horizon, the car skidding as I spun. The engine was screaming, struggling to get through the sand.

"Please," I whispered. "Please don't get stuck."

I revved the engine to compensate. I checked the rearview mirror. You were standing, still shouting, your arms raised toward me. Then you started running after the car, punching the air like a lunatic.

"No!" you shouted. "You'll regret this, Gemma!" You took your hat off and threw it at the car; then you leaned down and picked up rocks and sticks and whatever you could find and started hurling them, too. I felt the thump as some of the rocks smashed against the trunk. Your shouts were savage, like a wild animal . . . like you'd lost all control. I gritted my teeth and kept pressing the pedal. Then a rock pinged off one of the tires and the car started to swerve. I glanced in the mirror. Your body was crouched as you threw, aiming for the tires directly, as if you were trying to burst them. But I just kept my foot flat to the floor, swerving away from you.

I wouldn't let you stop me.

———————⟶———————

The car bounced over the land, hitting rocks and bushes. Somehow I managed to keep it straight, heading toward those distant shadows that I thought were the mine site. I should have changed gears, but I didn't trust myself. I needed to wait until those buildings were far, far behind me first; then I could do anything. The car strained and moaned. You must have heard it, too; each desperate whine of the clutch must have torn you apart.

The cluster of buildings got smaller as I drove, and eventually I couldn't even see your figure in the mirror anymore. I started to scream then, but God knows what I was saying. I'd done it! I was out there, alone . . . without you. Without anyone. I was free. I screamed with the car, whizzing across the land. I was driving into nothingness . . . driving toward everything.

A few times the wheels churned up the sand too much, and the car started to slow. I revved the engine hard, doing what I'd seen you do to get it moving again. Each time the car was strong enough to pull itself out. I changed gears when I smelled the engine burning. It was like the world's quickest crash course in learning to drive. Dad would have had a heart attack if he'd been in the car with me. I looked at the gas gauge. It was half-full, dot on the middle — half-empty, too. The temperature gauge didn't look too healthy, either; it was bouncing back and forth, edging farther toward the red section. I guess that meant the engine was overheating. One thing I did know, I was really fucking up your car.

I tried to ignore what was happening on the dashboard, and kept driving. I looked straight ahead, focusing on those shadows shimmering on the horizon. The land stretched on and on, never ending. No tracks. No telegraph lines. There was nothing to say that humans had ever been there. Only me.

———————

I got to the shadows eventually. Only they weren't the mine site like I'd hoped, or even a range of fertile hills. They were long, tall rolls of sand. Sand dunes, sculpted by the wind and held together with patches of vegetation. I'd realized this a long time before the car reached them, but I kept the vehicle pointed at them anyway. I don't know why. I guess I thought it was better than heading into the flatness of everywhere else. I thought there'd be something on the other side of them. As I got closer, the dunes began to tower above me. I couldn't drive over them. The car was already spinning and groaning, threatening to bog at any moment. I would have to drive around. I wiped my arm across my face, but it only added to the dampness. Every part of me felt hot and clammy, despite having the window open. The back of my T-shirt was as wet as if I'd jumped into a pool.

I hung my head out of the window and concentrated on keeping the car moving. The ground was getting softer. I revved the engine and the tires spun sand grains into my face. The car started to struggle, sand building up around the tires. I tried turning the wheel the other way, hoping there would be something to grip there, but that was a mistake. The tires hit the fresh sand at the edge of the track I'd made and stopped dead. I spun the wheel back, and tried again. No good. No matter how hard I pressed the accelerator, the car wouldn't move forward any more. It just sank deeper into the sand. I kept revving until I smelled burning again. Then I got out and tried pushing. But the car was heavier than an elephant. I was stuck.

The landscape began to blur in front of me, as though I was looking at it through water. The spinifex swirled like seaweed. I shut my eyes. But everything kept spinning. I leaned back into the hot panels of the car and slid down the door. My head was throbbing, my tongue thick and dry. I curled against the tire, my arms tingling from the warmth of the black rubber against my skin. The sun was scorching me, squeezing me. Drips of sweat ran over my face and onto the tire. I reached back to the darker space underneath the car. I wondered about crawling into it. I wanted to be a small insect, something that could dig through the hot sand and find somewhere cool below. I needed water.

I threw up then, just a small dribble of nothing down the side of the tire. I wanted to do more, but it wouldn't come. Everything spun and spun.

———————

When I opened my eyes, the sun had moved a little. My vision wasn't so fuzzy. I focused on the trees near me; three of them. I could hear their dry leaves scratching against each other, and flies whining around their trunks.

I dragged myself to the trunk. Before I opened it, I actually put my hands together and prayed. I never really believed in God, but right then I promised him everything. I was going to be the best God-lover in the world if only there was water and food inside that trunk, plus something to help me move the car out of the sand.

"Please," I whispered. "Please."

I felt for the clasp and popped it open. There was water. A two-liter plastic bottle of the stuff lay on its side in the middle. I grabbed it, fumbled the lid off, and poured the liquid down my throat. It was hot, but I gulped at it. Some of it spilled over my face and neck. I was like a sponge, soaking it all up. I had to force myself to stop, even though I wanted more. I'd already had nearly half.

There wasn't much else in the trunk. A towel. A tin can full of gasoline, by the smell of it. And one of your big animal-hide hats. There were some tools to fix the car with. But there was no food. Nothing that would help me move the car, either. I decided God didn't exist after all.

I got back in the car and started it again. But the wheels just spun deeper into the sand, bogging it further. I slammed my fists into the steering wheel. Then I thought of looking around the trees, maybe there were bits of wood I could put under the tires. If the car could get a grip on something, it might be enough to get it going. But those trees were tall, with branches too high up to reach. I pulled at the bark, but only small pieces came off.

It was then I saw the blood. At least, that's what I thought it was at first . . . hardened, ruby-red blood dripping down the bark of the trees. I glanced around quickly but there was nothing, and no one else, about. It was as if the trees themselves were bleeding. I picked at the blood with my fingernails, and it came off in crumbling shards, staining my fingers. I smelled them. Eucalyptus. It was sap after all.

I climbed the dune. My feet dug into the soft sand, and my muscles strained. Creatures rustled in the bushes as I passed. I stopped at the top, shielding my eyes to look out. There was nothing any different on the other side. There was no mine site, no people. There was only more sand, more rocks, more trees, and again, more shadowy dunes in the distance. As far as I could see, I was the only person out there. I hugged my arms to my chest and breathed cool air onto my burning skin. If I died right there on that dune, no one would know about it. Not even you. I walked back to the car. I would sleep for a bit. It was too hot to think right then.

---

The moon was out when I woke. I lay on the backseat and looked up at it through the window. It was plump and yellow, like the big, round cheeses Dad got from his office every Christmas. I traced out the man's face in it: two gouged-out eyes, then, below that the lazy smile, the craters that looked a little like beard stubble. It was a friendly moon, but so far away. The sky around it was a deep and clear lake. If there'd been an astronaut on the moon right then, I'm sure I could have seen him. Perhaps he could have looked down and seen me, too . . . the only one who could.

I was lying under the towel I'd found in the trunk, but I was still so cold. I rubbed my arms. They were pink from the sun, my upper arms peeling. I was too cold to sleep any more so I crawled through the space between the front seats to sit in the driver's seat. I reached back for the towel and covered my legs with it.

I turned the key, enough so I could switch on the headlights. The sand stretched out gray and ghostlike and illuminated, a column of light leading forward. It was like something a dead person would see, a tunnel leading toward heaven. I saw some movement at the edge. There was a small, long-eared rodent digging at the roots of one of the trees. It stared at the light, momentarily blinded, then hopped away into the darkness.

I turned the key fully until the car coughed back. I pumped on the accelerator until the cough turned into a roar. The noise was so loud in that silent night. Surely someone apart from me could hear it, too? I eased off the clutch, practically willing the car forward. And it did go, a little. For a second or two the wheels strained against the sand, almost getting a grip before falling back again into the churned up pit they'd created. I kicked the pedals.

"Stupid thing!"

My voice sounded so loud, it made me jump. I lay my head on the steering wheel and hummed a hymn we'd learned at school. But nothing hummed back. That silence sat hunched around me, menacing as a wolf. I wondered what was out there, in that blackness. My body started shaking and my eyes blurred. It took me awhile to realize I was crying.

I gathered together all the vegetation I could find or pick without slashing my hands too much and stuck it under the tires, but still I couldn't move the car. The wheels just ground the plants into the sand, unable to get a grip. I tried again, using small stones this time, but it got worse, the tires digging deeper. If I'd had someone else to push the car while I revved, then I might have done it, but with just me it was hopeless. I got out and kicked the tire a bit, but I knew it was a lost cause.

By the time I set off it was already getting light. I carried the bottle of water and shoved your hat on my head. It flopped down over my eyes, a little big. I knew it would be hot, walking in the daylight, but I didn't have much choice. I couldn't stay with the car; no one would find me then. And anyway, it was early. Still cool.

I trudged through the sand, keeping the dune to my right. I soon felt the strain in my upper thighs. I tried walking fast at first, trying to cover as much ground before the heat set in. But the heat came anyway. I noticed it when it became difficult to breathe deeply anymore and when each step felt like my boots were made of lead. I put my head down and focused on my feet . . . one foot forward, then the other. I was beginning to stink, my fresh sweat merging with the stale, dried sweat from yesterday. I sipped at the water. Each mouthful was never enough, but I wouldn't let myself take more.

I'd been walking for a while when I realized I couldn't see a tree. Not one. The tallest thing to aim for in that rusty-brown landscape was a clump of spinifex. I stopped, turned around, and looked at the endlessness surrounding me. Nothing but sand everywhere. How did anyone find anything? I sat on its warmth. I curled into the tiniest ball and rocked. I cried, then hated myself for it . . . for wasting all that water on tears. Hard grains of sand stuck to my cheeks and scraped against them. Farther away I could hear the wind, stirring up the grains and swirling them around. Dust slipped into my mouth and stuck to my teeth and tongue. The land was beating me, wearing me down like it had worn down the rocks. I was going to die. I'd been stupid to even hope I'd get anywhere.

But something wouldn't let me give up. Not yet. Not then. I pulled myself to my feet. I kept walking. I tried thinking about home. I imagined Anna was walking beside me, urging me on. But every time I turned to look at her, she vanished. Her voice was there, though, swirling around me like the light wind.

I sipped at the dregs of water. Then I licked around the top of the bottle, my tongue delving into the grooves. I chucked the empty bottle in the sand. I kept going. I was doing all right for a while. But then the sun moved higher and beat down right on top of me. I started to stumble. I fell down. I pushed myself back up. I stepped forward again, my toes dragging in the sand. I held my arms out in front and grabbed at the air, trying to pull myself on. The earth wanted me; it had arms waiting to grasp. I couldn't hold out forever. I stumbled again. This time I couldn't get up. I crawled forward on all fours.

I tore at my shirt, ripping it away from me, needing to do something, anything, to be cool. My boots came off next. I left them behind in the sand. And then my shorts. It was better crawling in my underwear. I even managed to stand and walk a few paces before I fell again. Then I lay on the sand, face up to the sun, trying to breathe. Everything was so bright and white. I turned over. I needed to keep moving. I stuck my fingers inside the elastic of my underpants and slipped them down over my legs. A few feet farther, I unhooked my bra.

I crawled forward. The sand scratched my skin, but I could deal with that. I was cooler. I pulled myself up again until I was standing. I could do it, just. My body wavered, my head drawing circles in the air. A fly flew up my nostril, desperate for moisture. I felt him crawling farther in. Then more came. They swarmed and settled on my body as if I were a carcass already. They were in my ears and mouth, between the tops of my thighs. To brush them off would have used too much energy. I took a step instead. The world spun. For a moment the sky was red, the sand blue. I shut my eyes. I took another step. I concentrated on the feeling of grains on the soles of my feet: hot, but not sharp. I walked like this, naked and sightless and covered in flies, just feeling my way. I no longer knew where I was headed. I no longer knew very much. I just knew I was moving.

Sometime later, I collapsed again. And that time, I knew I couldn't get up, no matter what I did. I rolled against the sand, and thrust my face into it. I wanted to be an animal, burying deep, deep down. I dug, trying to pull my body under, trying to reach the cool. But all my strength had sweated out of me. Everything had drained away. The sand had absorbed it all. I lay there, half-buried in the grains. I closed my eyes against the sun and sank down.

———————— ⟶ ————————

First my toes went, then my legs, my body, and finally my head . . . sinking down, down, deep beneath the sand. I fell through the grains. I kept going through earth and rock, past animal tunnels and tree roots and tiny digging insects, kept going until I reached the other side.

I was lying on my bed, back home. My eyes were stuck shut, but I could hear people talking. My TV was on. I recognized the voice of one of the news anchors.

"And today, London is getting hit by some incredible weather," he was saying. "Another crazy heatwave."

My duvet was pulled up tight around my neck. I couldn't push it down. It felt like it was sewn to my pillow, choking me with a blanket of heat. I could feel sweat pooling in the small of my back, sweat settling in my hair.

I smelled something. Coffee. Mum was home. I listened for her. She was banging things about in the kitchen and humming some stupid tune. I wanted to go to her, but I couldn't get my legs out of the duvet. My feet just kept kicking against the side, trapped. And my eyes were still shut, as if my eyelids were glued there. I started screaming.

"Mum! Come here!"

But she didn't. She just hummed louder. I knew she could hear me, though. The kitchen was the next room along and the walls were thin. I called again.

"Mum! Help!"

She stopped banging things for a moment, almost as if she were listening. Then she turned the radio on to something classical, blocking me out. I thrashed around, trying to pull myself up out of bed. But I couldn't get a grip on anything. I kept screaming for Mum to help. But she only turned the radio up higher. And then, suddenly, I understood why she wasn't coming. She'd sewn up my eyes and she'd sewn up my bed. She wanted to imprison me.

Then I felt arms reaching up from my mattress. They came up either side, and wrapped around my stomach, clasping together in the middle. They were strong, brown arms, arms with scratches all the way down them. They pulled me through the mattress, pulled me away from the sewn-up sheets. They dragged me down through the stuffing and then through the floorboards of my room, down through the concrete foundations of the house, and to the soft, dark earth beneath. There they just hugged me, cradling me against the earth's chest.

---

When I woke, it was cool. Almost too cool. Cloths soaking with water were lying over my body. On each side of me, a fan was whirring. A washcloth was flat on my forehead, its water dripping down my cheeks. I turned a little. My body stung as I did, and one of the cloths fell off my arm. Beneath it, my skin was bright red and blotchy, blistered in places. My arm went hot again immediately. Your hand reached across, picked up the cloth, and put it back, squeezing its water gently onto my skin.

"Thank you," I whispered, my voice barely escaping through

my swollen throat. Those two words hurt more than you can imagine.

You nodded; then you laid your head down on the side of the bed, inches from my arm.

And I slept again.

When I woke next time, you had a cup to my lips.

"Drink," you were urging. "You have to. Your body needs it."

I moved away from you, coughed. Pain seared through my limbs. It felt like my skin cracked every time I moved, opening up into sores. I looked down. There was a thin sheet covering me. Underneath I was naked, or I thought I was. My skin was too numb to really tell. But I could feel the cold cloths were no longer on my body. I tried moving my legs, but they were raised up, tied to the bed with soft cloth. I pulled at them.

"You said you wouldn't," I whispered.

You squeezed a towel, dripping water onto my forehead. "You've got bad burns," you said. "I had to raise your legs to reduce the swelling. I know I said." You stepped toward my feet, lifted the sheet up a little to look at them. "I can untie them if you like. You heal well."

I nodded. Gently, you put your hand around my right foot. You untied it, then lowered it to the mattress. You did the same with the other one, and covered them both with the sheet.

"Do you want more cold cloths?" you asked. "Are you hurting?"

I nodded again. You padded out of the room, your bare feet sticking to the wood floor. I looked up at the ceiling, testing different parts of my body, checking what hurt most. I tried to piece everything together. I'd been escaping. I'd been sinking into the sand. But then?

You'd been there. I'd felt your arms around me, scooping me up, cradling me against you. You'd been whispering something; I'd felt your breath on my neck, your hand on my forehead. You'd picked me up, so gently, as if I were a leaf you didn't want to crush. You'd carried me somewhere. And I'd curled into your arms, tiny as a stone. You'd splashed me with water. And then, after that, nothing. Blackness. Just blackness.

You came back in, with cloths soaking in a bowl.

"Do you want to do it, or should I?" You started to squeeze water from a cloth, then began to lift the sheet.

"I'll do it." I snatched the sheet from you. I lifted it and peered down at my body. Much of my skin was red and shiny, some of it peeling badly. I touched a blister on my chest. Around it the skin looked wet. I laid the damp cloths you'd wrung out over the worst parts, and it felt better immediately. It was as if my skin breathed out when the cloths touched it, then breathed in straight after, absorbing the water. It was hard to get to the burned lower parts without you seeing me naked, though I suppose you'd seen it all by then anyway. I shuddered as I remembered you carrying me in your arms. How had you touched me when I'd been like that? Was I brave enough to ask?

After a while, I gave up on the cloths. I lay back onto the pillow.

"How long have I been here?" I asked. "Like this?"

"A day or so. You won't be fully healed for a few days more. It's lucky I found you when I did."

"How did you?"

"Followed your tracks. Easy." You leaned your elbows on the mattress, too close to me. But it was too painful to move myself farther away. You picked up the cup of water and held it out. "I took the camel."

"How?"

"Rode it." You smiled a little. "She goes pretty fast."

Something dried up had settled in the corners of my lips. I licked at it. I let you pour the water into my mouth.

"You'll start to feel better soon," you said quietly. "If you're lucky, you won't even get any scars."

The water tingled in my throat. I gulped more. Right then, that water wasn't brown or full of grit; it was the finest champagne. I let the excess spill down my neck. I thought of the car, bogged down deep in the dirt.

"How did we get back?"

"I carried you at first, then I put you on the camel. We walked through the night." You nodded toward the cup. "Want more?"

I shook my head. "What about the car?"

"Didn't find it. You were heading back toward me when I found you."

"Toward . . . ?"

You nodded again. "So I figured the car had probably got stuck or died somehow, and you were just coming home."

"Home?"

"Yeah." Your mouth twitched. "Back to me."

Like you'd said, I felt better pretty quickly. The next day you gave me a small handful of nuts and berries. The berries tasted bitter and the nuts were powdery and sweet, both were unlike anything I was used to. But I ate them anyway. Then I felt between the mattress and the base of the bed. The knife was still there. I counted the notches on the wood, running my fingers over the grooves. Twenty-five. But how many more days had passed since then? I carved four more lines.

---

The next day, after I'd carved the thirtieth notch, I wondered about my period . . . why it hadn't arrived yet. Perhaps I had dried up, like the land around me, my body needing all the moisture it could get.

I got up and put clothes on, but the fabric stung as it touched my burned skin. I gritted my teeth and hobbled to the veranda. Even the feel of the floorboards against my feet hurt, and I had to hold my T-shirt away from my chest as I walked.

"You should have just gone naked," you said when you saw me. "Wouldn't hurt so much."

I stopped holding out my T-shirt. "It's fine."

"Here." You stretched your glass of water toward me.

"I'll get my own," I said.

I went to the kitchen. After I'd run myself some water, I stepped through the kitchen door and out the other side of the house from you. I leaned against the wall, keeping my body in the shade. From there I could see the camel, resting in the corner of her pen. Her head was down, the harness hanging loosely around her ears. She looked so docile now, like you'd sucked away her wildness. I shielded my eyes, scanning the horizon until I found the shadowy hills of the dunes: the hills I'd thought were the mine site. They seemed so far away.

I lowered myself onto the crate outside the door as it all sunk in. I'd always kept a small seed of hope alive, hope that I'd be able to escape. But suddenly I realized something. That view of sand and endlessness . . . that was it, that was my life. Unless you took me back to a town, that was all I'd ever see. No more parents or friends or school. No more London. Only you. Only the desert.

I rolled the glass of water against my forehead, then licked a drop from the side. I left my tongue momentarily against the cool. Maybe I'd wear you down, eventually. Maybe you'd take me back. Haven't there been cases where kidnapped girls have walked free, years later? Haven't there been rescues, too? But how long would it take?

There was movement to my left.

You were hunched over near the corner of the house, underneath the window where my bedroom was. Your arms were hanging down toward something, and you were bouncing backward and sideways. I looked closer. There was a snake. You were stretching toward it, trying to get a grip, then leaping backward when it went for you. Its head was up, challenging you. It was like a kind of courtship dance. You circled each other gracefully, eyes locked.

But you were fast. You darted toward the snake, confusing it, and grabbed underneath its head. The snake writhed, tried to turn its pink, wide mouth toward you. But your grip was firm. You lifted it from the sand and held it out in front of you. Your lips were moving, talking to it, inches away from its fangs. Then you started walking, taking it with you.

You went past me, straight to the second outbuilding. You backed into the doorway, the snake trying to wrap its tail around your wrist as you stepped into the building.

I dozed on the couch in the living room, only waking when the light changed from bright and white to muted and golden. I watched a beam of sunlight on the dark wood floor, turning the wood a copper color as it moved across the boards. Afterward, I wandered around the house. You weren't anywhere. I changed my clothes, finding a baggy T-shirt scrunched in the closet in the hall with the words SAVE THE EARTH, NOT YOURSELVES printed on it. It was loose enough not to hurt the burns too much. Then I went back to the crate outside the kitchen door, and waited.

A line of ants crawled over my ankles, and there was the high-pitched screech of a bird far above. My burned skin prickled, even though it was only the softer afternoon sun against it. I pulled at the T-shirt, trying to cover the back of my neck. I stretched my legs. After a while, I wandered toward the outbuilding where I'd seen you last. As I got close, I saw you'd left the door open a crack, the padlock hanging unlocked. I tried to peer into the darkness inside, but could only make out dull shadows. I couldn't hear anything. I pushed the door, letting the sunlight in. The room was full of boxes, all neatly stacked. There was a pathway through the middle, between them.

"Ty?" I called.

No answer. I listened. I thought I heard a soft shuffling, somewhere behind the boxes.

"Ty? Is that you?"

I took a step into the building. The cool darkness in the room felt good on my skin. I took another step so I could read the writing on some of the boxes: *food (tins), food (dried), tools, electricle wires*. . . . The writing was in pencil, spindly like a web. Yours, I guessed. Your spelling was terrible. I glanced back at the house. Everything was so still, more like a theater set than real life. I traced my fingers along some other boxes, sweeping away the dust as I went: *Medical supplys, blankits, gloves*. . . . I followed the boxes down the pathway. It was interesting, seeing these preparations, seeing what you thought was necessary for us to live. *Ropes, tools, gardning supplys, sewing, feminine higene* . . . you'd thought of everything. The farther in I went, the louder the shuffling noise became. It was soft and hesitant, more like an animal than you.

"Hello?" I tried again. "Ty?"

The path opened into a wider space. I squeezed sideways through the boxes and into it. The shuffling was louder, all around me. I turned. There were cabinets, on every side, from floor to head height. Some of them were made of glass, others wire. There was movement inside them, a quiet rustling. Creatures of some sort? I bent to look at them.

Tiny eyes looked back. A curled black snake raised its head lazily and a spider as big as my hand scuttled across its enclosure. I stepped backward. Breathing deeply, I studied the cages from there, checking all the doors were closed. A scorpion lifted its tail, rattling a warning. My legs were suddenly shaky. There must have been twenty of those cages around me. They mostly had snakes and spiders inside, a few scorpions, and some other cages that didn't look like they had anything in them at all. Why were they there? Why hadn't you told me? My eyes settled on a silvery-brown snake. It looked like the one you had caught that morning. Its tail still flicked angrily as it watched me, its tongue darting in and out like a dagger.

I forced myself to breathe. The cage doors were closed, everything shut in. The creatures couldn't get near me. But I could still hear them, scrabbling, clicking their tails and sliding. The noises made my heart falter. I steadied myself against the boxes and walked back down the pathway, feeling my way along. *GARdNiNg supplys, blankits, Alcohol . . .*

I paused at that box. I stood on tiptoe and looked at the top. The sticky tape was loose, barely fastening the cardboard sides. I glanced back at the open door, ready to jump into the sunlight if I needed to . . . if any loose creatures came my way; then I dragged the box toward me, bottles clinking as it moved. I pulled at the tape and the sides unstuck. Cautiously, I put my hand inside. My fingers were shaking. I was worried about what else might be in there, waiting for the soft tap of legs against the back of my fingers or the brush of snakeskin. I grabbed the first bottle I got a grip on and took it down, sneezing as dust landed on me.

BUNDABERG RUM. A one-liter glass bottle. I could do some damage with that. One way or the other, it could knock one of us out. I took it with me and stepped out of the building, glad to be out of there. I closed the door, resting it against the frame as I'd found it, the padlock still hanging. I breathed in the cooler air, checking for the camel. She wasn't in the rope pen, and I couldn't see her near the Separates, either. Perhaps she was behind the rocks. The sun was starting to dip, covering everything with a peach glow. It wouldn't be long until it was dark.

I went straight to my room and hid the bottle under my pillow. Then I sat for a while, listening. There was only the creak of the wood as the heat started to bleed out of the house. I did another lap of the rooms, checking for you, then went out to the veranda. The sun escaped over the horizon then, and quickly (it was always so quick) it got dark. I squinted at the fading light and at the sand that was slowly changing color from purple to gray to black. I could still make out most of the shapes around the house: the outbuildings, the trailer, the Separates. But your shape wasn't there; neither was the camel's.

I didn't know how to turn the generator on, so I went onto the porch and took down one of the lanterns instead. I unscrewed the glass casing, as I'd seen you do before, and smelled the cotton wick inside. It smelled like you'd soaked it recently in fuel, so I lit it and twisted the glass back on. Light! I was a little proud of myself for making it work. I twisted the knob on the side to increase the flame and carried the lantern back to the living room.

I sat on the couch and picked at a hole where the stuffing was falling out. My body was straining, listening for the slightest sound. A small part of me wondered whether everything had been leading up to this moment, whether you were finally going to play out your ultimate fantasy and kill me. Perhaps you were waiting until it was completely dark before you made your move. I listened for your footstep on the veranda, your cough in the darkness. If this had been a horror film, a phone would have rung at that moment to tell me you were outside, watching me.

But another part of me was worrying about something entirely different. Another part was wondering if something had happened to you out there.

"Stop being stupid," I said to myself out loud.

I waited for what felt like forever before I went back to my bedroom, taking the flickering lantern. I shut the door and dragged the chest of drawers in front of it. I kept the curtains open, watching for shadows outside. But the moon was still low, and everything was darker than usual. I put a pillow behind me and leaned against it. I watched the shadowy faces the lantern light made on the wall, all jagged and crooked-looking. I cradled the rum bottle. Then I grabbed it around its neck and rehearsed how to swing it if I needed to. I touched it against my forehead, imagining the blow it would give . . . feeling its weight. I spent some time unscrewing and rescrewing the lid, smelling it. Then I took a sip.

It was bitter, hard to swallow. But I was used to drinking raw alcohol after all those nights in the park with my friends. I used to be quite good at pretending that the liquid actually tasted nice enough to want to take another gulp.

I sipped again. It burned my throat like sunburn, only inside instead of out this time. I scrunched my face up, the way they do in the movies, as another sip went down. I looked out of the window. The desert was as still and quiet as it always was. Dead quiet. It's amazing how scary total quiet can be, how it can mess with your head if you let it. In London I was used to noisy nights, to the honks and shouts and whirs of a big city. London chattered like a monkey at night. The desert, on the other hand, slithered around me like a snake. Soft and silent and deadly . . . and quiet enough to keep my eyes wide open, always.

I tapped my teeth against the rim of the bottle. I kept swigging until the room started to spin, until I stopped thinking about whether that could be my last night on earth or whether that place would be the only place I'd ever see from then on. After a while, I stopped watching for shadows at the window. I stopped caring about the darkness. And the quiet.

I remembered then why all my friends liked to get drunk . . . it was the forgetting. The sweet not knowing of the future.

------- ⁊ -------

A scraping sound woke me. I opened my eyes. The chest of drawers was moving, being pushed forward by the door. Someone was trying to get in. I tried to sit up. I was half off the bed, the bottle still in my hand. The rum wasn't finished, but, judging by the wetness around me and the smell of stale alcohol, much of it had drained out into the sheets. I fumbled my way along the bed. I clasped the bottleneck tight, ready to swing.

The drawers shifted to the side, and your scratched arm came around the door. I lowered the bottle as you squeezed through the gap. I shrunk away, too weak, and still too drunk, to do much else. It was gray dawn-light, early. You looked me over, your eyes taking in the bottle, your nose wrinkling at the smell. I turned away from your frowning face.

"I had to get something," you said. "It took longer than I thought."

You tried scooping me up then, but I screamed at you to let

me go and bashed the bottle against your chest. So you stayed at the side of the bed, just watching. After a while, you took the bottle from my fingers and lifted the sheet up over me.

"I'll fix you breakfast," you said eventually.

I slept.

"It's on the veranda," you said.

I shook my head, pain searing through my temples. To walk that far, on that morning, seemed about as probable as escape. But I knew I needed food.

"Come on, I'll carry you."

I shook my head again, but your arms were around me, lifting me up before I could do anything about it. I shut my eyes, my head spinning, sickness in my stomach. You carried me like you carried branches, delicately, with your arms open wide to cradle me. You made me feel about as light as them, too.

You lowered me onto the couch on the veranda. As you did, I could see that your eyes were red and tired, with dark hollows around them. But the pale sun was on your skin, making it glow. The light made everything glow that morning. It seeped into the landscape and made the sand sparkle like popping candy.

It didn't make me glow, though. I felt more like I was fading away, like the world had forgotten me. As I stared at the glinting sand, I wondered if my disappearance was making the news. Was anyone still interested? I knew papers dropped stories when there wasn't anything new to report. And what could be new about my story, when the only thing that ever changed was the way the wind blew?

I'd been in your house for more than a month. Was anyone still searching for me? Just how dedicated were my parents anyway? They'd always been shrewd. "Good business sense" are the three most popular words in Dad's vocabulary. And maybe he was asking the question — was looking for me good business sense anymore? Was I a good investment? Right then, I don't think I would have put any money into my search.

You gave me a plate of small yellow fruits. You took one and showed me how to dig my nails in and eat it, sucking out the insides. I tried it. It was sour at first, but the taste became a little sweeter as I chewed. The seeds got stuck in my teeth and gums. You sucked on another one, before you spoke.

"You met the guys in the shed, then?" you asked.

I remembered all those eyes staring back at me, all those scales and legs. I shuddered. "Why do you have them?"

"To keep us alive." You reached for another of the yellow fruits. I gave you the plate. My stomach was too queasy for any more, even though I wanted it. You smacked your lips through the sour part, then picked the seeds from your teeth. "They're going to help me make antivenom."

I shook my head. "You don't get antivenom from a snake, you just get poison."

The corner of your mouth turned up. "You're just as clever as you look, smarty-pants," you said. "I knew it all along." You looked at me like you were almost proud. "You're right, though," you said, spitting seeds onto the floor. "Those guys are all poisonous. And antivenom comes from collecting an immune reaction to the poison . . . another reason why we need the camel. Soon I'll milk those creatures, inject their poison into the camel, then collect her antibodies, her immune reaction. I'll filter all that and make antivenoms . . . at least that's the plan. It'll take awhile, and I still don't know if I can do it, but I'm going to try anyway. That way we'll always have a fresh supply."

I frowned. "Won't the camel get sick?"

"Nah, she's immune, like lots of things out here. Us humans are the weak ones." You tore at the skin of another fruit, nibbling off the fleshy bits. "But what we should do first, before any of this, is start to desensitize you. If we inject a little of those creatures' poisons into your system, you can build up your own immunity."

"You're not injecting anything into me."

You shrugged. "You can do it yourself; it's not hard. Just prick your skin and put a little of the venom inside. I do it all the time."

"And if I don't want to?"

"Then you run the risk."

"Of what?"

"Dying, being paralyzed . . . poison's not much fun, you know?" You looked me over, one side of your mouth curling up. "But then, I suppose you know that already . . . what with all the rum you had last night. That was a year's supply, that bottle."

I avoided your gaze. It was the first time you'd mentioned the rum. I braced myself, waiting for you to be angry about me riffling through your supplies. But you just shrugged it off.

"With any environment, there's risks, I s'pose," you murmured. "It's all the same, really: poisons, injuries, sickness . . . just different triggers. The difference is that in the city they're caused by people, and out here it's just the land. I know which one I'd prefer."

My head was starting to spin again. I kept picturing those creatures in their cages, waiting with their poison to kill me, or to save me.

"How long have they been there?" I asked. "In those cages?"

You put the fruit down and wiped your hands on your knees. "I've been catching them since we got here. I've found most of them now, but some of them are bastards to find . . . still need a couple, actually."

"And they're all poisonous?"

You nodded. "Course. I wouldn't have them otherwise. Not all of them are deadly, but you still wouldn't want a little nip."

"Why haven't you been bitten?"

"I have. Nothing serious, though. I guess I've just learned to handle them; I know what makes them tick. Creatures aren't so dangerous when you understand them."

Again, you pushed the fruit toward me. "Come on, eat up." You grinned. "Anyone would think you've got a hangover."

———— ⁊ ————

You were nice to me after that. I mean, *really* nice. You kept the cold cloths coming and you fussed over me in a way that Mum would never have dreamed of. You even made me food you thought I'd like . . . or you tried to, anyway. (I guess it's hard to rustle up ice cream when the nearest freezer is hundreds of miles away.) But you watched me, too, all the time. It was as if you were constantly assessing me, gauging what was acceptable, what you could say or do that wouldn't upset me too much. I soon caught on to it. I started testing how far I could push you. And you let me push.

The next day I fed the chickens. You came with me, saying you needed to check the spring. When we reached the entrance to the camel pen, I slowed down and let you catch up. I let you walk in step. You glanced at me, checking if it was all right that you were there.

"You must really hate me," I said.

"What do you mean?"

"You must hate me so much that you don't care if I die . . . otherwise you'd just let me go."

You swung around to me quickly, so quickly that you stumbled on a rock. "That's the opposite of how I feel."

"Then why not let me go? You know it's what I want."

You were silent for four or five steps. "But I did let you go," you said quietly. "You almost died."

"That's because your car's a piece of crap and I don't know how to get anywhere out here. *You* do, though. If you really didn't hate me, you'd take me back to a town. You'd let me go."

"Don't start this again, please."

"But it's true, isn't it? You could let me go if you wanted to; you just don't want to. So that means you must hate me."

I plowed through a small shrub, my boots crushing its leaves. You stopped to straighten them.

"Things aren't that simple."

"They can be."

I stopped, too. You finished straightening the plant and stepped around it. You took a hesitant step toward me.

"Just give it a bit of time, please, Gemma. A few months more and you'll learn to appreciate all this, then . . ."

"Then what? Then you'll let me go? I don't believe you."

"Believe me, please. Just for once." You raised your arms toward me, almost begging.

"What will you do?" My hands were on my hips and I was trying to make myself look taller than I was. Even so, my head didn't go past your shoulders. You sighed.

"OK," you whispered finally. "Give it six months. Just six months. That's all you'll need. Then if you still hate all this, after that, *then* I'll take you back. I promise. I'll even take you to a town."

"I still don't believe you."

"Try me."

I kept staring at you. After a moment you looked down, putting your hands into your pockets. "I'm serious," you said, your voice breaking a little. "What's six months to you now anyway? What have you got to lose?"

You kicked the dirt. That dull thud of your boots was the only sound out there. I wiped the sweat from my forehead. I still wasn't sure I could trust you. I mean, who believes a kidnapper about anything? What had you ever done to make me believe in you?

"Even if you are serious," I challenged, "even if you do take me back, what's to stop you from doing all this again to some other girl?"

You ran your hand through your hair. "There is no other girl. Without you, I'll live here alone."

"You're disgusting." You flinched. I stepped toward you.

"You're just trying to flatter me, trying to get me to do what you want. You can't help yourself. There's always another girl. What do they say about dogs? Once they've got the taste for it — killing . . ."

"I'm not a killer."

"You're a dog, though."

You looked at me, your eyes huge. You were like a dog then, waiting for me to throw you a bone . . . waiting for something I could never give you.

"I love you," you said, simple as anything. You didn't blink. You waited for what you'd said to soak in. It didn't. It just bounced off. I refused to think about it at all.

"You're a bastard," I said.

I started walking. You spoke to my back, raising your voice as I marched farther ahead.

"The land wants you here. *I* want you here," you called. "Don't you care about that at all?"

I turned, incredulous. "You think I could care for you after what you've done? Are you really that crazy?"

"We need you."

"You don't need anything but help."

You gaped at me. As I watched, your eyes became wet, drowning as they looked back at mine. I shook my head, refusing to be sucked in.

"This is screwed up," I said. I spoke quietly, more to myself than you. You tried to speak, but I kept on, regardless, no longer scared. "You're seriously messed up, aren't you? And out here, I'm never going to get away from you. Not unless you take me back to a town."

"I don't want that."

"It's what I want."

You flinched away from my words as if I were physically harming you with them. You avoided my gaze, clearly embarrassed by your reaction.

"You're not so tough now, though," I said quietly.

I turned and walked fast toward the Separates. I could feel myself starting to shake. I was fragile then, almost in as many pieces as you were. I didn't want you to see. You didn't follow me; just stood, motionless, your head down to the dirt. I stumbled through the rocks, glad you weren't there. I could almost handle you when you were tough; I knew what to expect. But like that? I didn't know what to think.

<hr />

You were quiet that night, more thoughtful. You soaked cloths for my burns, infusing them with a plant mixture that made them smell like hospitals. After dinner you stood at the kitchen sink, looking out at the darkness. Your body was taut, like a hunter standing in wait. The lantern light made shadows on your skin. I cleared the plates from the table and took them to you. You turned and grabbed my wrist, almost making me drop everything.

"I was serious, you know," you began. "What I said today . . . I meant it. Just give this place six months, please. Can you wait that long?"

I stepped back, disentangling my wrist. I left the plates on the bench. A deep line formed on your forehead, creasing your skin like a gorge. Your blue eyes were bright underneath.

"Can you?" you whispered.

There was that familiar intensity about you, that seriousness. I could, almost, believe you. If you'd been anyone else, I wouldn't have hesitated. I moved my head. It wasn't a nod, but I wasn't shaking it, either.

"Three months," I said.

"Four." Your face twitched. "Just please don't try to escape again," you said. "Not by yourself, not until I can take you. You don't know this place yet." You took the plates, stopping to unwind the bandage that was still wrapped around your right hand before turning on the water. "It's just . . . to survive this land, you need to love it. And that takes time. Right now, you need me."

"I know."

You stared at me, as surprised as I was by those two words. But I did need you, didn't I? I'd tried escaping by myself, and it hadn't worked.

You sighed as you turned back to the dark window. "After four months, if you still want to go, I'll take you to the edge of a town. Just don't make me go in with you."

"I wouldn't want you to," I said. I frowned. As if I could make you do anything you didn't want to do.

You started to wash the plates, your shoulders drooping. Your fingers darted about in the water. I saw the pulse in your neck beating fast, that tiny bit of life under your tough brown skin. There were freckles around it, scattering down onto your collarbone.

"I don't have to turn you in, you know." I started speaking without really meaning to. "If that's what you're worried about, I don't have to turn you in. You could just let me go, then you could disappear, back into the desert. I could say I don't remember, that I've got heatstroke or amnesia or something. I won't even remember your name."

Your eyes flicked up to mine, but they were filled up with sadness, ready to leak.

⸻ ⸙ ⸻

There was a wind that night. I heard it as I lay in bed, picking up grains of sand and chucking them against the wood and the windows, spattering them toward me like gunfire. Or rain. If I shut my eyes I could almost imagine the sound was English rain, pelting down around me as if it were the middle of winter, quenching the gardens and fields, filling the Thames and the gutters around my house. I had forgotten how comforting the sound of rain was against the windows, how safe it felt.

You'd gone to your room before me that night. You'd been so quiet, disillusioned by me, I think. This whole adventure of yours hadn't turned out like you'd expected. Were you beginning to regret it? Were you thinking that you'd picked the wrong girl? Perhaps you'd only just realized for the first time that I was ordinary, no one special, just as much of a disappointment to you as I was to everyone else. I turned over and thumped the pillow, frustrated by still being awake, and by all those thoughts.

Then I heard you scream. The sound slashed through the silence, making me leap up in bed. It was a desperate, animal sound, as though it came from somewhere deep within you. It was the loudest thing I'd heard for days.

211

My first thought was that someone else was in the house. Someone had come to rescue me and was getting rid of you first. But that was a stupid thought. No one would rescue anyone like that, except in the movies. Certainly not in the desert. Out there, rescuers would come by plane and they would surround us with lights and noise first. We would have heard anyone else coming for miles.

Even so, I listened for sounds outside, steps on the veranda. But there were no bangs or bumps, nothing to suggest that anyone else was there. Only me. Only you. And the only thing I could hear were your screams.

You were yelling words as well as noises, but I couldn't tell what they were. In between, it sounded like you were crying. I got out of bed. I took the knife. I walked to the door on the balls of my feet, slow and soundless. When you screamed again, I pushed the door handle down, using your noise to mask the creak. I stepped into the hallway. Your screams were louder there, echoing hoarsely around the house. Your door was open a little. I tilted my ear toward the crack, listened.

There was silence for a few seconds, maybe even a minute or two. My ears rang with it. Then I heard you sobbing. It built up pretty fast, until it was uncontrollable and desperate, the way a kid sobs sometimes. I peered through the crack and into the darkness. Something was shaking on your bed: you. There was no other movement. I pushed the door farther open.

"Ty?"

You kept sobbing. I took a step toward you. There was a slip of light from the window falling on your face. It shone on the wetness of your cheeks. Your eyes were closed, shut tight. I took another step.

"Ty? Are you awake?"

Your hands were in fists, kneading the rolled-up sweater you used as a pillow. Your sheet had slipped down, exposing your back against the bare mattress. Stretched out like that, you looked too big for the bed. You had such a long, straight back, long like a tree trunk. But right then it was shaking like a sapling.

I left the door wide open behind me and glanced around the room. The window was closed, and there was nothing to suggest that anyone else had been there. Whatever you had been screaming about, you'd been screaming in your sleep.

Your sobs subsided as your face buried into the sweater. I stood there watching. You were sobbing like I had sobbed when I'd first arrived, quietly and desperately, as though you'd never stop. It was weird; it almost made me want to start crying again, too. I shook my head. You were tough and strong and dangerous. Maybe this was just an act.

As I watched, you curled your legs to your chest. You started rocking. And then the screams began again. They pierced right into me. I had to bring my hands up to my ears. I stepped closer. I had to make it stop. Without thinking about what I was doing, I grabbed you around the shoulders. Shook you. Your skin was clammy. Hot.

Your eyes snapped open, but you didn't see me straightaway. You saw someone else. You pushed me aside and dragged yourself backward along your mattress until you hit the wall. Your eyes were wild, moving from side to side as you tried to focus. Then you started murmuring words and sounds.

"Don't take me," you were saying. "Please, leave me."

I tried to find your gaze, tried to keep your eyes on me. "It's Gemma," I said. "I'm not taking you anywhere. Just calm down."

"Gemma?"

You spoke my name like it was something you only half remembered. You grabbed at the sheet, pulling it around you.

"You're dreaming, Ty," I said.

But you weren't listening. You crawled forward and clawed at my T-shirt. I stepped back.

"Stop it, Ty!"

I slapped your hands, pushing your fingers away. But your face was desperate.

"Don't take me," you sobbed, your voice like a child's. "Mamma was here, the trees, my stars . . . I don't want to go."

You grabbed my waist, throwing your arms around it. You sobbed into my stomach. Your eyes were open but they still weren't seeing me. You were kneading my back with your fingers, pulling my shirt. I touched your hair, and your crying subsided a little.

"It's Gemma," I said. "Wake up."

I felt the dampness of your tears on my stomach, your fingers grabbing tight around my waist, not wanting to let me go. I let you stay like that until your crying stopped altogether.

"I don't know where I am," you whispered.

"You're here," I said. "In the desert. There's no one else around."

You wiped your eyes against my T-shirt, then looked up at me. You saw me that time; you knew who I was. Your whole face relaxed as you focused.

"Gemma," you said.

I nodded.

"Thank you."

"You were dreaming; I just woke you up."

"Thank you."

———————

After a while you let go. You sat cross-legged on the bed and stared down at the floor. You were twisting your thumbs over each other, embarrassed, I think.

"What were you dreaming about?" I asked.

You shook your head, dismissing me. I stayed there, waiting. The wood creaked around us, and the wind battered the metal roof. You glanced toward the window as if checking it was still there.

"The orphanage," you said quietly. "The journey in the van, leaving the land." You glanced out at the night sky and the stars. I looked out at them, too. I thought I could maybe make out the straight line of the horizon, separating the black land from the graying sky. You sighed, running a hand over your face. "You probably think I'm a loony now, right?"

I looked down at you, huddled into yourself. "We all have dreams."

Your big eyes were shining in the darkness like a nocturnal creature, a creature that needed to be held. "What are yours about?" you whispered.

"Home, mostly."

"London?" You thought about the word, working out what it meant to you. "How can you dream about that place?" you said. Again, your eyes went back to the window. "How do you love it so much?"

"People love what they're used to, I guess."

"No." You shook your head. "People should love what needs loving. That way they can save it." You were quiet for a long time then, staring out of your window, just thinking. I walked softly to the door.

———————❧———————

Your bedroom was empty when I got up. I fed the chickens. On the way back, the camel lumbered up to me. I scratched her ears, pulling at the fine hairs inside them in the way you had shown me she liked. She rested her nose on my arm.

"He'll keep you, you know," I murmured to her. "When I go, in a few months' time, he won't let you go, too." I stroked the fur on her cheek, soft as a teddy bear's. She chewed in a circle, her rubber lips brushing the back of my hand. "How come you're so gentle?" I said. "You should be wild, worse than him." I touched her long, thick eyelashes with my fingertips. She blinked.

I took a couple of steps away from her, but she came with me, following behind. I walked around in a circle, the gentle thud of her hooves staying with me. I stopped and turned to her, wanting to try something.

"Whoosh down," I said.

I lifted my arm the way you did, and, after a bit of a moan, she tipped forward, her legs buckling underneath her. As her body hit the ground, she sent up a puff of dust.

"Good girl," I said.

I knelt down to her. Like that we were about the same height; her nose was huge and her teeth rotten. Her sharp, slightly stale smell was strong in my nostrils. She turned her head toward the outbuildings, closing her eyes against the sun. I shifted closer to her and put my arm over her wide, muscled shoulder. She rested her neck against my side. I could slip onto her back like this, roll onto her hump, and ride her. We could gallop off toward the sun.

I rested my head against her fur, and shut my eyes, too. Balls of fire danced behind my eyelids. Right then, for that moment, it was enough just to sit there.

———————⟶———————

You spent the entire day in your painting shed. It was midafternoon before I plucked up the courage to go and see you. You'd been so different the night before, almost vulnerable. . . . I wanted to see how you would react to me today. The door of the shed was open a little. I pushed it.

It was bright in that room, and hot; it took me a moment to adjust. The curtains that had been hanging from the window were torn down and bundled in a pile underneath. Sunlight was streaming in, and I saw that the previously fading walls had been repainted with vividly colored dots and swirls; streaks of reds and blacks and browns dashed across them. Leaves, sand, and branches were stuck to some of these colors, giving the walls a texture. If I stepped back and looked at it all as a whole, I could see patterns. A wave of yellow dots stretched across the floor like a sand dune, and circles of blue on the far wall made pools of water. The room looked wild, and reminded me of a story Mum had read, a very long time ago, where a kid's bedroom had transformed into a wilderness.

You were in the middle of it all, standing on top of a wooden stool, body thrust backward, painting the ceiling. You were wearing only a thin pair of shorts, the material torn and curling over your thighs. Your skin was almost the same color as the earthy brown paint on the wall behind you. You were painting the area above your head with thousands of tiny orange dots. After a while, you took another paintbrush from behind your ear and filled the space between the dots with swirls of white. Only when your paint ran out did you stop.

You turned. Your chest was glistening with sweat, smudges of earth-color all over it. I checked your face, looking to see if any of the previous night's anguish had stayed with you. But you seemed relaxed and happy. You stepped down from the stool and came toward me.

"Like my painting?" you said.

"What is it?"

"Everything around us. The land." You grinned. "It's not finished yet. Every bit of wall will be part of it; me, too."

"Why?"

"I want to capture this, all this beauty, I want to connect . . . I want you to see everything the way it is before . . . while you're here . . ."

Your eyes were sparkling. I turned, taking in all the colors and swirls and textures around me. My eyes lingered on a bundle of bright white dots on a black background in one corner of the ceiling. They almost looked like stars, tiny balls of light glinting. Is that what you'd intended? You took another step toward me and I could see grains of sand sticking to your shoulders and down half your chest. I reached forward to touch them. Your skin was as rough and as warm as the dirt outside.

"Doesn't that itch?"

"It's only the base coat," you said. "When it's fully dry, I can put on the patterns."

"What patterns?"

You smiled at my confusion. You reached up and pressed my hand against your chest, keeping it there. "Patterns of the land." You nodded toward the rest of the room. "Just wait until the sun sets," you said. "This whole room will come alive then."

"What do you mean?"

"You'll see."

My hand, beneath yours, felt the deep thud of your heartbeat. I quickly slipped my fingers away. You moved your hand from your chest, too, and ran it through your hair. A waterfall of sand fell to the floor.

"Sandstorm," you said. You shook your head, making more come down, making the sand fly.

———— ❧ ————

I followed you to the door, my head spinning a little from what I'd seen. You placed my hand against your back. Your skin was warm and damp, your spine stretching out underneath like roots.

"I can paint the front of me, but I need something to reach my back," you said.

I took my hand away quickly. "I don't want to paint you."

"You don't have to." You turned to face me. "There are leaves near the pool in the Separates, long leaves. Will you get one for me? While you're there, grab me a clump of moss, too."

You stepped back into the building, leaving me in the doorway. I balanced on the crate beside the door, rocking it back and forth.

"Come back when the sun starts to set," you called out to me. "I'll be ready then."

You shut the door. I wandered toward the Separates, pretending to myself that I wasn't really doing what you wanted. I walked slowly, stopping to look at things, pretending the little purple flower I noticed in the sand was the real reason behind my walk. I bashed through the longer grasses with a stick, as I'd seen you do, checking for snakes.

At the pool, I bent under the eucalyptus arm and crawled along the side of the water. I dipped my fingers in, enjoying the sudden cold on my skin. I reached the overhanging rock at the back, the thin dark slit where the moss was. Things rustled around me, but I didn't move away. I was strangely calm, just enjoying the afternoon laziness of that place. The rock was cool and shaded and I sat still, my bare calves resting against the stone. After a while I felt for the moss, reaching farther into the darkness of the rock and tearing off a clump. I waited as a tiny spider stepped in front of my fingers.

Crawling back around the pool, I saw the leaves you meant,

large and juicy-looking. I tore one away from its stem and a milky blood oozed out. I dabbed at it, trying to make it stop.

Heading back, I paused at the chickens. Dick was at the far end of his cage, but when I started talking to him, he strutted up to me. He stuck his beak through the wires and tore a triangle from the leaf I'd just collected.

"Ty won't like that," I chided.

But Dick only puffed his feathers up proudly and spat out the bits of leaf. I sat next to his cage, listening to the disapproving murmurs of the hens. Soon a group of frogs started to jangle and rusty-croak, building up into a frenzied chorus.

Then the sun started to dip. It was time. I meandered my way back to your painting shed.

———⋛———

I pushed open the door. The orange light from the setting sun shone through the window, lingering on the walls you had painted. The light picked out the sand grains, making them glitter and wink. All around me was color and sparkle, almost too much to take in. You'd worked quickly, transforming the space. You stood in the middle of it all, your painted body reflecting the light also. Your back was the only part of you not painted. There was a strong herbal smell, like the smell your roll-ups gave out. It was heavy and intoxicating.

You came over to me, reaching for the plants. You were naked. But you were so covered with paint and sand, flowers and leaves, that I didn't notice right away. The paint and textures covered you like clothes. Your face was a light red color with orange and yellow dots and swirls all over it. Your lips were dark brown. A gray, granite texture covered your legs. Your penis was painted dark amid a section of purples and greens and gray sprigs of leaves. I stepped away from you quickly, looking down at your feet. They were an ocher-brown, with white, veinlike swirls. I stepped back to the door, unsure whether to stay. You looked crazy like that, but beautiful, too.

"This is what I want to show you," you explained. "The beauty of this land. You need to see how you're a part of it." Your eyes were shining blue amid the orange. They seemed out of place, too, much like the sea.

You knelt on the floor next to a dish of red petals. You crushed them, adding water to make paint. You dipped the clump of moss in, then reached behind and sponged it on your back, putting red moss prints everywhere you could reach. Some of the paint ran, bleeding in long, thin rivers toward the floor.

I glanced around the room. There was no rope to tie me up, no weapons. The open door was behind me. I could leave, easily. But for some reason I didn't want to.

"Light's going fast," you said.

You grabbed the leaf, soaking its thick stem in a crumbly black substance, coating it thoroughly. You reached back and tried to press that to your skin, too. You sighed when you couldn't get it where you wanted, and held the stem out to me.

"Paint the patterns on me?" you asked. "With this?"

"I don't want to." I pushed your hand back.

"But the light is fading. I want to do this before the sun sets; then you can see what it all looks like." Your voice was impatient, firm. You took my hand. You cradled it in the dry warmth of your own, spreading the smudged color from your hands onto mine. The reds and blacks stained my fingers and made a bruise shape on my knuckles.

"Please," you said quietly. "Just do this for me. You know I'll take you back. I've promised."

Your eyes glinted with the light, your fingers gripping mine tighter. I extracted my hand and took the stem. I knelt behind your back and dipped the stem into the black paste.

"What should I draw?"

"Anything. Whatever you're thinking about this place."

My hand was shaking a little, and a small drop of paint fell off the stem and onto my knee. The end of the stem was sharp and jagged. I placed it against your skin, dug in, and made a dot. You flinched a little. A beam of sunlight streamed through the window, falling directly onto your back. I squinted, my eyesight blotchy.

"I can't see."

"Do it blind, then."

I dipped the stem into the black again. I drew a long, straight line across your shoulder blades, the stem scratching your skin as I tried to make the color stay there. I drew a mess of spikes: spinifex. Then I drew a person, with a stick-figure body and an uneven circle for a head. I drew eyes in the face and colored them in. On top I drew flamelike hair. Then I put a small dark heart in the middle of the body. You reached around and touched the edge of my knee.

"You finished?"

"Almost."

I painted a bird, flying across your shoulder blade. Then I drew a black sun at the base of your neck, shining over everything. You turned to face me, our knees touching, your face less than a foot away.

"Do you want some?" You dipped your finger into a puddle of bloodred clay, then spread a line onto my forehead. "I could paint you." You touched my cheek, smudging the clay there, too. "Red ocher," you whispered. "It intensifies everything."

You took the leaf from my hand and moved it toward my neck, but I coiled away.

"No," I said.

You shrugged, your eyes sad. Then you grabbed my hand, jolting me to my feet. I only resisted a little. We walked to the center of the room.

"Now we wait," you said.

"For what?"

"The sun."

You pulled me down onto a bed of sand and leaves, right in the middle of all the paint and color. The sun was shining through the window so brightly it was difficult to keep my eyes even half-open against it. And the smell was stronger there, too: leafy and herbal, earthy and fresh.

"Face this way," you said.

You turned to the wall at the back, and I did the same. With the sun behind us, I could see the way its rays picked out the lighter swirls and dots in the painting, making them look three-dimensional. You reached for a pile of dried leaves and crushed them in your hand, then picked out rolling papers from underneath a rock. You took a little ash from another pile and mixed it with the leaves, then sprinkled this into one of the papers. You sealed it tightly, your tongue darting quickly over it. When you lit up, there was that smell again, that heavy, grassy smell of burning desert leaves: the smell that clung to everything in the painting shed that day. You took a long, deep drag, then passed the roll-up to me.

It was like a tiny burning tree, burning up between my fingers. I rolled it there, watching the glowing red end. For once I tried it; I don't know why. I was more relaxed that day, maybe, more hopeful that you'd let me go. The burning leaves weren't as harsh as regular tobacco, but they weren't as grassy as weed. A subtle, sour herby taste soon filled my mouth and I felt myself breathe out gently, my shoulders easing down a little.

You leaned back onto your elbows. As the sun set farther, the colors became more vivid. A red washed over everything, brightening the darker sections in the painting. Shafts of light lit up the floor, illuminating the millions of painted dots and flower petals there. Reds and oranges and pinks intensified all around us, until it felt like we were sitting in the middle of a burning pit of fire . . . or in the middle of the sunset itself.

"It feels like we are in the center of the earth, doesn't it?" you whispered. "We're right there among the embers."

I could feel the heat against my back, sticking my T-shirt to my spine. I blinked to stop the colors from blurring. Black lines and shapes danced before my eyes like the edges of flames. Then the sun moved farther down. Its light reached toward your painted body, turning you golden . . . making you shine. The sand grains on your arms glistened. I could feel the sun on my skin, too, turning it a peachy orange, making it soft. The whole room bathed in light.

You watched me, your blue eyes floating in the gold. I noticed the black markings on your left cheek, tiny animal tracks making their way toward your hair, walking right over your scar. You reached out and touched the skin on my arm, your sandy fingers brushing against me. It was where the sun was hitting me, where my skin was warmest. You pressed the tips of your fingers against it.

"The light's coming from within you, too," you said. "You're glowing."

I turned my head and tried to take in all of the painting at once. My head was reeling a little; from the colors and the light, or your cigarette, I don't know. That room was so different from all the other paintings I'd seen with Mum, so much more real somehow. And yes, I admit it; it was beautiful. Wildly beautiful. Your fingers traced patterns on my arm: circles and dots. The touch of them didn't scare me anymore.

———⁊———

Then, so quickly, the sun dipped down beneath the window and the colors disappeared. You passed the roll-up to me again as shadows crept over the walls. We sat there a little while longer, until the colors faded altogether. I blinked, passed the roll-up back. The room had turned murky and it was getting harder to see the objects on the floor. I stood up and stumbled toward the door.

"Here, I'll show you," you said.

You took my arm. You walked confidently, eyes nocturnal. When we reached the doorway, I felt the coolness of the evening pinching at me already. I wrapped my arms around myself and you went back inside for your clothes. You handed me the holey woolen sweater you'd been wearing that morning.

"Put it on," you said. "You'll warm up."

Your smell of sweat and eucalyptus and dirt filled my nostrils as I put the sweater over my head, the wool scratching at my arms. You had your shorts on when I looked back at you. You took my arm again, grabbing me around the elbow, and led me outside.

The stars were already bright against the fading gray sky. The moon was a slender fingernail. I let you lead me. We were quiet. The only sounds were my boots, and your bare feet, upon the sand. Far, far away something made a single ghostly howl, like a banshee in the dark.

"Dingo," you whispered.

There were so many thoughts in my head right then, so many emotions. Your hand was close and tight around my elbow, guiding me straight. Some small part of me almost liked it there. I blinked, shaking my head, not wanting to admit it. But it was true, wasn't it? A part of me was starting to accept you. I wondered, if I gave in to that part, if I leaned into you in return, where would it lead?

"Are you hungry?" you asked.

I shook my head. I stopped and looked around at the sky. It was actually nice, right then, to look at that blackness. It was kind of soothing after all those colors.

"I just want to sit for a while," I said. "Out here."

"Alone?"

"Yeah."

"I'll get a blanket."

You padded toward the house. I watched your back fade into the dark. I rubbed at my elbows, feeling the sudden chill there. I walked away from the buildings, farther out into the sand. I found a smooth patch with no plants or rocks, and lowered myself onto it. The sand was still warm. I buried my hands underneath the top layers and felt the heat that was stored in the grains seep into me. I pressed my wrists into the warmth. Another howl echoed around the land, and that time there was a reply, another moaning spirit in the dark. I looked up at the stars. More were appearing now, populating the blackness like it was rush hour. I suppose it was, for the stars. There seemed to be as many stars in that sky as there were grains of sand around me. My fingers dug deeper into the grains as the crickets began their rickety whirring around me.

I felt the vibrations of your steps as you returned. You had a gray blanket wrapped around your shoulders and another draped over your arm. You hadn't cleaned the sand or paint from your body. But the paint had smudged away a little anyway, near your mouth and eyes, on your arms. . . .

You wrapped one of the blankets around me, then handed me a cup.

"What's this?"

"Just herbs and water. It'll keep you warm."

"I'm not cold."

"You will be."

The smell of clean, fresh tea tree wafted up on the steam. It was too hot to drink right away, but it was comforting just to hold it in my hands. I bent my head over it and inhaled. I took that bush smell with me as I looked up at the stars. You glanced up, too, scanning the sky like you were reading a map. You nodded a little, but at what I don't know.

"Got everything you need?" you asked.

You turned toward the house, but hesitated before you took a step. You hovered there for a moment, waiting for me to say something . . . wanting me to. You clasped your fingers together and twisted your thumbs. I gave in.

"What do you see up there?" I said. I threw my hand toward the sky.

You smiled, grateful. "I can see anything you want."

"Do you know the patterns?"

"You mean constellations?" You shrugged. "I know *my* patterns."

"What do you mean?"

You crouched down to me quickly. "I know the pictures *I* see up there. I can trace people's faces, the lay of the land . . . anything, really. If you look for long enough those stars will tell you everything you want to know: directions, the weather, time, stories. . . ."

You didn't stand up again, move away, back to the house. Instead you sat down next to me and buried your hands under the sand. You grinned when you saw my boots were buried also. You buried your feet, too. It reminded me a little of when Anna and I used to be tucked up together under the same duvet, sharing the same bed. Those times felt like a million years away.

We were as quiet as the shadowy moths that flitted around us. I reached out and grabbed one; it fluttered against my closed fist. When I opened my hand it stayed there for a moment, bruised, on my palm. It was the color of my skin, tanned and peachy. The moonlight caught the delicate patterns on its wings, swirly and faint. It had tiny furry antennae. Its legs started to twitch, tickling me. How could this thing survive? It seemed so delicate. I shook my hand and it flopped down onto the sand. I pushed at it and it flew away, slightly lopsidedly, ready to fumble around us again soon.

"That moth is early," you said. "It's not normally out for a few weeks. You've been lucky."

You smiled, your eyes crinkling at the corners. I looked away quickly, wanting to hold your gaze but nervous of it, too. Some of the stars were winking at me, others were still. I heard the high-pitched *chip-chips* from dark bat silhouettes, their wings sweeping soundlessly across the velvet sky. Right at that moment it was as if we were the only two people left in the whole world. And I don't mean that to sound corny; it just honestly did. The only sounds were the droning crickets and *chip-chips* of the bats, the faraway wind against the sand, and the occasional distant yowl of a dingo. There were no car horns. No trains. No jack-hammers. No lawn mowers. No planes. No sirens. No alarms. No anything human. If you'd told me then that you'd saved me from a nuclear holocaust, I might have believed you.

You lay back into the sand, face up to the stars. You were so quiet and still, you might have been asleep, or dead. I prodded you.

"What?" You half smiled. "I'm thinking about the stars."

"What about them?"

"How everything is both eternal and brief."

"How do you mean?"

You talked up at the night sky. "I mean, that star far up over to my right is blinking at me madly now, but for how long? An hour or two, or for the next million years? And how long will we sit here like this? Just another moment, or the rest of our lives? You know which one I'd prefer. . . ."

I ignored your comment, glancing instead at the stars myself. "If you remember, *I* was the one who came out to sit here, you just followed me."

You propped yourself up onto your elbows. "Do you want me to leave?"

Your face was less than an arm's width from mine. I could lean across to you, or you could lean into me. We could kiss. You watched me, and I felt your hot, leafy breath settle on my skin. Your lips were parted slightly, dry and cracked around the edges. They needed a little moisture to soften them. I reached across and rubbed away a bit of paint still stuck in your short beard. You held my fingers to your chin. I froze, feeling the warmth of your hand on one side and the tiny beard prickles on my fingertips. What was I thinking? I turned back to the stars. After a moment you let me slip my fingers out from yours, away.

"I just want to sit here," I said shakily. "You can do what you like."

"I want to stay."

I kept looking at the sky, not trusting myself to look back at you. There was a cluster of particularly bright stars, sinking down toward the horizon. They were like a small city made up of winking lights. A highway of bright stars led to them. You saw where I was looking.

"The sisters," you said. "That's what some folks call them."

"Why?"

You sat up, surprised at my willingness to talk. "Those stars were beautiful women once," you said. "The first women on this land. As they walked through this country, trees and flowers sprouted up behind them; rocks emerged. A river soaked into their footsteps. But then, while the women were bathing in their river, a spirit man watched them. He decided he wanted to keep them as his wives. He chased after them and the women ran. They fled to the only place they thought was safe, the sky. They turned into stars. But he chased them up there, too, turning into a star himself, always following behind."

You raised your arm and pointed out one of the brightest stars in the sky. "See? He's there." Then you traced a line between that star and the cluster of stars you called the sisters. "See it?" you asked. "He's always there, following the sisters, chasing them eternally . . . but he never quite catches up."

I shivered suddenly. "The sisters can never get away from him, then?"

"True." You tucked my blanket tight around my shoulders. "But they'll never be caught, either. He's just behind them, always watching . . . wanting them. He chases them all around the world. You could have seen him chasing them in London, if you'd been looking."

"You know you can't see the stars in London, not really," I said.

You flopped back down into the sand. "Maybe not. But he's there all the same. Behind the clouds, behind the lights . . . watching."

———— ✦ ————

We sat there longer, me drinking the tea you'd brought and you talking more about the stars. You were right about the tea. Its liquid seemed to spread out under my skin and warm me. "Should I build a fire?" you asked. I shook my head, not wanting anything to pollute the light show above us. You shifted nearer, making me warmer anyway. You showed me some of the pictures you saw in the sky. You pointed out a small cluster of stars you thought looked like the boulders of the Separates, then traced across to two brighter stars for the outbuildings and another for the house; then you pointed out two blue-tinged stars that you said were us. I squinted, tried to see it, too. But all I saw were stars.

"Can you see London?" you asked. "Up there?"

"What do you mean?"

"Can you see the city? The skyline? The bridges? Can you trace them in the stars?"

I scanned the sky. There were so many stars, with more emerging by the second. There were too many stars for anything to seem clear. I followed a few stars up in a line and tried to trace Big Ben in the way you'd traced the shape of the Separates. You rolled over and looked at me.

"It's funny, isn't it?" you started quietly. "How you look up there and find a city, and I look at London and see a landscape?"

I frowned, glancing back at you. "What do you mean 'landscape'?"

"Just everything underneath, I guess." You rubbed your fingers against your beard, thinking. "All that earth and life, always just under the concrete, ready to push back through the pavement and take over the city at any time. All that life beneath the dead."

"London's more than just a pile of concrete," I said.

"Maybe." Your eyes glinted in the dark. "But without humans, the wild would take over. It would only need a hundred years or so for nature to win again. We're just temporary, really."

"But we're there all the same," I said. "You can't ignore the humans and buildings and art and everything else in a city. You can't take that stuff away. There really would be nothing then . . ."

I broke off, remembering what I'd left behind; thinking about my route to school on the double-decker bus, past the museums and iron park gates. I thought about those two old ladies who sat in front of me and talked about *EastEnders*. I clasped my arms tight around my shins as I imagined what was happening back home. School would be starting again, Anna and Ben would have returned from their vacation, summer would be over. The leaves would be fading from green to brown and settling in the playground. The school corridors wouldn't yet have the heat turned on, and the cavernous school cafeteria would be freezing in the mornings. Did they miss me there? Was anyone even collecting notes for me? Or had they given up on me by now? I pressed my mouth into the tops of my knees, the tears already on my cheeks. I tucked my face inward, not wanting you to notice. But you sat up anyway and moved closer behind me.

You pressed your hand onto my shaking back. It was warm and solid.

"You're right," you whispered, your breath on my neck. "Perhaps there are good things in a city sometimes . . . beautiful things."

Then you pulled me toward you. The way you did it was gentle and soft, first picking me up around the shoulders and then guiding me back. I fell into you, and it felt like I was moving in slow motion. You wrapped your warm arms, and the blankets, around me, cocooning me in a snug darkness. I thought of the moth I'd caught in my hand: safe, yet trapped, in the dark of my fingers.

"I'm sorry," you said. "I didn't mean to upset you."

I could feel you shaking, too. You held me tighter, pressing me to your quivering body and against the sand and plants and paint there. I buried into you, for once wanting something back. Your eucalyptus smell smudged onto me. You reached down and dabbed at my cheeks, wiping wet paint sideways into my hair. I stayed there, curled up into the warmth of your body, under the blankets, like something soft in a shell. Your arms were firm as rock around me. I felt your lips on my hair, brushing against it. Your warm breath on the tips of my ears. I didn't move away. I thought carefully about the words I wanted to say.

"If we were back in London," I began, "before any of this, knowing me as you do now . . . would you still steal me?"

You were silent a long time, your body stiff around me. "Yes," you whispered. You brushed my hair behind my ears. "I can never let you go."

You wrapped the blankets around me tighter. I felt your

warm, dry hands around my shoulders, your fingers grasping at my skin. After some time, you leaned back into the sand, bringing me with you. I didn't have the energy to fight you anymore. And you were warm, so warm. You leaned into the sand, and I stayed with my head against you, my cheekbone against your chest. I felt your body relax and soften. I pressed myself into the sand, too. There was still heat in it, even then. You cradled me with one arm and stroked my hair with the other. And you talked. You whispered stories about how the desert was created, sung up by the spirits of the land. You told me how everything was twined together, the whole world around me balancing on a moth's wing. I shut my eyes and let your voice lull me. Its rhythms were like a stream flowing. I felt your lips again, fluttering against my forehead. They were soft, not dry. And your arms pulled me down toward you, down deep into the earth.

And we slept, like that.

———⟩———

A pale pink awoke me. Dawn. I felt the lack of your heat beside me before I opened my eyes and found you gone. I missed it. I stretched my hand out along the sand: The grains where you'd been sleeping were still faintly warm. Perhaps you hadn't been gone long and the sand was still storing your heat. The shape of you was indented into it. I traced my fingers down the hollow where your head had been, then your broad shoulders, your back and legs, the sand firm and compacted from the weight of your body. Traces of paint had rubbed off, lingering on some of the grains.

I pulled the blankets around me, shutting out that cool

freshness of morning. But already the light was intrusive. My eyelids glowed orange when I closed them. I sat up. Sand was all over me. A wind must have been blowing in the night. Funny, I hadn't even felt it. I shook out my clothes. There was a line of stones, leading out to a smoother section of sand a few feet away. I followed them.

There were words there, finger-written in the sand. I stood at the bottom and read.

Gone to catch a snake. See you lata. Ty x

I knelt down beside the message and traced my fingers through the *x*. I rubbed it out, then drew it again. You didn't seem like the kind of guy to write an *x* in the sand, a kiss. My stomach twisted, though for the first time it wasn't from fear.

I stood, needing to move. I looked across to the house, but I didn't want to go in there. Not yet. What I really wanted was to have your hard, hot arms around me again. I craved your warmth. I hugged myself, rubbing my fingers up and down. I guess people are like insects sometimes, drawn to heat. A kind of infrared longing. My eyes roamed across the land, looking for the heat of a human. One particular human.

I blinked, rubbed my eyes. I was being stupid. But I couldn't figure it out. I did, and yet I didn't, want to be near you. It didn't make sense. Without stopping to analyze it, I started walking toward the Separates.

I paused by the camel. She was sitting and sleepy. I reached my hand to her forehead and rubbed between her eyes. Her eyelashes blinked against my arm. I sat beside her, nuzzling into her warm dusty fur, and watched the pink and gray of the sunrise. The morning was perfect, still. I heard shrieks from a flock of birds as they arrived at the Separates for their morning bath. I took my boots off and dipped my toes into the sand. I rubbed them against the grains, scratching them. I tried being still for a moment, tried relaxing into the camel and the morning. But I wanted to find you.

I walked barefoot. I tiptoed carefully around the prickly plants and played stepping-stones with the rocks as I made my way around the Separates. Then I saw fresh prints in the sand. Yours. I put my foot inside one of them, the print of your toes and heel surrounding mine entirely.

I brushed my fingers against the rock as I walked slowly around the outcrop. I touched the wavy streaks embedded in the surface, left by ancient streams. A black bird cawed at me from high in a tree, a grating, warning call in that stillness. Perhaps he was warning his flock about me, a clumsy human stumbling across his territory.

I kept going. There was a jagged bit of rock coming up, sticking out from the base of a boulder. I couldn't see past it. But I could see a pathway around it, a collection of large, smooth rocks to step across. I rested my arm against the boulder for balance, and started to step from rock to rock. The cool stone felt good beneath my feet.

When I had almost climbed around the jagged part, I heard movement on the other side. A grunt or two. Then, silence. It could only be you. I paused, grasping the boulder, my breathing suddenly quicker. Should I step around and show myself? Or just wait there, listening? My ears strained for sounds of you. I heard a faint rustling of leaves. A muffled swear word. Then, silence again. I hugged the boulder.

"Gemma?"

Your voice startled me so much I almost fell. But I clung on and got myself around the rock. You were standing, facing me, your arms outstretched. For a second I thought you'd been waiting for me like that, waiting to hug me to you, enclose me like you had done the night before. The sun was bouncing full onto your chest, making your skin bright. There were still traces of paint on you. I wanted to run toward you, but something in your eyes held me back.

"Where are your boots?" you whispered.

I frowned. Then I remembered what you were supposed to be doing. "The snake."

You nodded. "I thought I found it, but then I heard you coming. I wasn't expecting you to follow me." Your eyes were soft as they looked at mine, curious. You smiled a little. "It's OK," you whispered again. "This snake's not aggressive. You just need to stay still . . . stay there and don't step onto the sand, OK?"

"Really?" My voice was suddenly shaky. I coughed, not wanting to sound nervous. "Maybe I should go back to the house?"

"No, it's better if you keep still. It's somewhere near; I don't want it distracted by your movements." You looked me over. "Just sit on the rock there, be still, watch. I'll keep looking for it." You flicked a piece of hair out of your eyes. "Don't worry, Gem; I've caught hundreds of these guys before."

I did as you said and knelt down cautiously on the rock. You stepped slowly, moving like a crab. You stuck one foot out first to feel the sand carefully before moving the rest of your body.

"What are you doing?"

"This snake hides. He buries himself underneath the sand so

nothing can see him. He's shy and clever. His prey comes to him — he never really has to hunt."

As you stepped closer toward me, the small black tip of a tail darted up from a bundle of dried leaves near my rock. I started backward.

"He's here," I whispered.

"Don't move."

My body tensed, wanting more than anything to race back to the house. I looked at where the tail was. Around the leaves was a smooth lump of sand. The snake was underneath. You crouched a little, coming toward me like a ninja, eyes focused on the patch of sand in front of me. "It's OK, he's looking at me," you said. "He knows I'm the threat."

You shuffled toward that small mound in the sand, getting just a couple of feet away. Then the snake raised its head, throwing off its camouflage. My breath faltered. Its body looked long, its skin the same color as the sand, with thin yellow bands circling its middle. It hovered there, watching you . . . each of you waiting to see what the other was going to do.

"Be careful," I whispered.

Those words made you glance up at me. The snake saw. He chose his moment to escape. Unfortunately that escape path was back toward the rock I was sitting on, and the snake slithered quickly in my direction. I saw the length of its body, the large triangular lump of its head, and the darting of its tongue. With the snake looking at me, you took your chance and stepped toward it. But the snake felt your vibrations; it turned back. Its tongue was darting in and out constantly, trying to find the threat. When it found you, it moved its head backward, its body curling into an *S*, ready to strike. You stopped, your arms outstretched. There was only a pace or so between you. One movement was all it would take. The snake wavered a little, watching. You were ready to spring. But the snake surprised us both. It spun away from you and again slithered fast across the sand toward me. You lunged at it, grabbing the black tip of its tail. But it slipped through your fingers easily. It picked up speed, swishing from side to side across the sand.

"It's trying to get away," you shouted as the snake got closer. "Don't move. Stay exactly where you are. It's just scared."

But I couldn't help it. The snake was only inches away. Its head was bobbing slightly, its pink tongue stabbing in and out. I pushed myself backward and leaped toward the surface of the boulder, trying to claw my way up it. I got a foothold with my right foot.

But the snake was going in the same direction. I felt its heavy body slither over my other foot. I looked down at it, screamed, then lost my balance. My foot slid down the rock face. I tried to push myself into the rock, tried to stop my foot from falling farther. The snake was sliding fast toward a crevice at the bottom. But not fast enough. My foot slammed down hard on its tail and it twisted around toward me. I saw its huge triangular fangs, its jaws open wide, warning me. I arched backward, trying to get away, but the snake didn't like the movement. Its head darted toward me. It sank its fangs into my leg.

Then it disappeared into the crevice in the rock.

———— ~ ————

You were at my side immediately.

"Did it get you?" You reached for my leg, turning it over. "I saw it strike."

You held my leg carefully, pressing gently at the skin. You felt all the way up to my knee and back down. Then you found what you were looking for. There were small scratches on the skin above my ankle, as if I'd brushed against a sharp thorn. You ran your thumb over these, then over the skin around them. You looked at me.

"I need your shirt," you said.

"What? Why?"

"It's either your shirt or my shorts, you choose. I need to stop the venom from going up your leg."

I looked at your serious blue eyes. "Take the shirt."

"Don't worry," you whispered. "I know what to do. I have antivenom." You tried a smile, but it didn't look that genuine. I just stared back at you, still in shock, I think. You moved closer to me, sitting beside me so that I could lean against you. "Come on, your shirt." You tugged at the bottom of it.

I crossed my arms and pulled it over my head. You took it from my hand instantly. I wrapped my arms around my bra, but you didn't stare once at my body; you just found a long, straight stick and pressed it to the bottom of my calf.

"Hold the stick there," you said.

I pressed it against my skin and you tore my shirt down the middle. You wound it quickly around my leg, securing the stick by pulling the material tight.

"I can't feel anything," I said. "Are you sure it got me?"

"It got you." You frowned. "But maybe it didn't release any venom. Let's hope so. But if someone had stood on me that hard . . ." Again, the forced smile when you couldn't finish your words. You took my head in your hands, suddenly serious. You stroked your thumb against my cheek. "From now on, you must tell me everything you are feeling . . . headaches, sickness, numbness, general weirdness . . . anything. It's important."

There were beads of sweat on your forehead. I reached out and wiped them away.

"OK," I said. "But I feel fine now."

"Good." You grabbed my hand. "But you need to stay calm and still, don't move too much. Whether there's venom in there or not, we need you relaxed."

I nodded. I didn't like the seriousness in your tone. I glanced at my leg. I thought I could feel a numbness starting around my ankle. I closed my eyes and tried to keep myself from panicking.

"Keep your leg as straight and as still as possible," you said.

Carefully you fed your arm underneath my knees and placed your other arm beneath my shoulders. You stood, slowly, lifting me up. You held me out, slightly away from your body, trying to keep me as flat as possible, holding me steady. I could see the muscles in your arms twitching with the effort.

"I'm taking you back to the house," you said.

You walked carefully, choosing a route between the rocks and plants. You winced as you stepped on a pile of twigs.

"I won't let anything happen to you," you whispered.

You hurried past the camel, your breathing becoming more labored. I could feel your muscles shaking with the effort of holding me like that. I shut my eyes against the sunlight. The rays were so bright and piercing. I turned my face to your chest, pressing my forehead into your skin.

"What's wrong?" you murmured. I felt the words rumble in your chest. I whispered back.

"I'm starting to get a headache."

You let out a quick breath before moving on. "I'll fix it," you said. "I promise I'll fix it. Just don't panic."

I didn't say anything. There was a dull pain in my ankle, working its way up my leg. I concentrated on that.

---

You backed through the doorway and carried me quickly into the kitchen. You laid me gently on the table. You disappeared for a moment and I heard you in the hall, throwing open the closet. The light was bright through the door so I turned away toward the kitchen cabinets. You came back with a couple of towels. You rolled one up and placed it underneath my head.

"How do you feel?"

"A bit weird."

"Weird how?"

"Just weird. I don't know. Like I'm getting a cold or something."

You swallowed. "Anything else? Pain around your ankle? Numbness?"

I nodded. "A little."

You felt for the pulse in my wrist and touched the back of your hand to my forehead. Lightly, you pressed the skin around my ankle. You shook out the other towel and frowned as you laid it over my chest.

"Maybe I should get you a T-shirt, huh?"

"What?"

You nodded toward my chest and bra, your cheeks pinking slightly. "Wouldn't want you to be uncomfortable." You raised an eyebrow, then forced that smile upon your face again. "And I've got to concentrate here, too, you know."

You went to get the T-shirt. Through the open door I heard the squeal of a bird, circling high above the house, but that was it. I felt along the top of my leg. Just how serious was this snakebite? I couldn't figure out whether your joking tone was because you weren't worried about it, or because you were trying to mask your fear.

You were back quickly, handing me a shirt, supporting me while I put it on so that I didn't have to move my leg too much. You left and returned with a metal box. You flung it open, took out a roll of bandage, and started winding it over the shirt on my leg. You wound all the way from my foot to my hip, rolling up my shorts to get to the top of my thigh. My skin tickled as you touched it. You pulled the bandage tight.

"I can't believe I was so stupid," you muttered.

"What do you mean?"

"I let you get bit, didn't I?" You placed the metal box on the floor and rifled through it loudly. Gauze and bandages and rubber gloves fell out as you searched. "I should've caught that snake days ago," you continued. "I should at least have tried to desensitize you to it. But, well, snakebites never happen to me, and I guess I kind of hoped . . . I thought we had time for all this. . . ."

Your words faded away as you found what you were looking for. You took your hand from the box. As you uncurled your fingers, it looked like they were shaking. Inside them was a key. As you stood, I saw how pale your face was. It reminded me of how you'd looked when you'd had the nightmare. I had a sudden urge to touch it. I stretched my fingers a little toward you.

"I stole antivenoms from a research lab," you explained. "You'll be OK."

You strode to the locked drawer beside the sink, stuck the key in. You rifled through it, your back preventing me from seeing exactly what was inside. You took out several small glass vials with different colored lids and a plastic bag full of clear liquid and put them on the bench; then you took out a strap and something that looked like a needle. You left the drawer open while you turned back to me. You grabbed my arm and slapped at the veins. I glanced back at the vials. They were the same ones I'd seen once before, spread out before you on the kitchen table . . . the ones I'd thought contained drugs.

"Do you know what you're doing?" I whispered.

"Course." You rubbed your forehead. "You'll be OK. The snake's not that dangerous anyway. . . ."

"How dangerous?"

"I'll be able to fix it." You wound the strap around my arm, pulling it tight above where you'd been pressing my veins. "Look away," you urged.

I looked toward the open drawer. I heard a crack as you opened something. I felt the jagged prick of the needle go in, the jolt as you attached the plastic bag . . . the release as you undid the strap on my arm. Then a rush of fluid, straight into my veins.

"What is that?" I asked, still looking toward the drawer.

"Saline solution, also from the research lab. I've mixed the death adder antivenom into it. It should start filtering into your veins right away; you should start feeling better."

I turned my head back to you, registering your words. "Death adder?"

You stroked the side of my cheek. "His name's worse than his bite."

I looked at the bag of fluid slowly seeping into my body, at the tube stuck into my arm. "How do you know how to do this?"

Your eyes darted away from mine. "I practiced on myself." You tapped the side of the bag, checking how fast it was flowing.

"Now what?"

"Now we just wait."

"How long?"

"About twenty minutes, dunno. Until the bag's used up."

"And then?"

"Then we see."

You scraped a chair from under the table and sat beside me. You ran your finger lightly over the needle in my arm.

"Will I be better after this?" I asked, nodding at the bag.

"More or less." Again I saw the sweat on your forehead. I saw your temple pulsing quickly.

"You're worried," I whispered. "Aren't you?"

You shook your head. "Nah." Your voice was breathy and

your mouth fixed in a smile. "You'll be 'right. I have another vial if you need it. You'll be fine, though. Just relax, wait."

But your eyes were unsettled as they looked at me, twitching slightly at the corners. You breathed out, deliberately slowly, and pressed your fingertips to the twitch.

"What's going to happen to me?" I whispered. "What are you hiding?" I felt my breathing speed up, my throat tighten around it.

"Nothing," you said quickly. "Just don't panic; that's the last thing we need. When you panic, your blood travels faster, speeding up the venom." You pushed your hands against my shoulders, rubbing at the muscles in my neck. "Relax," you whispered.

But I couldn't calm down, not properly. I just kept thinking about dying out there, on a kitchen table, in the middle of a billion grains of sand. My breathing sped up further, and you put your hand against my mouth to shush me. You stroked my hair.

"Don't worry, it's OK," you were saying, over and over. "I'll keep you safe."

I shut my eyes. I saw darkness behind my lids. Perhaps that might be all I'd ever see again. Perhaps the numbness that was taking over my leg would soon be taking over my body, then my mind, and then that would be it. My heart would stop and an everlasting numbness would replace it. I'd be under the sand then, grains below and above and all around me. I gripped at the table, scratching my nails into its wood.

"Calm down," you murmured.

I'd thought about death before, so many times. But the death I'd imagined would be violent and painful and caused by you, not numb and clinical.

"You won't die," you whispered. "You just need to wait it out. I'm here, and I know how to help. Just don't panic." You stroked the edge of my face. "Gem, I won't let anything happen, not to you."

You peeled the sweaty strands of hair away from my forehead.

"You're hot," you murmured. "Too hot."

About half of the bag's fluids had gone into me, but I could still feel a dull ache at the bottom of my leg. Was it from the snakebite, or from the bandage being too tight? You checked my pulse again.

"Do you want to be sick?" you asked.

"Not really."

"Any pain in your stomach?"

"No."

You put your fingers over your mouth, thinking. You looked carefully at my bandaged leg. "This is still sore?"

"Yes."

I thought I could feel that dull ache around my knee now, traveling slowly up my thigh. I stretched my hand down and touched near to where I could feel it.

"It's there," I said. "The pain's there."

You shut your eyes for a second. Again, there was that twitch at the side of one of them. You pressed your hand against where I was feeling, then ran your fingers down to my ankle.

"Venom's traveling fast," you whispered, to yourself, I think. "It's all swelling up." You glanced at the bag of fluid, then tipped it to see how much was left. "I'm putting the other vial in." I watched you use the needle to draw up the antivenom. Then you injected it into the bag and swirled it around. "This will give you a rush," you said. You tried grinning, but it was a crooked grimace instead.

"That's the last one, isn't it?" I asked.

You nodded, your face tight. "It should be enough."

You started wiping my forehead again, but I reached for your hand. I didn't want to be alone right then, I guess. I didn't want you to be alone, either. Your eyes opened wide when you felt my fingers touch you. They looked over my face, my cheeks and mouth, skimming down over my neck. I was the best view you'd ever seen. It gave me a buzz, the way I made you look, right then.

"Are you dizzy?" you asked.

"A bit. It feels a little like I'm floating."

I gripped your hand tightly, wanting some of your strength to seep out into me. You held my gaze. There were questions in your eyes, and thoughts behind them.

"The antivenom should be working by now," you said. "I don't know why it's not."

"Maybe it takes time."

"Maybe."

I could feel the tension in your fingers. You glanced at the fluid bag. Then you got up quickly and stood beside the open door. My fingers went cold as you left them. I blinked. The kitchen cupboards were fuzzy around the edges. Everything was slightly fuzzy. I was floating in a haze. You were pacing around it.

You picked up the empty vials, squinting as you read their labels.

"What is it?"

You sighed, crushing a vial in your palm. "The only thing I can think is that these aren't working properly. Where I've stored them . . . I'm worried it's been too warm."

"What does that mean?"

You came back to me, stumbling onto the stool. You placed your damp palm against my shoulder, your eyes searching for mine. "It means we've got a choice."

"What choice?"

"We either stay here and ride it out — I've got other, natural, substances that could help you — or we . . ."

"What?"

You wiped your forehead with the side of your hand. "Or we go back."

"Back where? What do you mean?"

You took a ragged breath. You spoke slowly, staring straight ahead at the kitchen cupboards, not wanting to think about the words you were saying. "There's a mine site, I told you about it once. I could get you back there before you —"

"Why would you do that?" I interrupted. "I thought you didn't want to let me go."

"I don't." Your voice cracked a little.

I watched you, looking at me. I saw my face in your eyes, reflected double.

"You said four months?"

You had to swallow your emotions before you could speak. "It's up to you. I'll do what you want now."

"You said it was hundreds of miles to the next town?"

"It is . . . to the next town."

"Then what . . . ?"

"The place I can take you is that mine site; there's just men and a big hole there. But they have a clinic and an airstrip. They can help you; they could stabilize you. . . ."

"How far?"

"It's far." You smiled at me, a sad smile. "But I know a shortcut."

Then your face twisted away again, your expression tortured.

"You'd really take me back?" I whispered. I moaned a little as I felt a sharp stab in my guts.

You nodded, running your hand down my cheek. "I'll get the camel ready."

I laid my palms against the smooth, cool table as I waited for you to return. I looked across at the fluid bag, empty and deflated and unhooked from my arm. Earlier I'd been walking across the sand, eager to find you. Two hours later I was staring up at the kitchen ceiling with venom coursing through my body. My eyes wanted to shut. I almost let them. It would be so easy just to sink back into that haze that was threatening to engulf me. I focused on the pain in my stomach and listened to you outside, calling to the camel. I didn't know how you'd get me out of there, still didn't know if you really would. The room started spinning slightly and sick rose in my throat. I turned sideways and spat.

I pressed my hand to my chest. I could feel my heart. *Boom, ba-boom, ba-boom.* It was going to beat right through my ribs, cracking them all. I tried slowing my breathing. To do this, I tried to determine exactly where my heart was. Left side, or right? We'd learned that at school once. I pressed around, trying to find it, but it felt like my whole chest was made of heart. My whole body was beating. And it was getting faster. It felt like I was going to explode.

I looked over at the cupboards, wanting to focus on something else . . . anything but death. My eyes latched on to the open drawer. There were sheets of paper spilling out of it from where you'd been searching. I blinked, tried to focus. There was that photograph: the one I'd seen before of the girl and her baby. It was sticking up between the pages.

"Gem?"

Your voice jolted me back. You were coming through the door, your arms full. You let the things you held drop to the floorboards and the noise reverberated around me. You came to my side, saw where I was looking, and extracted the photograph from between the papers. I caught one last glimpse of it before you slipped it into the back pocket of your shorts, seeing the long hair of your mother and the smallness of you.

You hesitated before shutting the drawer, then took out something else.

"I made it," you said gruffly, "for you."

You shoved it onto my finger. It was roughly carved, shaped from a lump of something colorful and cold . . . a ring made entirely from a gemstone. It was beautiful. It glinted emerald greens and blood reds over my skin, and had tiny flecks of gold threading through it. I couldn't stop staring at it.

"Why?" I asked.

You didn't answer that. Instead you touched the ring gently and looked at my face, unsaid questions in your eyes. Then you turned my hand over and checked my pulse, leaving your fingers resting against my skin. They felt like flames.

"Now listen," you said more firmly, your voice in control again. "I've got a plan."

I tried to concentrate on you, but your face was going a little wobbly around the edges. You picked up something from the floor. I blinked when I realized what it was — a long metal saw. Its teeth looked rusty and sharp.

"What are you doing with that?" I said. I felt down to my bandaged leg. You noticed.

"Don't worry, your leg's safe." You nodded toward the table. The corner of your mouth came up in a half smile. "The ones on that aren't, though."

You reached into the metal box and pulled out more bandages, starting to unwind them. You placed one across my stomach. Then you stepped back, looking at me like you were measuring me up.

"What now?" I asked.

"I'm going to tie you to the table," you said. "Then I'm going to tie that to the camel. Then we're going to walk to where you left the car and get it started."

There were too many things to object to, so I focused on the car. "You'll never find it."

"I will."

I remembered my last image of the car, stuck deep in the sand.

"You won't start it," I said. "It's bogged."

You shrugged. "I thought it would be."

"I don't want to die out there," I whispered.

But I don't think you heard me. You started moving quickly around the room, pulling out another metal box and filling it with different containers of medicine, water bottles, and food. Then in one swift movement you scooped me up and laid me gently on the floor.

"Just while I chop the legs off," you said, smiling apologetically.

A draft wafted up from a crack in the floorboards, making the dust swirl and tickle in my nostrils. You picked up the saw and started cutting the first leg. I felt the vibration in the floor as you cut, and the saw blurred into a copper fuzz. One leg came off. You started on the next. You worked quickly. But I wanted you to work faster.

Soon the legless table lay on the floor beside me. You lifted me up and placed me on it. Using the bandages you'd taken out just before, you tied my body tightly to it.

"It's too hot, too tight," I complained.

You dabbed at my face with a towel; then you laid it across my body. You got me a glass of water and forced me to drink.

"It'll only get hotter," you said.

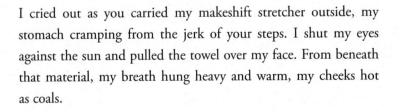

I cried out as you carried my makeshift stretcher outside, my stomach cramping from the jerk of your steps. I shut my eyes against the sun and pulled the towel over my face. From beneath that material, my breath hung heavy and warm, my cheeks hot as coals.

I tensed as you lowered the table to the sand. The camel was beside me, kneeling. I could hear her chewing, and I could feel her body heat. I stretched my arm out sideways and touched the fur of her belly with my fingertips. You were on the other side of her. I heard you there, attaching something: the box you'd just packed, I guessed. Then you slung a rope over her hump and across to me. You wrapped that around and underneath the table, tying me and my stretcher to the side of the camel. You pulled hard on the rope, and the stretcher moved across the sand, drawing me closer to the camel's stomach so that I was lying next to her. I was so close I could smell the stale dust of her fur and hear the rumblings of her stomach. I pressed my arm against her side, and a tiny insect jumped from her skin to mine.

Then you told the camel to stand. I heard her moan start deep in her belly, rumbling all around me. From somewhere farther away, I heard your words of encouragement, urging her on. Then my body jolted backward as her front legs rose. I cried out, grabbing at her fur. The pain was worse when she straightened her back legs. But somehow the stretcher remained horizontal, with me flat on my back, tied tightly to the camel like a heavy saddlebag.

"Hang in there, Gem," you said, laying your hand on my shoulder. "This whole thing's going to hurt a bit."

The camel took a couple of hesitant steps. I braced myself, gripping the table edge. My body shifted back and forth, sending out stabs of pain. And then we were on our way. Once she was moving, the camel seemed to forget about the weight she was carrying and strode forward easily. I peered out from under the towel. You had a lead rope in one hand, attached to the camel, and a long stick in the other. You were walking fast beside us, almost jogging to keep up with the camel's huge steps. Sweat was pouring down your bare chest, washing away the last of your paint.

"Up, girl, up," you called. "Faster . . ."

The words you spoke were a little like a song, the dull thud of the camel's steps the beat. The sounds blurred in my mind, getting softer, softer . . .

I tried to breathe slowly, concentrating on that rather than the cramps in my stomach. The light was burning my eyes, burning them blind. I pulled the towel back over them. You'd put a bottle of water on either side of my head and I leaned my cheek against one, cooling my skin slightly. But soon the bottles were as warm as I was, the water swishing loudly against my ears. My whole body jolted and hurt with each step. My head was pounding, too.

At one point you slowed the camel enough to push something into my mouth.

"Chew this," you said. "It will help with the pain."

The substance was soft like gum, but it tasted as bitter as leaves. An earthy smell rose up into my nostrils. A numbness spread out around my lips. I listened to the sound of the water swishing, the camel plodding, and you panting beside us. There was a fly somewhere, too, whining on the other side of the towel. The heat was smothering me, making my breathing shallow. I think I slept.

I was back home, walking down my street. It was a warm spring day. On my neighbor's front lawn, some kids were splashing about in a paddling pool. I went around the side of the house, leaping the fence and heading for my bedroom window. If I jiggled the window latch in just the right way, it would open. But it didn't. Not this time. I kept pushing at the window, trying to force it. I slammed my fist against it. A thin crack appeared in the glass. I brought my hand to my mouth and sucked it, checked for glass fragments. Then I looked through the window into the room.

There was a child in my bed. She was about ten years old, with coppery-brown hair and green eyes. She even had my pink rabbit tucked in beside her. Her fingers were clutching the covers tightly around her, and her eyes were open very wide. She was staring at me. As I watched, she glanced toward her bedroom door, assessing how far it was to run to it. She could do it. It was only five steps to that door, and another ten to the kitchen. She reached toward the intercom, but I knew already what was going to happen. Her hand brushed the glass of water beside the bed, knocking that to the floor instead. As her mouth opened into a scream, I pressed a finger to my lips. I shook my head.

"No," I mouthed. "It's OK. It's only me."

The girl stopped then, mouth open, looking back at me like I was an alien. I gave her a little smile. Then I took something out of my pocket — a bird's nest — and I placed it on her windowsill.

And then, I knew. I was *you* placing the bird's nest. But I was *me* looking out, too. I was us both.

———— ≷ ————

There was water on my forehead. The towel was stuck to my skin. I forced my eyes open. I moved my arm from under the towel and felt the water drop onto my hand. I thought I was still dreaming. I grabbed the towel and pulled it from my face. The water dripped onto my cheeks and mouth, cold and fresh. It almost sizzled as it hit me. I stuck my tongue out and licked at it. The sky above me was gray and it wasn't so hot anymore. I could breathe.

My body was moving more than before. The camel had picked up pace. I turned my head and cried out as pain shot up my neck. It was the first I'd felt since you'd given me the soft leaves to chew. You were jogging beside us, your legs stretching out to keep up with the camel, your eyes darting back toward me. You saw me watching you. I wanted to ask how long we'd been traveling, but my throat and voice were thick and useless.

"Not much farther," you said, your voice breathless from running.

I looked up at the drops of water, falling more frequently. You grinned, sticking your arms out and twirling as you ran.

"Rain," you said. "The sky's crying for you."

You clicked your tongue and tapped the stick against the camel's back legs, and she broke into an even faster pace. It made me slip farther back and forth on the stretcher, made me wince. You noticed and slowed the camel. I tilted my head and looked at where we were headed. We weren't far from an outcrop of rocks and trees. The rain started to get heavier. The towel glued itself to my body with the downpour. The rain ran over you in streams, turning your hair dark. You shook it out of your eyes, flicking more drops in my direction.

"We're going to need to wait this out," you panted.

The rain pattered against the sand like tiny claps, or muted drumbeats. I tried to focus on that sound, rather than on the pain in my leg that was becoming worse. My stomach was cramping badly again. But we got to the trees. Quickly, you whooshed down the camel and unloaded the supplies. You made a makeshift shelter from tarpaulin and rope and tree branches. Then, carefully, you carried me to it. You laid me on a blanket inside it. You took the wet towel from me and replaced it with something warm and dry, crouching down beside me.

"You're feverish," you said.

You pulled at the tarpaulins you'd tied between the trees, trying to block the rain that was coming in at us sideways. I felt the weight as you put another blanket on top of me. For a moment I thought I heard thunder; a deep growl from the sky. You moved my head so that it was lying in your lap.

"Keep your eyes open," you said. "Stay with me."

I tried. It felt like I was using every muscle in my face. But I did it. I saw you from upside down, your lips above my eyes and your eyes above my lips.

"Talk to me," you said.

My throat felt like it was closing up, as if my skin had swollen, making my throat a lump of solid flesh. I gripped your hand.

"Keep watching me, then," you said. "Keep listening." You glanced out at the weather, looking at the sky. "It's not a full-on thunderstorm, only the side effects of one nearer the coast. Hopefully it won't be long until it passes."

I frowned, wondering why it was raining in the desert. You read my expression.

"It doesn't normally," you muttered. "Only when it needs to."

Your words made your face blur. Your eyes swam in a round brown pool of skin. I gasped for more air and a raindrop fell in my mouth. You smoothed wet strands from my face.

"I'll tell you a story," you said. "I'll tell you about the rain." You poured a little water into my mouth. I almost coughed it back up again. You took a sip of water yourself, before continuing.

"Rain here is sacred," you began. "More precious than money or gemstones. Rain is life."

You pressed your fingers to my temples. That small amount of pressure made it easier to look at you, easier to keep my eyes open.

"When rain falls in this country," you said, "it mixes with the sand and makes new rivers of red. Riverbeds that have been dry for months come alive and run with bloodred water, making veins in the sand . . . bleeding life over everything."

You stuck your hand past the tarpaulin into the rain, then pressed it down into the ground. When you brought it back to me it was stained with red clay. You stroked it across my forehead, down my cheeks, and across my mouth. I felt sand grains smear across my skin, and smelled the iron-earth and freshness from the rain. Somehow it helped me stay awake.

"When rain falls here," you started again, "animals that haven't been seen for months, years sometimes, crawl up out of the earth and live again. Plants stretch up from the sand. Roots flower."

Your fingers moved over my chin. I could feel your short nails against my skin, pattering like the rain, keeping me awake. When you spoke next, you whispered. I had to strain to catch your words before they were lost in the drumming of the downpour.

"Traditionally, women dance when the rain falls," you said, "splashing at the edge of the flowing red rivers. And as they dance, they let blood run down their legs, the rain-blood, and their own. It's not only the land that bleeds out here . . . we do, too."

Your fingers darted up, brushing over my lips. I could taste the salt on them. A grain of sand slipped inside my mouth. You smoothed the red clay down over my neck and onto my collarbone, massaging it into my skin. A raindrop fell on my forehead and I felt it take the clay with it as it dripped down my cheek. For a moment, I felt like the trees I'd seen bleeding when I'd been lost in the sand dunes, with streams of ruby sap on my skin.

Again there was that distant rumbling sound, like the earth was opening up somewhere far away, like it was swallowing something. And quickly you turned your head from me, toward it. You glanced at the tarpaulins, checking everything was secure.

"So, you see," you murmured, "rain is the desert's way of changing. All around us, plants are spreading out, insects are mating . . . things living again."

Your face swirled. You talked more, but I could no longer hear the words. Your lips were just caterpillars, wriggling on your face. And I was slipping, my skin heavy and swollen like a grub's, a dull ache traveling through my muscles. I needed the rain to make me live, too.

Then you were loading me onto the stretcher again, tightening bandages and rope around me. Pain crunched my insides, as if someone had a hand in my stomach and was twisting.

"Open your eyes," you were saying. "Open them."

Your hair was hanging down toward me. Strands of it dripped drops of water onto my nose. You called to the camel to stand. She rumbled like the thunder, protesting. You tapped the stick against her and I felt her surge forward, first her front legs rising, then her back ones.

"Come on now, lady," you called.

It was still raining, but only a little, the drops light like summer sprinklers. I opened my mouth and felt the water against my tongue and teeth. I think it was the only thing that kept me going then, that rain. Each drop was like some sort of remedy, healing me . . . keeping me conscious.

The rain fell, and the camel ran.

After a time — I don't know how long — we got to the car. You whooshed down the camel underneath the small collection of trees nearby and untied me. Then you led the camel away. I heard the strain and grumble of the engine as you tried to move the car; I heard moaning from the camel. I tried desperately hard to keep my eyes open. I looked at the sky — blue-gray again — and I looked at the trees. The veins of blood were still on the bark, just as before. Insects were feeding there, drinking up the red sap. There were flies on my own skin, too, buzzing and stepping all over me. I smelled the moisture of freshly rained-on earth. The car roared and snarled, churning the sand. You were shouting to the camel. A stick snapped somewhere.

You came back to me with blankets and water. Made me drink. You spoke constantly, but your words were just background noise; like wind against the sand, or radio static. Then you grabbed my arm and stuck something sharp into it. I felt something rushing into my veins. I woke up a bit after that.

"We've got to hurry," you were saying.

You lifted me and carried me to the car. There was oil and dirt and sweat on your skin. You smelled like gasoline. The car was growling, expectant. You paused before placing me inside.

"Do you want to say good-bye?" you said.

You clicked your tongue and the camel came toward us. Her huge face came right up to me as she sniffed at my cheek. Her harness was gone. I reached out and touched her velvet nose, but the soft sensation didn't fully reach my fingers until I'd moved them away from her.

"This is it," you murmured.

"How will you find her again?" I tried to say. "How will she find you?"

You didn't answer. You just kept staring straight ahead at the camel, your eyes slightly glazed.

"Good-bye, girl," you said softly.

You clicked your tongue again and the camel rumbled in reply. She stepped back, away from the car. You bundled me into the backseat, leaning me against the window to keep my leg straight. You shut the door. I saw you pat the camel's neck one last time as you passed her.

You revved the engine to get the car moving, your foot pumping the accelerator. The tires spun on the sand. I watched the camel through the window. As the car edged off, she started trotting. You went faster and she moved into a lope. She ran beside us. I leaned my cheek against the window and thought things to her. I didn't want her to be left, to be on her own again. How would she find her herd? How would she find you?

Eventually, you pulled away. She stumbled in the sand, trying to keep up, then she slowed to a trot, getting farther and farther behind. She tipped her head back and moaned as we went. I wanted to moan then, too. If I'd had the energy, I would have. I turned my head, watching her until she became a tiny speck in the distance. She stood, still watching us.

"Good-bye," I whispered.

The car bounced and slid in the sand. Stones flicked up and hit the window. I gripped the seat. Every swerve and sway sent a stab of pain through my muscles.

"Hang in there," you said.

But it was difficult. After a while, my eyes closed again. I felt myself sinking down in the seat. The venom traveled up my body, poisoning me quietly. It turned my limbs stiff and hard. It made me dream that my feet grew through the car door and sank down into the sand. My skin turned into dry bark and my arms into branches. My fingers were soft whispering leaves.

I was vaguely aware of something shaking. My body was moving sideways, but I didn't know how. The movement kept going. Something was speaking to me. The wind, or the sand, or something, was calling my name.

"Gemma . . . Gem," it said. "We're almost there."

But my body wouldn't respond. I tried to open my eyes.

Nothing worked. My body was rigid. My fingers twitched and swayed with the breeze. Then I felt your hand on my cheek, cool and dry.

"Wake up, Gem," you were saying. "Wake up, please."

I tried moving my face again, straining the muscles in my forehead. And this time I did it. I slid my eyes open. Just a crack. But it was all I needed. I saw you. You were twisting around from the front seat, one hand on the wheel, one hand on me. Behind you, through the windshield, towered a huge mountain of dirt.

"The mine site," you said.

———⋦———

Again you forced a tablet of soft leaves into my mouth, much more bitter than the last.

"Chew," you said. "Stay awake."

You turned back to the front and suddenly the car stopped jerking so much. We'd hit a dirt track. It was hard and well used. My head pressed against the window as you put your foot to the floor, dust rising up around us. Compared to the rough ground that I'd got used to, the car felt like it was flying. As we got closer I could see huge trucks moving on top of the mountain, towers and chutes and large metal tanks beside it. There were more buildings around the base, white dust in the sky. Red dirt was everywhere else, and other colors, too . . . browns and whites, oranges and blacks. There were piles of stones. No trees.

I chewed, tasting the antiseptic bitterness of the leaves. I blinked and forced my eyes to stay open. I'd been dreaming of that moment for weeks, that first glimpse of life outside your desert home. But right then, it didn't feel real. Buildings, telegraph poles, trucks, and rubble blurred into the same thing, all swirling into a red smudge behind the window. Everything looked hot and burned.

You skidded, wheels spinning, toward the buildings. I gasped as the force of your turn spread pain into my shoulders. It felt like barbed wire under my skin. You roared down a street with small square buildings on either side. Houses? It got harder for me to breathe. It was hotter in that place; the air was thicker somehow, heavy with mine dust. My eyes started to shut.

You swung into a driveway. There was another squarish, makeshift building there. I gasped as the pain hit me again. I closed my eyes and pressed my cheek against the cool glass of the window. Every breath was more difficult than the last. You leaped out of the car, not bothering to turn it off. You were yelling something toward the building, but I don't know what. My hearing was fading now, too. Everything was slower and quieter around me. My body was closing down, shutting up shop. Everything was fuzzy, like a dream. Nothing was real.

I heard another voice yelling, too. Then the door I was leaning against opened and I fell back. Your arms were there, catching me. Something pressed against my nose and mouth. There was a smell of something clinical. And then, suddenly, I could breathe a little better. You were leaning over me, lifting me up. But I couldn't really feel you. Only your skin brushing against the tip of my fingers. I could feel that.

You took me into a room. Laid me on a table. A man stood over me. I saw him when he pulled open my eyelids. He said something to me. Then he put something into my arm. From somewhere far away, I felt a small jab of pain. Then a mask went over my face. And I could breathe again.

Then we were driving fast. I could see sky through the windows: blue, with orange streaks of sunset. You skidded to a stop. The door opened. And you were picking me up again. You were running, my body swaying in your arms. But I wasn't in pain. From very far away I heard the sound of your feet, slapping against tarmac. There was another sound, too. A rhythmic grumbling. Mechanical thunder. Someone in white was waiting.

"Name? Age?" I heard a lady's voice, again from a long way away, like she was talking from another world.

You carried me inside the plane, laid me on something soft. Then you started to pull away. I reached out and grabbed your hand, locked my fingers around yours. I wouldn't let go. I didn't want to be left alone with these strangers. I looked up at you, found your eyes. You hesitated, glanced back outside at the tarmac and flatness and red land beyond . . . then back at me. You nodded slightly as you sat. You started talking to me. I don't know what you said. But there were tears in your eyes.

My ears felt thick, and the machine moved around me. The person in white was back. Another mask on my face. Air. More things jabbed into my arm. I just kept watching you. You were the only thing that could keep my eyes open. But my chest was sinking, down through the soft mattress, down through the plane's floor . . . I was under an avalanche. The sky turned orange around us, the land red beneath us. We were flying into the sun.

Then the plane was dipping down and bumping and I was being pushed out of it. Wheeled across tarmac. It was dark, but lights were winking in the distance. The mask was taken from my face. You were running beside me. Running like you'd been running in the sand beside the camel. This time you were holding my hand, your fingers tight. Your eyes never left mine. There was a building. I went through a set of sliding doors.

Then we stopped. A man was asking you questions, pushing you back. You were shouting, pointing. Then you looked at me . . . *really* looked at me. Your eyes were desperate, wanting something . . . finding something. Maybe. Your eyes became wet as they traveled over me, lingering on my legs, my face, my eyes. I tried to speak, but I couldn't. You turned back to the man, yelled something at him. Then you stepped up to my stretcher. You leaned over me. Stroked my face.

"Good-bye, Gem," you whispered. "You'll be OK."

You touched the ring on my finger as you started to pull away. No. I shook my head. No.

I grabbed at you. Got a hold on your elbow. My fingers grasped at your skin. And with all the strength I had, I pulled at you. I pulled you toward me. You let me. You came down easily. And then, suddenly, you were right there. I ran my fingers up your arm onto your bare chest, feeling for your heat. I gripped the back of your neck, my fingers twisting in your hair.

Then, with my final bit of strength, I pulled your face toward me. My head left the pillow to get to you. Your skin was almost touching mine. Your mouth so close. I felt the roughness of your beard. I felt your warm breath, smelled the sour eucalyptus. I tasted your dirt and salt and sweat. Your lips were soft against my skin.

And then, you were being pulled off me. You were being held. And I fell back. I looked for you, found your eyes as I was wheeled away. I could still taste your salt on my lips.

You didn't cry. You didn't move. You just stood there, like a rock, watching me, while the hospital staff closed in around you. You were the hunted one now. I wanted to lift my hand, wanted to say thank you. But I could only watch as I was wheeled backward through a flapping door. Plastic edges fluttered against my arms as I was pulled through. I pushed myself up, wanting to keep you in sight. You brought your hand to your mouth. You opened your fingers and blew something at me. It looked like a kiss. But I saw the sand hang in the air for a moment before it fell toward the floor.

Then the plastic doors shut and other, colder, fingers felt for my face. Another mask went over my mouth. Plastic straps pinched my cheeks. And then, breathing became easy. But it didn't matter. The world all went black anyway.

I sank down. Everything was cold, and dark, and very far away. A blurred hum of machines surrounded me, the distant drone of voices . . .

"Who is this girl anyway?"

"She's fading on us . . ."

"Bring her into intensive . . ."

Then,

nothing.

---

A sharp chemical smell. Stiff sheets against my skin, heavy on my chest. Wires plugged into my arms. Something was beeping. When I tried to find it, it started beeping faster. I was cold. My body wasn't so numb, more sore. Kind of empty. There were four shadowy walls around me. No windows. When I looked at one wall, it felt like the others were closing in.

It was such a tiny room. You weren't in it.

Only me.

---

Another time I felt someone's fingers, cold against my arm, wrapping something around me.

"Where's Ty?" I said.

"Who?" It was a lady's voice, oldish.

"Where's Ty?"

The fingers stopped moving. A sigh.

"You don't have to worry about him anymore," the voice said gently. "He's gone."

"Gone where?"

The fingers slipped down to my wrist and pressed against it, their tips so cold. "Your parents are on their way."

---

I slept.

---

There was blood between my legs . . . my period, arrived at last. Only a few weeks late. They say fear dries it up sometimes. I lay there, too numb to feel embarrassed, watching the nurse change the sheets.

---

I slept again, wanting a dream.

---

I heard Mum's voice first, high and shrill, echoing down the corridor toward me.

"We left as soon as we possibly could," she said. "Where is she?"

Her heels clicked quickly, getting louder.

Dad's voice was quiet in the background, talking to a third voice.

"She's been in a venom-induced coma," that voice was saying. "She'll feel strange for some time."

Then suddenly, they were all in my room: Mum and Dad and a white-coated doctor. There was a policeman at the door. Mum was grabbing me, smothering me with her soft wool cardigan and expensive perfume. She was sobbing into my shoulders. Dad was standing behind her. He was smiling, his whole face wrinkling up with it, which confused me for a moment because Dad never used to smile like that. Not at me anyway, not that I can remember. Then everyone was talking, asking questions, and staring. . . . I looked from Mum to Dad to the doctor. There was too much noise. I watched their mouths, opening and closing, but couldn't take in their words. I shook my head.

Then, almost at the same time, they all went quiet. They stared at me, expectantly, waiting for me to respond.

Mum pulled back, studying my face. And I opened my mouth. I wanted to speak to them. I wanted to talk. I did. A part of me, a large part, was so glad to see them that I wanted to burst into tears. But I couldn't cry, couldn't say one word. Nothing would come out. I couldn't even raise my arms for a hug. Not then. Not right away.

Mum made up for me, though, releasing floods of tears. "Oh, Gemma, it must have been terrible for you," she sobbed. "But now we're here, I promise it will be all right. You don't have to worry. You're safe."

There was something awkward about the words she said, as if she were trying to convince herself more than me. I tried to smile back. I really did. Every muscle in my face hurt from the effort. And there was pain thudding through my forehead. The lights in that room were so bright.

I had to shut my eyes.

———————❧———————

Later, Mum came back in by herself. Her eyes were red and tired-looking. She'd changed her shirt to a peach-colored one, freshly ironed and sweet-smelling.

"We shouldn't have all come together," she said. "It must have been difficult for you . . . after having no one for so long, no one except for . . ."

She couldn't say your name; her face curled up in pain as

soon as she even thought of you. I nodded, motioning that I understood, and she continued.

"The doctors have told me how hard it is sometimes for people to adapt back to one's real life. I know I can't expect you to . . ." Her face wrestled with an emotion I couldn't read. I frowned. "I don't even know what he's done to you," she whispered. "You seem different somehow." She had to look away, biting her lip. She breathed deeply until she regained her composure. "And we were so very worried, Gemma," she added, "thinking we'd never . . . that you'd never . . ."

Tears were on her face again, making her mascara run. In a previous life she would have hated that. I watched the black lines streak down her cheeks. She reached across to my hand, and I let her take it. Her fingers were cold and thin, her nails long. She felt the ring that you had given me. I stiffened, watching her twist it around my finger, seeing the colors glint.

"Did you have this before?" she asked.

I nodded. "Got it on Portobello Road," I lied. "It's fake."

"I don't remember it."

Silence settled between us. Mum bit the edge of her lip. Eventually she leaned back, twisting her fingers in her lap. I put my hand under the sheets. I brought my other hand across and pulled the ring off my finger. Mum looked at me carefully, concern frowning her face.

"The nurse said you were asking about him," she said.

"I was wondering . . ."

"I know, it's understandable." She leaned across and stroked the side of my face. "But you don't have to wonder anymore, love, you don't even need to think about him."

"What do you mean?"

"They have him, Gemma," she whispered. "He turned himself in at the hospital. The police will need a statement from you soon."

"And if I don't want to . . . ?"

"You have to. It's the best thing." She tucked the sheets around me tighter. "Once you've given your statement, the police can charge him. We'll be one step closer to getting that monster locked up. And that is what you want, isn't it?" Her voice was hesitant.

I shook my head. "He's not a monster," I said quietly.

Mum's hands went stiff around the sheets as she looked sharply at me. "That man is evil," she hissed. "Why else would he have taken you from us?"

"I don't know," I whispered. "But he's . . . not that." I couldn't find the right words.

Mum's face went pale as she studied me, her lips pinched and tight. "What did he do to you?" she asked. "What did he do to you to make you think like this?"

---

The next day two police officers came: a thin man and a young-ish lady. Both carried their hats in their hands. They were baseball caps, so much more casual-looking than the police hats in the UK. My parents stood at the back of the room. A doctor was there, too. Everyone was watching me, assessing me. I felt like I was in a play, with everyone waiting for me to say my lines. The thin policeman took out a notebook and leaned close enough for me to see the pimple on his chin.

"We realize this is difficult for you, Ms. Toombs," he began. His voice was nasal and high-pitched, and I disliked him immediately. "Captives often go through a stage of silence and denial. Your parents say you've not been speaking much, to anyone, about your ordeal? I don't wish to push you, but . . ."

I stayed silent. He paused to glance up at Mum. She nodded at him, urging him on.

"It's just, Ms. Toombs, Gemma . . . ," he continued, "we are holding a man in custody. We have reason to believe that he is your kidnapper. We need you to give a statement to confirm this."

"Who is he?" I said. I started shaking my head.

The thin man checked his notes. "The accused is Tyler MacFarlane, he's six foot two inches in height, blond hair, blue eyes, small scar on the edge . . ."

My stomach turned over. Literally. I had to reach for the bedpan to be sick.

---

The police kept pushing. Every day they were back with their questions, each time phrased in a slightly different way.

"Tell me about the man you met in the airport."

"Did he take you against your will?"

"Did he use force?"

"Drugs?"

There was only so long I could hold out. I had to speak in the end. Mum was always there beside me, urging me on. After a while, they showed me photographs. Some of you. Some of other men.

"Is this one him?" they asked over and over, flicking the photographs. They wouldn't let up.

You were so easy to spot; the only man with any fire behind his eyes. The only man I could really look at. It was as if you were looking into the camera lens just for me; as if you knew I would be studying those photographs later, looking for you. You were proud in that shot. As proud as you can be in front of a smeared police wall. There was a cut under your eye that hadn't been there before. I wanted to keep that photograph. But of course the detective slipped it back into the brown paper envelope with the others.

It all dragged on. A couple more days, at least. But I gave them their testimony eventually. I had to.

The time was a blur of injections and interrogations. I had become public property. Anyone could ask me anything they wanted, it seemed. Nothing was off-limits. The lady detective asked me whether we'd ever had sex.

"Did he make you touch him?" she asked.

I shook my head. "Never."

"Are you sure?"

I talked to psychologists, therapists, counselors, doctors for this and doctors for that. A nurse took blood every day. A doctor checked my heart for tremors and palpitations. They treated me for shock. None of them left me alone. Especially not the psychologists.

One afternoon a lady with a short bob and a dark blue suit sat at the side of my bed. It was toward the end of the day, and I'd been waiting for the rattle of the dinner cart.

"I'm Dr. Donovan," she said, "clinical psychiatrist."

"I don't want another shrink."

"Fair enough." She didn't leave, though. She just leaned across to the clipboard at the end of my bed and started flicking through it. "Do you know what Stockholm syndrome is?" she asked.

I didn't answer. She glanced back at me, before writing some notes of her own on the clipboard.

"It's when a victim emotionally bonds with his or her abuser," she explained, still writing. "It may be as a survival mechanism, so that you feel safer with your captor when you are getting along, for instance, or it may happen if you start to feel sorry for your abuser . . . perhaps he's been wronged at some point in his life and you want to make it up to him . . . you start to understand him. There are other reasons, too: Perhaps you are isolated with him; you have to get on, or you suffer tremendous boredom . . . or perhaps he makes you feel special, loved —"

"I don't know what you are getting at," I interrupted. "But that's not how I feel."

"I didn't say it was. I was just wondering if you knew about it." She looked at me carefully, raising an eyebrow. I waited for her to keep going, mildly curious. "Whatever he did," she continued softly, "whatever Mr. MacFarlane did or said to you, you know he hasn't done the right thing, don't you, Gemma?"

"You sound like my mum," I said.

"Is that so bad?"

When I didn't answer that, she sighed deeply and took a thin book from her briefcase.

"They'll discharge you soon," she said. "But doctors will keep quizzing you until you understand, until you realize that what Mr. MacFarlane did —"

"I know Ty did the wrong thing," I interrupted quietly. And I did know that, didn't I? But it was almost as if a part of me didn't want to believe her. A part of me understood why you'd done it, too. And it's hard to hate someone once you understand them. I felt so mixed up.

Dr. Donovan paused, looking at me, not unkindly. "Perhaps you need some help working through your thoughts?"

I was silent, looking straight ahead at the pale gray wall. She put the book on my bedside table. It said something about Stockholm syndrome on the cover. I didn't look at it any more closely.

"You'll have to talk to someone at some point, Gemma," Dr. Donovan urged. "You're going to have to figure out your real feelings soon . . . what's true."

She dropped her business card on the table. I took it and put it inside the drawer, next to where I'd placed your ring. Then, when she left, I stared at the ceiling. I wrapped the blankets around me, suddenly cold. I felt naked . . . as if I'd shed my skin in the desert like the snakes do. As if I'd left a part of me behind somewhere.

I wondered if you were being interrogated, too. I shivered as I pulled the blankets over my head entirely, enjoying the darkness they gave.

---

Mum and Dad handled the reporters. They made the appearances on the news and spoke to the papers. I was grateful for that. Right then the thought of a camera in my face was enough to start me hyperventilating.

When they were both at a press conference, I got out of bed. I paced around the room that I'd been trapped in until slowly I made my limbs work again. The leg that had been bitten was still stiff and sore. It felt good to move it.

I tried walking down the corridor, testing how far my leg would carry me before the pain got too bad. Could I walk right out of the hospital? Two elderly patients stared hard at me as I passed. They knew who I was. Their looks almost sent me running straight back into my room. It was almost as if I were famous. I swallowed and forced my legs to keep walking.

I continued to the foyer, to the flapping plastic doors where I had last seen you. I touched their hard edges, and stepped through them. There was a pregnant lady waiting at the reception desk. She looked up, too, as I passed, but I ignored her. I walked to the sliding doors leading out of the hospital. I stood in front of them, and the doors slid open with a purr. It was hotter outside, and sunny. I blinked at the brightness. There were cars and lampposts and people, and birds twittering in the leafy trees. The blacktop of the parking lot rolled out before me. And beyond that, flat, red dust.

I took one small step. But almost immediately, there was a nurse at my side, placing her hands on my arms and not letting me go.

"You haven't been discharged," she whispered.

She turned me around and walked me back to that room. To that tiny, tiny room . . . so much like a cell, with its gray walls and lack of light. She tucked me back under those sheets, and pulled them close around me.

Later, Mum came in with a plastic bag. Inside were hundreds of articles, all clipped carefully from the newspapers.

"I don't know if you realize how big it's all been," she said. "The whole world knows about you." She placed the bag on my bed and thumbed through the pages of words. "These are just the pieces I've collected since we left Britain. There's more at home. I just thought . . ." She paused, choosing her words. "I thought you might want to catch up, see how people care."

I pulled the bag toward me, feeling the weight of the papers on my legs. I pulled out a bundle. The first thing I noticed was the photograph. The last school photograph that had been taken of me was blown up, huge, on the front cover of *The Australian*. My hair was tied up in a ponytail and my school shirt tight around my neck. I hated that shot, always have. I flicked through some more of the articles. That photograph was nearly always with them.

"Why did you give them that photo?" I asked.

Mum frowned, pulled the bag back toward her. "You look pretty."

"I look young."

"The police needed a recent shot, sweetheart."

"Did it have to be a school photo?" I thought of you then, sitting in a cell somewhere. Had you seen all those articles, too? Had you seen the photograph?

I read bits of the stories.

Gemma Toombs, the 16-year-old abducted from Bangkok airport, has been admitted to a remote West Australian hospital, apparently taken there by her captor. . . .

Anxious parents of Gemma Toombs charter a plane from London to be by their daughter's side. . . .

Mum's face was blotchy and tear-stained in the accompanying photograph, Dad with his arm around her. Anna was in the crowd behind them, staring worriedly at the camera.

The articles went on and on, mostly saying the same thing. I flicked through the headlines:

## Gemma: Found!
## Gemma Toombs Released From Desert Drifter!
## Is This the Face of a Monster?

I paused at that one. It was dated the day before. In the middle of the article was a line drawing of you. Your head was bowed and you were sitting in a courtroom, your hands in handcuffs . . . your blue eyes not sketched in. I skimmed for the details. The article stated it was your preliminary hearing, and had lasted just a few minutes. You'd kept your head bowed the whole time. You had said two words only: "Not Guilty."

At that, I looked up at Mum.

"I know." Mum shook her head. "He must be mad. It'll never hold up. The police have witnesses, video evidence from the airport, and you, of course. How can he even think to plead not guilty?" She shook her head again, annoyed. "It just proves he's insane."

"What else has he said?"

"Nothing, for now. We'll have to wait for the trial. But the police think he'll say you came of your own free will, that you wanted to join him." She stopped abruptly, wondering if she'd said too much. I could see in her eyes that she still wasn't sure how affected I was by you.

I smiled, thanking her, trying to reassure her. "You're right, that is insane," I agreed quietly.

Mum started fussing then, tidying up the clippings around me before I'd finished reading them. "Would you like to go back to London?" she asked. "Until the trial? Then we can really prepare ourselves. Maybe you'd like some time to sort out your thoughts, to be with your friends?"

I nodded absently. "I just want it to be over," I said. "All of it."

We would change planes in Perth before flying back to London. We'd wait there, in our house, until the trial. Until then, the police would gather evidence against you, and I'd work on my statement. I would return to school if I thought I could handle it, and I'd continue talking to the shrinks. Mum made it seem so straightforward when she told me.

"In a few months, life will start to get easier," she said. "You'll see. Things will work out."

I hadn't found out much about you. I knew you were in a high-security unit, somewhere in Perth. You had a solitary cell.

You hadn't been allowed bail, and you weren't speaking to anyone. That's all the police could tell me. Apparently.

I took the window seat on the flight to Perth. It was a small plane, specially chartered for us, and it rattled and shook as the wheels left the ground. It was strange, being the only ones. Apparently the British government had paid. I called the airline attendant and asked for a glass of water. It came right away.

I pressed my hand against the plastic windowpane as we started to gain height. Dad took my other hand and held it tightly. His solid gold wedding ring was cold against my fingers. He was talking to me about life back in London, about my friends who'd sent messages and would be waiting to see me . . . about Anna and Ben.

"You can invite them all round, perhaps," he said. "Have a kind of . . . party?"

His voice was questioning, so I nodded; I wasn't really listening. I just wanted to stop his questions, however well meaning they were. I shut my eyes as I realized something: No one seemed to have any clue about me, about what I was really thinking. It was like I existed in a kind of parallel universe, thinking thoughts and feeling emotions that no one else understood. Except for you, perhaps. But I didn't even know that for certain.

I leaned my head against the window and it juddered against my temple. I watched the land move by below. From up there, the desert was made up of so many colors . . . so many shades of browns and reds and oranges. White dried-out creek beds and salt pans. A dark river, curling like a snake. Burned-out blackness. Swirls and circles and lines and textures. Tiny dots of trees. Dark smudges of rocks. Everything stretching out in an endlessness of pattern.

It took two hours to cross all those hundreds of miles, all those billions of grains of sand, all that life. From up there, so far above, the land looked like a painting, one of *your* paintings. It looked like your body when you'd painted onto yourself. If I squinted, I could almost imagine the land was you . . . stretched out and huge, below me.

And then I realized something else: I knew what you'd been doing, all this time, in your outbuilding in the desert. You'd been painting the land as it looked from above, just as a bird would see it, or a spirit, or me . . . your swirls and dots and circles drawing out the pattern of the land.

---

The reporters were waiting. Somehow they knew we had to switch from the domestic terminal to the international; they knew we had three hours to wait until our flight back. They crowded around us, closing in on me, their camera lights flashing.

"Gemma, Gemma," they shouted. "Can we have a word?" They spoke as if they knew me; as if I was a schoolgirl who lived down the road from them.

Dad tried shielding me, tried pushing them all back, but they persisted. Even the ordinary people at the airport — the other passengers and taxi drivers and coffee shop staff — even they knew me. I actually saw some of them snap photographs, too. It was ridiculous. In the end Mum took off her jacket and put it over my head. Dad got angry — well, angry for Dad anyway. . . .

I think he even told someone to fuck off. That surprised me, and I paused for a moment to study Dad's face. He really did care for me then; he really did want me safe. He held me close to him as we passed a TV crew.

But something was clear: I was no longer just an ordinary schoolgirl. Instead I'd turned into a celebrity. My face sold papers. Millions of them. It made people tune into the news. But, right then, with a coat over my head and all those men in leather jackets yelling at me, I felt more like a criminal. They were like leeches, wanting to suck up every tiny thing that had happened between you and me in the desert . . . wanting to know it all. You'd made me famous, Ty. You'd made the whole world fall in love with me. And I hated it.

We made it to the other terminal. There were reporters there, too, and onlookers, and police, and noise and noise and lights and noise. My breathing sped up. I just kept thinking of that huge plane, on the runway, waiting to take me back to England and the cold and the city and the gray . . . waiting to carry me away from you. I felt the sweat on my skin, the way my clothes stuck to me.

I couldn't do it. I broke away from Mum and Dad. And I ran. Mum was grabbing on to my cardigan, but I slipped out of it, leaving her holding the empty sleeves. I ran straight past the reporters with their flashing lights and noise. I ran past the shops and other passengers and straight into the restrooms. I found an empty stall. I wedged the lock shut. I kicked the door so I was sure it was secure. Then I sat on the toilet lid and leaned my head against the toilet paper roll. I stuck my mouth against it to stop myself from crying, to stop myself from shouting and screaming and tearing the place down. I breathed in its chalky, fake-flowery smell. And I just stayed there. I couldn't face them, any of them. Everyone wanted answers I wasn't ready to give.

Mum found me. She stood on the other side of the bathroom door with her red shoes pointing in toward each other.

"Gemma?" she said. Her voice was shaky and weak. "Come on, love, just open the door. There's no one else coming in. I've made Dad block off the entrance. It's only us."

She stood there for ages before I pulled back the lock. She came in and hugged me, awkwardly, with me sitting on the toilet lid and her kind of crouching beside me, kneeling in the dirt and scraps of toilet paper and old splashes of piss. She pulled me into her lap, and for the first time since she'd arrived, I hugged her back. She leaned against the toilet bowl, covering me with her jacket, and I wondered something. This Mum, hugging me close, didn't seem like the same Mum you'd been telling me stories about. For the first time, I wondered if all the stories you'd told me in the desert were even true; all those conversations you'd apparently overheard about my parents moving away or being disappointed in me. Had you been lying all along?

Mum gently stroked my hair. I whispered into her shoulder.

"I can't go back. Not yet. I can't leave."

And she held my head tight to her chest and wrapped her arms around me.

"You don't have to," she said, rocking me. "You don't have to do anything you don't want to do, not anymore."

And I cried.

———— ⚮ ————

None of us talked on the taxi ride into the city. I stayed curled up, in Mum's arms. My head was buzzing, recalling the way you'd spoken, remembering the things you'd told me about my life. You'd said my parents didn't care, that they were only concerned about themselves and money; you'd said they wanted to move away. You'd made it sound so convincing.

I had to force my mind to go blank. I didn't know what I would do if I started thinking again. I probably would have rolled right out of the taxi and got myself killed. Dad busied himself with the luggage and with sorting out somewhere to stay. I focused on the concrete shooting past . . . the pavement and buildings and pavement, the occasional tree. I focused on the faintly sweet smell of Mum's blouse.

The driver pulled up outside a block of dark gray apartment buildings.

"Serviced apartments," he grunted. "They're new. No one knows they've opened yet." He waited for a tip.

We walked in, my blank expression masking what was going on inside me. Mum took the key and led me through the foyer, Dad did the explaining. My legs shook as Mum helped me up the stairs.

Once inside the apartment, I snapped. I slammed the door and reached for the first thing I could find — a lamp — and I hurled it against the freshly painted beige wall. Its china base shattered on impact, shards flying everywhere. Then I picked up something else — a vase — and hurled that, too. Mum ducked for cover. Her eyes were wide and shocked as she started moving toward me, but I grabbed the next nearest thing and held it out at her before she got to me. It was a small electric fan, still plugged in with its blades whirring. The cord was taut over my arms. I was ready to throw that, too.

"What's wrong?" Her eyes didn't leave mine.

I shook my head, tears running down my face. "Tell me something," I whispered. "Did you want to move away, next year, without me? Did you ever talk about that with Dad?"

"What?" Mum's eyebrows shot up. "No, of course not! Who told you this?"

She moved toward me, but I held the fan between us, ready to throw it at her face. The plug was straining in the socket. She saw in my eyes not to come any closer. Every part of me was shaking, every part of me going mad.

"I hate it, all of this," I screamed, my voice breaking. "I even hate him, even him." A huge sob came up from my chest.

And I did, right then. I hated you for everything; for making me feel so helpless everywhere I went, for making me lose control. I hated you for all the emotions in my head, for the confusion . . . for the way I was suddenly doubting everything. I hated you for turning my life upside down and then smashing it into shards. I hated you for making me stand with a whirring fan in my hand, screaming at and questioning my mum.

But I hated you for something else, too. Right then, and at every moment since you'd left me, all I could think about was you. I wanted you in that apartment. I wanted your arms around me, your face close to mine. I wanted your smell. And I knew I couldn't — *shouldn't* — have it. That's what I hated most. The uncertainty of you. You'd kidnapped me, put my life in danger . . . but I loved you, too. Or thought I did. None of it made sense.

I growled in my throat, frustrated at myself. Mum took a cautious step toward me.

"It's all right to be confused," she whispered. "The people we . . . care for . . . aren't always the ones we should . . ." She frowned, wondering if she'd got it right.

A noise came through my teeth then, from deep in my chest.

"Don't tell me anything," I snarled. "No more words!"

I yanked the fan from the plug, holding it between us, keeping her away from me with it. I pushed it toward her, and she jumped backward, stumbling over the coffee table.

"But, Gemma!" she whispered. "I love you!"

And I threw the fan, in the same direction as the lamp, its blades still whirring as it hit the wall.

---

We stayed in Perth. Even with the stuff I smashed, they let us keep the apartment.

It's still more than a month until the trial, despite the court agreeing to prioritize your case. And the apartment complex couldn't refuse the money Dad offered for keeping things quiet.

My emotions bounce. Some days it feels better knowing you are here, in the same city, knowing you are close. Some days that same thought fills me with fear. But either way, I think of you in your cell every night. My stomach still twists when Mum opens the windows and lets in the eucalyptus smell from outside.

Our full-service apartment feels a little like a prison, too, with its gray colors and cleanliness; the way that I can't leave it without someone taking my picture. From its windows I stare out at the city . . . at the concrete and buildings, cars and suits. Some days I imagine the land that lives beneath it all, red and dormant; the land you love. I imagine it coming alive again one day. Then my mind drifts back to the desert; to the open spaces of color and pattern. I miss it, that endlessness.

The police officer in charge of the case has visited me twice already. After my fan-throwing incident, Mum called Dr. Donovan, too. She comes most days, and I don't mind talking to her. She doesn't push me too hard, just lets me talk when I want to . . . when I can.

———————⁂———————

It was Dr. Donovan who suggested I write this, actually. Only, she didn't suggest that I write it to you. Course not. She just gave me the laptop. She just told me to write.

"If you can't speak about your experiences, write them down," she said. "Get all your thoughts out, anyway you can, start a journal, maybe . . . whatever makes it easiest. You need to try to understand this whole big thing that's happened to you."

And I'm trying to, believe me. I'd love to understand all this. But the only way I can is to write this journal — this letter — to you. After all, you were the only person out there with me . . . the only person who knows what happened. And something did happen, didn't it? Something powerful and strange. Something I can never forget, no matter how hard I try.

Dr. Donovan thinks I've got Stockholm syndrome. They all do. I know I scare Mum when I say something good about you, when I say you're not as bad as people think, or that there's more to you than what the papers write. And if I say anything like that in front of Dr. Donovan, she just makes lots of notes and nods to herself.

So I've stopped saying these things. Instead, I tell them what they want to hear. I tell them you really are a monster, that you are screwed up. I tell them I don't have any feelings for you other than hatred. I go along with everything the police say I have to say. And I've written the statement they want me to write. I try to believe it all.

I wish I had amnesia so I could forget what you look like. I wish I felt good about letting you go to prison for ten or fifteen years. I wish I could believe everything the papers write. Or that my parents tell me. Or that Dr. Donovan says. It's not as if I don't understand where they're all coming from. I've also wanted you dead.

And, let's face it, you did steal me. But you saved my life, too. And somewhere in the middle, you showed me a place so different and beautiful, I can never get it out of my mind. And I can't get you out of there, either. You're stuck in my brain like my own blood vessels.

I've just taken a small break to walk around the garden at the back of the apartment complex. It's not much of a garden; just paved, with a few potted plants and shrubs. I sat on the tiles and looked up at the skyscrapers around me. I could almost feel you, somewhere in this city, not far away. I could almost hear your soft cough. You were thinking of me, too. I shut my eyes and tried to imagine what it will be like. Will I be scared when I see you, or will I feel something else?

You will be chained up, your strong arms still. You won't be able to hurt me, or touch me. Will your eyes plead, or will they bore into mine with anger? How have they treated you, in there? Have your nightmares returned? One thing is certain: When we next meet, I will be looking at you with the whole legal system between us.

I thought that when I got to this point in this letter, I'd understand something. I'd realize why all this has happened, why you came into my life . . . why you chose me. Sometimes I think you're still just as messed up as that first day I met you in the park. And sometimes I think about your plan of living out there in the heat and the endlessness and the beauty, and whether it would have worked. Mostly I don't know what to think.

But writing all this down is doing something. When I write this in bed, I can almost hear the echo of the wind over the sand, or the groans of wooden panels around me. I can almost smell the dustiness of the camel, taste the bitterness of saltbush. And when I dream, your warm hands cover my shoulders. Your whispers carry stories and sound like the rustle of spinifex. I still wear that ring, you know . . . at night, when no one is watching. It's in my pocket now. I'll hide it before the police officers come this afternoon.

They want to discuss what I'm going to say when I get up in the witness box. And I suppose I should think about that. It's just . . . I'm not yet sure what exactly it will be. That day in court could have two different endings, but it will start the same way.

———— ≷ ————

It will be a Monday morning, just before nine. The media will be waiting. I'll be sandwiched between Mum and Dad, keeping my head down, and we will have to push through the reporters and commuters and onlookers. Some of them will grab at me, shove microphones in my face. Mum will be holding my hand so tightly that her nails will dig into my skin. Dad will be wearing a suit. Mum will have chosen something black and sensible for me, too.

We'll step inside the High Court, and it will be quieter there immediately. That big grand entrance hall and all those suits will somehow muffle us. We'll find Mr. Samuels, the prosecution lawyer. He'll ask if I've had a chance to reread my statement. Then he'll usher my parents into the courtroom, the main courtroom, and I'll hear talking and movement for a moment before the door thuds behind them. Then I'll be left outside, on a cold leather chair, with nothing but my thoughts.

After some time, a time that will feel longer than it is, the door will open again. Then it'll be my turn. My testimony. The air will be tense like a trampoline, waiting for me to bounce. Everyone will look. Even if they think it's impolite, still they will look. The court artist will begin drawing my face. But I'll only be looking at one person.

You'll be sitting in the dock, your hands clipped together. Your eyes will be searching for mine, too, wide as the ocean. You'll need me now. So I'll make my decision. Then I'll turn my face from you.

And it will start just as it should. They will ask my name, my age, my address. Then it will get interesting. They'll ask me how I know you.

In the first instance, I'll tell them exactly what they want to hear. I'll tell them how you followed me, how you . . . stalked me . . . from such an early age. I'll tell them how you came to the UK to look for your mother and instead found drink and drugs . . . and then me. I'll tell them about your inability to fit in, about your deluded thoughts about the desert and me being your only escape.

Then the lawyers will ask me about the airport, and I'll tell them that you drugged me and stole me. I'll tell them that you shoved me in the trunk of your car and held me against my will. I'll tell them about the long, lonely nights in that small wooden shack and about being locked in the bathroom . . . how I waited for you to kill me. I'll tell them about your angry outbursts and instability, your lies, and I will tell them how you grabbed me so hard sometimes that you made my eyes water and my skin turn red.

And I won't look at you through that testimony. I'll just say what they expect.

"He's a monster," I'll say. "Yes, he kidnapped me."

And the judge will bash the little hammer and hand out a sentence of fifteen years or so, and everything — everything — will finally be over.

———————⟶———————

But there is another way.

I could tell the courtroom a story about the time we met in a park, so long ago, when I was ten and you were almost nineteen. When I found you under a rhododendron bush, with its foliage wrapped tight around you and the pink buds just beginning above your head. I could tell them of how we became friends, how you talked to me and looked after me. I could tell them of the time you saved me from Josh Holmes.

Mr. Samuels will try to interrupt, of course. His face will be red, and his eyes bulging with surprise. He may tell the judge that my testimony is unreliable, saying that I'm still suffering from Stockholm syndrome. But I'll be composed, calm, able to explain clearly how I'm not. I've done my research. I know exactly what it is I need to say in order for them to believe me.

So the judge will let me go on talking, just for a while. Then I'll really surprise them. I will tell the courtroom how we fell in love. Not in the desert, course not, but winding through the streets and parks of London two years ago, when I was fourteen and looked so much like your mum.

The courtroom will rustle, murmur. Mum will probably cry out. It will be hard to look at her after the next bit, so I won't; I'll look at you. I'll say I wanted to run away.

You'll nod at me a little, your eyes alive again. And I'll tell them of your plan.

You said you knew the perfect place to run to. A place that was empty of people, and buildings, and far, far away. A place covered in bloodred earth and sleeping life. A place longing to come alive again. It's a place for disappearing, you'd said, a place for getting lost . . . and for getting found.

I'll take you there, you'd said.

And I could say that I agreed.

———— ≷ ————

My hands shake as I type this. The tears are rolling down my cheeks, and the screen is a blur before my eyes. My chest hurts, trying to stop the sobs. Because there is something that pulls at me, something that's so hard to think about.

I can't save you like that, Ty.

What you did to me wasn't this brilliant thing, like you think it was. You took me away from everything — my parents, my friends, my life. You took me to the sand and the heat, the dirt and isolation. And you expected me to love you. And that's the hardest part. Because I did, or at least, I loved something out there.

But I hated you, too. I can't forget that.

Outside it's so dark, with the tree branches tapping against the window . . . tapping like fingers. I'm tucking the sheet around me, even though I'm not cold, and I'm staring at the blackness behind the glass. You know, maybe if we'd met as ordinary people, one day, maybe . . . maybe things might have been different. Maybe I could have loved you. You were so different and wild. When the light made your bare skin glow on those early mornings, you were the most beautiful thing I'd ever seen. To put you in a cell is like crushing a bird with an army tank.

But what else can I do, other than to plead with you like this? Other than to write down my story, *our* story, to show you what you've done . . . to make you realize that what you did wasn't fair, wasn't right.

When I get into court, I'm going to tell the truth. *My* truth. I will say that you kidnapped me, of course. You did. And I will tell them how you drugged me, and of your mood swings. I won't shy away from the evil you can be.

But I'll tell them of your other side, too. The side I saw sometimes when you spoke softly to the camel, and when you gently touched the leaves of the saltbush, only picking what you needed. And the times you rescued me. I will tell them how you chose prison rather than let me die. Because you did, didn't you? You knew, right from when that snake bit me, it was all over. When I asked you to stay with me in the plane, you did it knowing you were turning yourself in. And I am grateful, Ty, believe me, I am. But I gave my life up for you, too, once . . . back in Bangkok airport. And I had no choice.

The judge will sentence you. I can't stop that. But perhaps my testimony may influence where they send you . . . somewhere near your land, a room with a window this time. Maybe. And perhaps this letter may help you, too. I want you to see that the person I glimpsed running beside the camel, running to save my life, is the person you can choose to be. I can't save you the way you want me to. But I can tell you what I feel. It's not much. But it may give you a chance.

You told me once of the plants that lie dormant through the drought, that wait, half-dead, deep in the earth. The plants that wait for the rain. You said they'd wait for years, if they had to; that they'd almost kill themselves before they grew again. But as soon as those first drops of water fall, those plants begin to stretch and spread their roots. They travel up through the soil and sand to reach the surface. There's a chance for them again.

One day they'll let you out of that dry, empty cell. You'll return to the Separates, and you'll feel the rain once more. And you'll grow straight, this time, toward this sunlight. I know you will.

———⸙———

It's not long now until dawn. The smell of eucalyptus is thick in this room, seeping in through the open window and traveling into my lungs. In a moment, when I'm ready, I will turn off this computer and that will be it. This letter will be finished. A part of me doesn't want to stop writing to you, but I need to. For both of us.

---

My eyelids are heavy as stone. But when I sleep, I'll have that dream again. I haven't wanted to tell you about it, until now.

I'll be in the Separates, and I'll be digging with my bare hands. When I've made a hole deep enough to plant a tree, I'll place my fingers inside. I'll slip off the ring you gave me. It will catch the light and glint a rainbow of colors over my skin, but I will take my hands away, leaving it there. I'll start to sprinkle the earth back over it, and I will bury it. Back where it belongs.

I'll rest against a tree's rough trunk. The sun will be setting, its dazzling colors threading through the sky, making my cheeks warm.

Then I will wake up.

*Good-bye, Ty,*
*Gemma*

*Bonus! A special sneak peek at
Lucy Christopher's next novel:
In a dark wood, Emily takes a chance on
a wild boy she can't stop watching . . . and
faces the truth about her troubled dad.
Coming soon!*

As soon as the final bell rings, I'm out of there, charging through the school passageways toward the gates.

"See you over the weekend!" I yell back at Joe and Beth.

They'll be standing in the hallway staring after me, probably getting annoyed at me again, but I don't care. There's someplace else I want to be right now. I don't take the bus; don't want to be squashed between limbs and schoolbags like some sort of sandwich filling. I jog down the main road instead. My whole body is almost trembling to get into the trees. I take a shortcut across the golf course, skirt around the edge of the park and the garbage dump, and then I'm there.

The woods.

I jump over the turnstile to the footpath and stand under the first trees. I breathe in. There's something about this place in late spring. It's bursting with life and possibilities, as if it's desperate to be sucked down deep into my lungs to take root. If I could become anything in the world, it would be a tree. I'd dig my toes into the earth, shut my eyes, and be still. I wouldn't have to worry about all the things Dad wants me to be. Or that Dad's done. I wouldn't even have to worry about Dad. I could let all of me stretch down into the dirt and that would be all I'd need. The Damon-ache in my chest wouldn't be there anymore. I smile at the ridiculousness of that thought. The Damon-ache has been with me so long now I'm sure it's taken root, working its way around my heart.

Maybe the ache will blossom one day. Maybe it will grow into a huge elm branching out from my chest. Or perhaps a little bird will fly down into my heart and pluck the ache out, fly off and build a nest with it.

Who knows . . .

Two swifts pass by as I'm thinking this, circling and whirling and screeching for sex. They flap their wings against each other; feathers scatter to the ground.

I take off down the path. I'm heading for the Leap. Of course I am. I want to know Damon's secrets; this is the only way to find out. Every step I take toward it makes the tingle in my stomach grow. He could be there. A part of me thinks — *knows* — he will be. What would I say when I see him?

I don't let myself stop and think about this. If I do, I know I'll get scared and turn back. I've never spoken to Damon before. What if my mouth forgets how to talk?

For a second I want to call Beth and ask her what to do. I want to say, "You know that feeling? That feeling you had with Marcus at Jess's party last year? I've got it now, tingling and twisting right down deep in my gut." Maybe deeper.

She'd tell me to go for it.

I follow the edge of the quarry, huge rock on one side of me, the tallest trees in the wood on the other. Each step makes me imagine what it would feel like to be walking here with him.

I think I'd do it with a boy like Damon, right here on the forest floor. Right now on a Friday afternoon. I'd give myself to someone like that.

I say his name out loud — just whisper it, really. I love the way the *m* in the middle bounces off my lips. And then I laugh, and it sounds loud among the birdsong and tree rustles. A wood warbler—or something small and chattery—laughs back. The bird's right, though. Damon won't even look twice at a girl like me, even if I am the only girl around to look twice at. What am I thinking?

I move away from the quarry and onto the main bike track. The woods are empty today. No kids riding their bikes. No dog walkers. The sky is gray as charcoal. Rain soon, then. I hope it'll hold out till I get to the Leap.

I reach the row of pine trees where I hid yesterday: the place where I watched him. I look up the hill. No movement through the bracken today. No beautiful boys weaving like grass.

A deep, heavy lump settles in my stomach. He's not here.

I squint until my eyes water, trying to see the flag up on the ledge. But if it's there, it's too far away to make out. Or too well hidden.

Maybe Damon's up there with it, hidden too.

I find the deer path he jogged up yesterday. Check around me. But the trees are empty and silent. Someone's been here, though. There are footprints. Loads of them. The ground is all churned up near where the bracken starts. Heavy boot prints, like the tracks near the bunker. I bend down, touch my fingers to the edge of one, push in its muddy ridge. I should tell Dad about them. I know, though, even as I think it, that I won't. He'd just worry more about the war, about the fighting coming close, so close it's here. Right here. I keep pressing the mud, wondering what it would be like to hide, knowing that if someone finds you, you're dead. Playing hide-and-seek for real.

A gust of wind whips up through the bracken and I feel two light raindrops brush my cheek. I'll look at the boot prints more closely on the way back down. I dig my toes into the bank instead, begin up the deer path. It's not long before my school shoes are slipping in the mud-rivers that have started racing downhill. I grasp at clumps of gorse, yank myself up. I still can't see the flag. The rocks are cold and damp now; I clamber over them. With the rain that's softly falling, the birds have gone silent too. There's only the sound of my breath, heavy and ragged.

Then the smooth, flat ledge is above me. The Leap. I stand under it for a moment, enjoying its shelter. Damon could be standing on top of me with only this sheet of rock between us. I press my hands up against the cold, hard surface. If I could push them straight through the stone, I'd be grabbing his ankles. But I can't, so I reach up around the rock and haul myself onto the ledge. There's a moment when I think I'm going to slide right off it, tumble all the way back down to the bracken, but I get a foothold and crawl, belly against rock, until I'm lying spread-eagled on its surface. I quickly look around.

No Damon. He's not anywhere.

But for the first time, I'm actually glad about that: glad he didn't see my clumsy entrance, anyway. I lie on the rock with the rain tapping my cheeks, catching my breath.

The flag is still here. It's blowing to the side, facing away from the ledge, just like yesterday. After a minute or two, I get up and crouch beside it. The only thing that's different is a fresh gash, carved into the sapling above the first one. Another deep, straight line. I run my fingers over the bark and a dribble of sap sticks to my nail. I touch it to my nose and smell it. Trees always smell better in the rain.

The clouds crack above and all around, like the whole sky is splitting open. Then the rain really hits me. There's no shelter here. I lower myself off the edge and skid down the rocky path again. And it really is a skid. I slide on my butt nearly the whole way. But I get to the bottom, leap across to the main path until I'm under the trees again. I glance back at where the boot prints were, but there's no point looking at them now. They'll be sinking into a pond of brown.

I find the oak I was hiding behind when I first watched Damon, and I lean against its trunk. My entire body is shaking with the cold. I can't believe it's spring; it should be warmer than this. I press right up against the tree, wishing it were a body with warm arms to wrap around me, wishing it were Damon. He would smell like boy deodorant and coffee. Real coffee. But the tree smells wooden and dank and dark; alive in a festering sort of way. Wet bark: Mum's favorite smell. Dad's too, I think. Maybe even mine. So there is something the three of us have in common after all. Wet trees. Awesome. I shut my eyes and try to remember a time when we were all in these woods together. It must have been years ago, maybe even before the first time Dad went on tour. Dad and Mum met in a wood. That's what Mum told me once, anyway. Maybe we'll all meet in one again someday. Though I'm glad Dad's not here with me now. Here, he'd only hear gunshots in the thunder, see firefight in the lightning.

I tilt my head and look at the topmost branches of the oak. There are taller trees on either side of this one. If lightning strikes, it'll hit those first. Even so, I should move.

I'm an idiot for thinking Damon would be back here. He's probably sitting in his nice warm house, probably watching TV or doing whatever it is boys like him do on Fridays after school. Why would he be in the woods in the middle of a thunderstorm? He may be gorgeous, but he's not stupid. I push myself away from the bark. Open my eyes.

And there he is after all.

Damon.

It's as if he's heard my thoughts, as if I've drawn him to me.

He's looking at me from across the clearing, still and silent from the edge of the trees on the other side of the path. He's not wearing a mask this time, and the expression on his face is perfect and beautiful. The wind whips the hair across his eyes, though he doesn't move to tuck it back. He just watches me. Even from here I see the frown in his forehead. His eyes run over my school shirt to my face, taking it all in, stopping my breath for a moment. It's the first time, ever, he's really seen me. I think I could pause this moment and play it over and over for the rest of my life. Suddenly I don't care about the rain and the thunder and the swaying trees and the chance of lightning. I want to stay right here. I want to get closer.

I start forward, even half-smile at him. My heart's hammering inside me like some sort of epileptic woodpecker. But he doesn't move in response; doesn't smile back. I look behind me. Maybe he hasn't seen me through the rain. It's dark here, under my oak. But no, he's staring right at me. It has to be me he's looking at. There is no one else. Did he see me on the Leap? See me with the flag? Maybe he's mad at me somehow for that. I bundle my nerves up tight and . . . just go for it.

"Hi!" I call out. My voice sounds shaky and young. "I go to your school. It's Damon, right?"

What a lame first sentence. Heroines in films always have something witty and seductive as their opening lines. I know I'll think of the best line when I'm lying in bed later.

My words don't inspire him to answer. Of course they don't. But he does keep staring at me. Trying to figure me out, I can tell by his expression. So I stay where I am. I don't want him to stop looking, I don't even want him to blink.

It's him that moves. He takes two steps toward me, out into the clearing so he's in full view. He's dressed in army fatigues; a little like Dad's old uniform. They're exactly the color of the trees. He's still not smiling, still not doing anything other than watching me. I try a small wave, my hand feeling heavy and awkward.

Still no response. I have a sudden urge to run toward him, push him back beneath the trees, away from the lightning. He's the only tall thing in that open piece of ground. A target. But there's something in his expression that keeps me rooted to the spot.

"You shouldn't have followed me."

His words echo around the clearing, punch me in the stomach. I don't have a response. If he'd asked me *why* I was following him, then I might.

Because you're beautiful.

Because I've been in love with you since forever.

Because my dad wants me to.

Because, Because, Because . . .

But my mouth hangs open and no words come out.

Some sort of emotion flickers across Damon's face.

"You'll regret it," he says. Though this time his words are so faint above the rush of the wind, I hardly hear them. It's more like I see the shape his mouth makes when he speaks. I'm still floundering, mute. I want to say that anything that involves me and him and a deserted part of the wood isn't possible to regret, but Beth's words from this morning are still stuck in my head. *Not cool, Emily, not cool.*

He shrugs when he sees I'm not going to respond. Then, very slowly, he raises his right arm. Curls his fingers so that his hand makes the shape of a gun. Squints, and sweeps his hand across until he's aiming that gun at me. I stand stock-still, almost as if it's a real gun he's pointing and if I move, he'll shoot. I don't know how long we stand there like that — him looking down the barrel of his arm toward my face, me trapped in the firing line. All I know is that each of my heart-beats feels like a bullet. And each time one hits, my heart explodes a little more.

My eyes move from the barrel of his finger, up his arm and to his face. I look at the wink of his left eye, the concentration in his brow. He is utterly perfect. I want every single inch of him.

And then he smiles. His mouth tilts up crookedly and his whole face transforms with it. I didn't think it was possible for a heart to explode and still keep beating. Or possible to become a million pieces of shrapnel somehow held together in one body. I feel my lips moving before I even know I'm smiling back.

Then he jerks his fingers upward in one quick movement, and he shoots.

"Don't come here again."

I'm still standing there as he turns and walks away, his army fatigues disappearing into the browns and greens of the trees.

**LUCY CHRISTOPHER**'s novel *Stolen* was named a Printz Honor Book by the American Library Association and received England's Branford Boase award and Australia's Golden Inky for best debut. In a starred review, *Publishers Weekly* called it "an emotionally raw thriller . . . a haunting account of captivity and the power of relationships." She is also the author of *Flyaway*, a novel for younger readers, which *Booklist* described as "compelling" and "sensitive" in a starred review. Lucy grew up in Australia, and now lives back in South Wales, where she was born. She is currently writing her third book, a psychological thriller for teens — as well as a fourth one about a horse! Visit her website www.lucychristopher.com and follow her on Twitter @LucyCAuthor.

# this is teen

## Want to find more **books, authors, and readers** to connect with?

Interact with friends and favorite authors, participate in weekly author Q&As, check out event listings, try the book finder, and more!